# Once Burned

## by

## Susan Vaughan

*Task Force Eagle, Book Three*

Cover Art by *Lisa Dawn MacDonald*

The Wild Rose Press, Inc.
PO Box 708
Adams Basin, NY 14410-0708
Visit us at www.thewildrosepress.com

Publishing History
First Edition, 2024
Trade Paperback ISBN
Digital ISBN

*Task Force Eagle, Book Three*
Previously Published Gullwood Press 2013
Published in the United States of America

## Dedication

To the other writers and to the law enforcement experts
of Crime Scene Writers for your advice and
information. And many thanks to my husband, who has
my back—always.

Chapter One

*May, Dragon Harbor, Maine*

JAKE WESCOTT OPENED the driver's door and eased his bad leg out of his SUV. The muscles had tightened up. Too damn much. After his punishing run on the Middle School track, he should've done the damn stretching exercises his physical therapist had prescribed.

He ought to have more improvement by now. Ought to be a hundred percent. They'd cleared him for duty—light duty, which this gig was supposed to be. He dug his fingers into the thigh muscle and kneaded. When the spasm eased enough, he gathered his mail and the *Bayport Chronicle* from the passenger seat, stood, and locked up.

In the harbor, power and sailing yachts as well as fishing craft bobbed around the three rocks that gave the town its name. At low tide, they were a boating hazard, but now at mid tide, the massive rocks formed the undulating back of a mythical beast.

The salt-scented air and the waves lapping against the pilings brought back memories of carefree summers. He half expected to see his dad like he was back then, young and tall and strong, waving from the stern of his lobster boat. Something about returning here gave life to the dead and clarified what was important.

1

As he made his way onto the docks, Ed Pascal waved a greeting. "How much distance you puttin' in now, Jake?"

"Made three miles today." He nodded to the harbormaster.

Pascal lifted his khaki ball cap and resettled it on his dark hair. Touching a finger to his flat nose, he grinned, digging creases around his eyes, squinty from forty-some years on the water. "Makin' progress. Not too shabby for a guy who could barely walk when you got here."

Jake thanked the man as he passed the harbor office, a one-room shingled building by the docks and floats. The finger docks took him to the boat slip where the *Amy Jo* sat in calm water. Once Uncle Joe's lobster boat with the typical high bow and roomy cockpit, she'd been retrofitted for cruising. Peeling paint and worn teak showed her age, but she was seaworthy.

Living on board was only temporary but not too tough a lifestyle to take. Despite the reason for his return to town, life on a boat soothed his soul. Living here supported his cover story—fixing up Gram's house to sell and looking out for his mom—which was truthful as far as it went.

He climbed aboard, gratified he could swing his left leg over the toe rail with minimal strain. A check of the companionway found no disturbance of his low-tech security—two paint chips stuck across the gap between the padlock and the hatch frame. Probably unnecessary here but taking no chances was good procedure. Especially if his investigation turned up anything.

Either investigation. Hell, looking into the fire by printing out news articles on the old Cameron fire hardly qualified. Stopping by Gail's grave had gotten him thinking. Probably no chance he'd find anything new. He had skills and experience now he didn't have twelve years ago. Maybe that's why he itched to have all the facts.

Below deck, he deposited the items he'd carried aboard on the small dining table. He glanced at his watch. Overdue to check in. He opened his lock box and moved his ATF ID and service pistol aside. He took out his laptop, ready to take notes, before tapping the number into his phone. The receiver clicked after three rings.

"About time, Wescott." Holt Donovan's western drawl stretched out the syllables like a rubber band. "Partyin' on that yacht instead of working?"

Jake chuckled at his contact's characterization of the *Amy Jo*. The DEA agent had never been Santa, but he morphed into Scrooge when schedules fell apart. Agents in Jake's Boston ATF office had joined with other federal agencies in Task Force Eagle to work on a smuggling case involving multiple jurisdictions.

"Yeah, Donovan, I just kissed the last of the girls good-bye and threw out the empty champagne bottles." A snort was the reply. Ginning, Jake said, "You got anything for me?"

Muted voices and computer hums of the big office filled a moment of silence. "I got a couple things on my end. Report from our man inside says at least one Dragon Harbor local, maybe two, are part of the smuggling ring. We've IDed one of El Águila's men in the Northeast, Hector Vargas. Vargas has moved explosives into Maine. Might be the C-4 you were hunting in New Hampshire."

"The same C-4 they used on us. You know how

much I want these guys." Too often lowlifes murdered innocent people and destroyed property with impunity. Jake knew from painful experience. The primary reason he'd joined the ATF. He keyed in the new information before asking, "Anything else? What about Ruiz?" ATF Special Agent Ruiz was deep undercover with the Mexican cartel offshoot in New Hampshire.

"They seem to be waiting around for more. Ruiz said talk is it's AR-15s and Bushmaster assault rifles, more like the ones we rounded up in Portland back before you— Sorry, don't mean to keep reminding you what happened after that."

Jake rubbed the scar on his thigh. He didn't need reminding about the biggest fuck-up of his career. He had let the gang sucker him. The same bomb that had injured him also blew apart his partner. He swallowed past the clog in his throat. "No problem. What do you know about this Hector Vargas?"

"Not much. Vargas may be an alias. Ruiz has never seen the man, so we're nada on a description."

I'll keep an eye out, but a Mexican would stand out on this lily-white peninsula like a cactus in a pine grove. Any progress on tracking down the drug lord himself?"

"Inch by fucking inch," Donovan said. "Task force's cutting a deal with the Federales for a joint op, some sort of a trap. I'm itchin' to get in on it."

Jake balled one hand into a fist. "That could take months. Won't do any good to catch the sons of bitches here in Maine if El Águila's free to set up shop somewhere else."

Donovan put him on hold for a call on another line.

No one else should suffer because of those Mexican thugs. He had to connect the Dragon Harbor link to them and seal up this harbor to the smugglers. If Donovan and the others could capture El Águila, the whole cartel would go down. He relaxed his fisted hand as the other agent returned. "Does Ruiz have any idea of a deadline here?"

"Hard to tell when the shipment will move. Make it three, four weeks. They know we're pressuring them. They could move up the timetable."

"Won't Ruiz let us know?"

Donovan cleared his throat. "That was my other call. Ruiz is dead."

The announcement blasted through Jake like a Nor'easter. "Dammit! How?"

"He was driving back to the compound after reporting in. A sniper shot from an overpass. Bullet went through the windshield. Cops found nothing. Said it was probably a hunter out of season. The SAC figures the cartel made Ruiz. Don't let that happen to you."

Jake's temples pounded. "I got this one. No problem."

**\*\*\*\***

*June*

Lani Cameron parked her car in the Birch Brook Farm driveway. She put the house and attached small barn behind her and crossed the pasture. As she'd done twice a day since her arrival a week ago, she stopped at the splintered frame of the burned-out horse barn's doorway.

She turned her face to the late-afternoon June sun, absorbing brightness before lowering her gaze to the blackened remains. Not much left after twelve Maine winters. She bent to pick up a scrap of pine board. Her fingers clenched around the charred wood.

The remembered smell of creosote turned her stomach. If she closed her eyes, she could feel the searing heat. Hear the roar. But she couldn't see more, couldn't see Gail's body, limp on the floor, couldn't— She dropped the wood as if it was scorching her hand.

The sun shining through the structure's skeleton cast eerie shadows over the witch grass and daisies. Cow vetch twined its way up one of the posts. Green life amid the ashes—a mockery.

She needed to sell the farm, but without that phone call from Nora, she might not have had the courage to return to Dragon Harbor to do it herself. When school had ended the second week of the month, she finished her students' final reports and booked it out of Concord. She prayed braving the scene of the fire would end her nightmares and help her remember, but the dreams were haunting her nightly, becoming more vivid. More real. The murderous fire monster, bigger and more frightening, woke her up in a cold sweat. She rubbed her arms in the sudden chill of memory.

Dammit, she would put up with a lack of sleep if her efforts led to answers.

She strode toward the farmhouse, seeking comfort in its white clapboards, peaked roof, and front door painted shut because everyone used the side-porch entrance to the kitchen. Repairs had to be done before the real estate agent would list the property.

As she reached the pasture's edge, a blue SUV pulled into the driveway and parked behind her car. A tall man in jeans and a faded University of Maine tee-shirt emerged.

She held up a hand to shade her eyes from the sun and watched as he ambled toward her. Light-brown hair and strong boned features with bold planes and angles made her pulse flutter. He stopped a few feet from her and raised his gaze.

Her heart drummed, slamming against her ribs. *Jake Wescott.* The same blue eyes, but older, wiser, sadder. She'd expected to see her twin's old boyfriend, planned on it, but not yet. She'd wanted this first meeting on her own terms. Never mind. She would deal.

"What are you doing here?"

"I was just—" His mouth dropped open, and he took a step back as if a horse had kicked him in the gut. "*Gail.*" Shaking his head, he blew out a breath. "Lani, is that you?"

Her throat closed. How long had it been since someone mistook her for her twin? A cruel joke, except he wasn't joking.

*The best defense is a good offense.* She cocked a hip and flapped a hand at the scar on the left side of her face. "Who else would it be, Jake? Mrs. Frankenstein? And I repeat, what *are* you doing here?"

Tension crackled in the air between them. Her heart pounded like a kettledrum.

His face was a blank mask. Time had changed him. He was taller and broader shouldered. Lines etched into his cheeks added more than the three years he had on her. No familiar crooked grin, the one that used to melt every girl in Dragon Harbor. Including her. Although she'd kept it to herself. Back then he'd been open—funny and kind. But that wasn't the Jake here today. She didn't know this Jake with the unreadable, hard eyes.

"I'm living on my boat in the harbor while I take care of some family business. Fixing up Gram's house to sell it, for one."

Not what she meant but she'd get to that. "Nora told me you've been here since March. That you're in the FBI."

"Not FBI, ATF. Bureau of Alcohol, Tobacco, Firearms, and Explosives. I'm on leave. You mind me looking around in the horse barn, what's left of it?"

"No problem. Knock yourself out."

Chapter Two

PERMISSION RECEIVED, IF grudgingly, Jake strode toward the rectangular black scar stitched up by a few stubborn two by fours. He hadn't expected Lani to follow him but behind him, her sneakers swished through the grass, stirring up green smells of the freshly mown grass. If she noticed the awkward hitch in his stride, she said nothing.

She stopped at what was left of the barn doorway. He wondered if she *could* step inside, breaching some emotional barrier. She stood by stiffly, watching him meander through the charred wood.

"What are you doing? Looking for something?"

Not the first time he'd looked, but doubtful any clue to that horrible night would still be here. He kept hoping for insight. He kicked aside a board and bent, coming up with mangled metal. "A bicycle wheel. Yours or Gail's?"

"I don't know. Both of them could be in there. Gail called bike riding juvenile, but I considered it healthy exercise. I rode to my job at Dragon Stables that summer. I still ride a bike." As if she couldn't bear to look anymore, she turned her back.

Seeing the wheel revived memories of that summer. The summer that had changed all their lives. His throat tightened. He couldn't bear to see this anymore either.

He dropped the wheel and dusted off his hands as he joined her. "I'm surprised you came back. Seeing all this has to be doubly painful for you." He made a sweeping gesture.

As if considering her answer, she sighed and set out toward the house. The two of them walked silently away from the scorched relic of their past.

She turned to him, her eyes solemn and guarded. She was still smart-mouthed but not the light-hearted girl he'd once known. "Guess I thought it was time to face down my demons. The house is going up for sale. Granddad left the farm to me because of… well, you know. The caretaker kept the house in shape until he became too old. He died last year and I decided to sell. Porch needs shoring up, among other repairs. I'm doing some of the interior painting."

His return was more complicated than fixing up a house to sell, but he couldn't tell her his reasons, not all of them anyway. "Your grandfather used to paint the shutters every summer. They look crusty."

"I'll add it to the list for the outside painter. I can't afford everything, but my father's covering me until the sale."

"Maine saltwater farms sell for millions these days, especially ones with hundreds of acres and deep-water frontage. You'll have to wait for the right buyer."

"Only a major developer could afford it. Ugh." Her shoulders moved in a shudder of revulsion. "No, I'm negotiating to transfer most of the acreage to the Coastal Land Trust, which will preserve it, maintain the fields, and allow some recreational use. The house and these two acres by the road will go separately."

"I'm glad," he said. "I can't picture condos or resorts on your grandfather's farm."

As they reached her car, she stopped him. "When I

asked you earlier why you were here, I meant *here*, at Birch Brook Farm."

At the emotion in her voice, his throat tightened. "I need to know exactly what happened that night. Late to find much of a clue, but I had to see what was left."

"Nora also told me you'd been reading up on the fire. You're investigating? Officially?"

He shook his head. "Nothing official. I've read over all the old news stories. That's all."

"If I'd gone out to the barn with her, if I'd seen the fire earlier…"

He knew all about survivor guilt. The beast clamped him in its jaws. If he hadn't left, Gail would still be alive. And a mottled, white puckering wouldn't mar the skin of Lani's face. Other, more recent, images flashed through his mind, and pain jabbed him.

Forcing away the onslaught, he said, "Too many ifs. Neither of us can go back. A guilt trip gets you nowhere. No replay or do-over."

He drew in a breath, harnessing the emotions kicking around in his chest. Lani's perception had made him angry at himself because the elegant curve of her neck—identical to Gail's—and the pain in her eyes made him ache to touch her. No, the attraction was merely a flashback, a reaction to Gail's lookalike. He'd hurt her, calling her by her twin's name. If he ran into her again, he'd be more thoughtful.

He didn't know how to deal with this new Lani. Twelve years ago, she hadn't tempted him. He'd been so blinded with lust for Gail. Teasing, seductive, partying Gail. He'd laughed with Lani, traded barbs with her, but hadn't known her well. The twins shared identical drop-dead gorgeous looks, but Gail and Lani had very different personalities.

And this Lani was different from that one. He couldn't have prepared for the change. Not the scarring, but the change in Lani the woman—hazel-gold eyes sharp enough to score glass. And her voice—low and smooth, like whiskey chased with honey. Sexy, even when she was skewering him.

Scars remained beneath the surface too, judging from the flashes of pain in her scorched-earth eyes. Defensiveness, and some bitterness, for damn sure. Who could blame her? The knowledge of what she'd suffered—still suffered—curled around the muscles of his chest and made it ache. He began edging toward his ride.

She collected her keys, handbag, and a folder from the car's front seat. She slung the bag onto her shoulder and held up the folder, stuffed with papers. "After I got here, I decided I should read those news articles myself, the coverage I couldn't bring myself to look at back then. And I asked myself why a federal agent would check into a twelve-year-old tragic accident."

He opened his mouth to spout some inane answer but she held up a hand.

"Possibly this agent—who I now discover is an *arson* expert—suspects the accidental fire might have been something more. Am I warm? Hot?"

Her words seared him. "Lani—"

"Wait, there's more. I come home to find this expert digging for clues at the scene of the *accident*." Cheeks pink with emotion—temper or excitement, hard to tell—she charged onward. "Jake, if you suspect arson or some other foul play, I want in. I want to help, to *do* something. Gail was my twin, identical DNA. I need to *know*."

"The fire was declared an accident." Except what he'd read raised doubts of that as fact. He wasn't ready to speak that aloud to anyone, especially to this woman. He made it two more steps down the driveway.

She huffed in disgust. "Remind me to invite you to my next Texas Hold'em game. I'll clean up."

"I have no information that indicates it *wasn't* an accident." The less he said about it, the better. Another few steps and he could escape before she could talk him into deputizing her.

"Official speak. Like that spokesman for the state police. 'We have no information at this time pending the investigation.' Bull crap." She jabbed a forefinger his direction. "You're the arson expert but I'm pretty good at research. I'll read the rest of these news clippings and go from there."

"Let me do the investigating. Stay out of this." Shit, he'd given away too much by warning her. "Okay, here's how you can help. Tell me what you saw that night."

Pain flashed in her eyes. "I would if I could. I can't tell you squat."

"But you must—"

"I must nothing! Ever since I woke up in that hospital bed, I've *tried* to remember. I thought coming back here, living in this house would bring it all back."

"But not yet, I take it."

She shook her head. Her mouth quirked up on one side. "So why do you want to shut me out? What's the risk in researching an *accident*?"

"Man, I'd forgotten what a hard bargain you drive. I'll share whatever I find with you."

"Good. Then we'll plan *our* next move." She beamed him a smile that rocked him back on the heels of his boat shoes. "Good to see you again, Jake. Don't be a stranger."

He said goodbye and hustled into his SUV. Watched her trot up the porch steps and swing through the door into the mud room. Sat staring at the closed door.

He shouldn't let her get involved even in a small way. Every time he saw her—saw Gail's face—would be another log on the burn in his gut. If someone had set the fire that killed Gail, the arsonist was a murderer and might do anything, *anything* to keep his crime secret. He wasn't worried for himself but he couldn't protect Lani. Not that she'd ask.

A scream from inside the house yanked him from the driver seat. He raced to the porch and slammed into the house. "Lani, what's wrong?"

She stood as if planted beside the table in the center of the big kitchen. Hands at her throat, she trembled, wide eyed and mute, her cheeks pale beneath the veneer of light tan.

*The fire, she's flashing back to the barn fire.* Seeing her so vulnerable drew him in, tugged at something inside he thought had atrophied. He clasped her shoulders and turned her to face him.

Underneath the sharp smell of pine cleanser, he registered a smoky odor. And more, a rotten stench that stirred nausea in his belly. Dread tightened his chest. When he pulled Lani into his arms, she made no resistance. Behind her, he spotted what had terrified her.

A mangled form lay on the counter. A cat or a rabbit. Tendrils of smoke rose from its patchy, blackened fur. Jake dragged his gaze upward. On the cabinet door above the creature, someone had daubed crude lettering that dripped dark red.

*LEAVE OR THIS COULD BE YOU*

Talking softly to Lani, he led her away from the disgusting tableau and into the living room, where he lowered her onto the sofa. She blinked up at him as if roused from sleep or a hypnotic state, but said nothing as he took out his cell phone and called the cops.

A uniform arrived within fifteen minutes, a fresh-faced kid who looked to be barely out of high school. Jake waited while the officer asked questions, took photographs and samples from the lettering. The jagged warning seemed to have been written in a mix of paint and ashes—not blood. He stowed the burnt critter in an evidence bag. A cat, the cop surmised.

"I'll help you clean up the cabinet," Jake said when the officer had left.

"You don't have to stay. I'm okay now the... thing is gone," Lani said, embarrassment for her panic attack evidenced by the faint wash of pink on her cheeks. Understandable. So was her terror of fire.

Rather than push her, he gave her his cell number and left. On the drive back to Dragon Harbor, he reflected on her reaction to the cruel warning. Given what she'd already been through, he figured she could handle almost anything, and did, alone.

Except one.

If the barn fire had been arson, his poking around and her return might have someone scared. Scared Lani's visiting familiar territory would jog her memory. Scared she'd remember something incriminating.

If her chagrin at his witnessing her panic kept her from inserting herself into his investigation, so be it. But now that she had the bit between her teeth, he doubted she'd give it up. Shit, he wanted answers, and her poking

15

into the old case might stir her memory.

If he dragged her in, he'd have to protect her. His gut clenched.

\*\*\*\*

The next morning Lani bought the same cabinet paint as in the old can in the attached barn, more of a garage, matte enamel in an eggshell cream. She pried off the lid and stirred the thick mixture as she contemplated the reunion with Jake. Did his ATF work make him naturally suspicious or had he found something in those news stories? If it wasn't an accident, why would someone set the barn afire? A pyromaniac, a drifter, maybe, not knowing Gail was there?

Yesterday afternoon, once she'd recovered enough to talk to the policeman, sick revulsion morphed into anger. The cop reassured her the animal was an apparent road kill, and the crude letters were paint, not blood. After he and Jake left, she scrubbed the sink nearly through the enamel. But the message remained. And had forged anger into determination.

She would read the remaining printouts tonight and find out exactly what Jake saw in them. After she painted the ruined cabinet door. Unfortunately, it meant repainting the rest of the cabinets to match.

The slam of a car door announced her expected company. Lani looked out the kitchen window to see Nora Meagher and her two sons. Her best friend from the old days had volunteered to help with the painting on her day off from nursing duties.

Dressed in faded jeans and a blue work shirt, Nora gestured to her little boys to stay within sight. They wagged their heads as if to say, "Jeez, Mom, we know," before carrying a baseball, mitts, and a bat from the car into the pasture.

"Hey, girlfriend," Nora called as she breezed into the kitchen. Her wild red curls were the same as always. Her rosy cheeks, along with the rest of her, were plumper than they used to be, although she claimed her boys ran her ragged. Ironic and awkward that Nora had married Lani's ex-boyfriend, but for friendship's sake, she hid her animus toward Kevin the wimp.

"Hey, thanks for coming to help." Lani hugged her friend, glad to have the support.

Nora gaped at the lettered warning, *LEAVE OR THIS COULD BE YOU*, now smeared and faded, but still dramatic enough to send chills down Lani's spine. "Gawd, no wonder you want this gone as fast as possible. And you think it was just a teenage prank?"

"That's what the nice officer said. What else could it be?"

Nora rolled her eyes. "And the flaming dollhouse?"

Three days before the painted warning, vandals had left a burning dollhouse on the front lawn. The last thing Lani wanted was for her mother to find out about this and the other reasons she'd returned to Dragon Harbor. The nightmares were one thing, but looking into the old fire? Hope Cameron Nash would pitch a hissy fit.

On a sigh, she waved a hand in dismissal. "Bored teens, the first officer said. Same deal. But they'll get tired of harassing me and give up. I'm going nowhere. Now do you intend to rag on me or help paint?"

Nora spread the newspapers she'd brought on the table and poured paint into first one and then the other paper bucket. "Oh, I'm ready to work, but I don't intend to let you get away with this blasé attitude. You could be setting yourself up for real danger out here alone. Did you at least tell Jake about the dollhouse?"

The policeman hadn't mentioned it and neither had she. She'd learned the hard way to depend only on herself. When things got tough, other people—read: male species—wimped out. Whining to him would only arm him with ammunition to shut her out. So no, she'd keep to herself the burning dollhouse and any future stupid stunts. She had to press Jake to cooperate with her. Like him, she needed answers, and soon.

"Of course not," she insisted. "The vandalism is *my* problem, not his. I'll handle it myself."

"Until you can't. Okay, where do you want me to start?"

"How about you work from left to right, from the fridge toward the middle? I'll do the ruined door? Paint remover ruined the finish but not the or-else memo. Sanding didn't take it off. One coat or ten, I'll slap on as much as necessary."

"You got it," Nora said, dipping her brush into the bucket. "You know, you can paint over this obscenity, but glossing over your fears about what it might mean won't work. Maybe Jake could help. He's a trained investigator, not like our local yokels."

"So paint already." Lani carried her paint container to the cabinet, dipped in the new brush, and swiped the first stroke over the mocking abomination.

Chapter Three

"MA, YOU HAVE that number. I-14, see?" Jake set his mug on the blue woven tablecloth as he pointed to the spot on her Beano card. If only he could communicate better with her, get through the fog that encased her mind.

His mother said nothing, staring blankly at the marker she should put on the spot. Did she even see the card or hear the volunteer caller? Pine View was nice, as nursing homes went, clean and more homey than institutional. And less expensive than the swanky facility in Portland near his brother Hank. Relatives and local volunteers came in often to visit the patients, play Beano or checkers with them, and entertain. But Grace Wescott was becoming increasingly hard to reach no matter what anyone did.

In her day, Grace had suited her name. She'd run the library and her all-male family with lively warmth, a steel backbone, and contagious humor. Seeing her now in this wheelchair, barely able to communicate, dressed in pink sweats that hung on her bony frame, tightened Jake's chest until it might implode.

"My boys don't come to see me," she said suddenly, her tone petulant. She peered at him with watery blue eyes that used to be the same color as his. "When's Henry coming?"

Jake's heart thumped. "He was here this morning.

He brought you this dog." No sense telling her that her husband of forty years wasn't coming to see her. Ever.

His dad's accidental death years ago had scraped him raw, but seeing early-onset dementia steal Ma away brain cell by brain cell ripped him bloody every time he visited her. She was only seventy-three.

"I remember now." She cuddled the stuffed hound Jake had placed in her lap. Ma used to love her dogs, the last one, a yellow Lab mix named Hilly, long gone. Her lips curved in a wistful smile and her eyes lost focus, turned inward. Maybe to old memories. Her hand fell away from the toy. Her mug sat untouched on the table.

"Don't you want your tea?"

"Not my…" Grace faltered for the words, pushing away the mug.

He heaved a sigh. His visit had taxed her energy. "That's okay, Ma. I'll come back tomorrow." He'd pick up a tin of Earl Gray in Bayport.

Rising, he wheeled her back to her room, away from the abandoned Beano game. He kissed her papery cheek and left her by the window where she sat most of the daylight hours. She liked to watch the bird feeders in the courtyard. At least, she appeared to. Hard to tell these days.

She was slipping away little by little every day. If he'd been in Maine, could he have made a difference? The doctors said no but accepting that was hard. He could barely reach her now, and soon…

His throat closed. If only he could do something to bring her back. He made a fist, but he had no target to punch but air.

After climbing into his vehicle, he opened his cell phone. When his brother answered, he said, "Just left

Ma."

"I'll try to get there on the weekend. How's she doing?"

"She knows me sometimes, but today she's confused. I'm not sure who she thought I was. Sometimes Dad. Yesterday she thought I was you. If it makes her happy, that's okay with me."

A high-pitched squeal rose in the background. "Hold on a sec." A clunk as Hank deposited the receiver on a table.

The joyful sound would be Hank's two-year-old son Zack. Jake had met him for the first time when he brought Grace to Pine View. The little guy was a pistol.

His brother came back on. "Zack says hi to his uncle. He wants to show you his new truck. Nicole went out of town. An advertising conference in Boston. I get to take care of my big guy for a long weekend."

"Give Zack a hug from me."

"Will do. How are your projects coming along?"

"Gram's house, slow progress. Porch is shored up. I've started on the living room. On the Cameron fire, nothing yet." His ATF connections had given him cachet with the state fire marshal. He'd gotten some reports by e-mail that morning and was waiting for the rest. But he wasn't ready to talk about any of that. "Basically, I need a crystal ball."

Hank laughed. "I'd look into mine but the damn thing lets me down all the time. You're on your own, bro."

An apt description of his situation. Especially with wild card Lani Cameron in the mix. Ma was never going to remember much, but if Lani would…

\*\*\*\*

The door of the Wheelhouse Bar and Grill swung shut behind Jake. He stood to one side adjusting to the dim glow. Plastic boat lanterns and lobster-shaped party lights shed a dim glow on the happy-hour crowd of fishermen and other working stiffs. Odors of ripe bait and the lather of hard labor mingled with those of beer and whiskey.

He'd just left a half hour with DHPD Chief Galt, giving him a heads-up on a conversation he'd overheard, some guys plotting sabotage of another lobsterman's trap line. After Galt said he'd advise the Maine Marine Patrol to keep an eye on the situation, the chief suggested Jake curb his interest in the Cameron fire.

"With minor exceptions like fishing disputes, Dragon Harbor's a peaceful town," Galt said in his Down-East drawl. "Probing an old tragedy's like dredgin' the harbor. Raises old mud and old stink. Gossip won't do much for folks' peace of mind. Bad ambiance for the tourists." He'd regarded Jake with the kind of level stare that must wring confessions from felons. "Take a little friendly advice and let the matter drop."

Friendly advice? Not likely. And less likely Jake would drop his probe.

As his eyes became accustomed to the gloom, he spied Kevin Meagher around the side of the bar. The position suited him. Back to a wall, not to the crowd or the door, so he had a good view of the room.

Kevin had been a teenage heartthrob in the old days. He was still burly but now puffy flesh padded what had once been an angular face and an athletic build. A paunch strained the buttons on his checked shirt. He was running for Congress, like his old man. J.T. had lost.

Maybe Kev would do better. Hard to think of him as a mover and shaker, but there it was.

Kevin was talking to a ruddy-faced man in work-stained khakis. The pair seemed to be arguing.

Tall tales and complaints swirled through the low-ceilinged room, about the day's catch or engine troubles or the Red Sox as Jake made his way to the bar. Glasses and bottles clinked.

"Hey, Kevin." He clapped a hand on his friend's shoulder.

"Jake! Man, great you could make it. Take a load off." Kevin beamed the eager smile that had once charmed teachers and coeds.

The ruddy-faced man said good-bye and melted into the crowd.

"Didn't mean to chase your friend away."

"Don't worry about Brandon. He had to leave anyway." Kevin waved to the bartender. "He drives a bulldozer part-time. Problem with his paycheck."

Part-time could mean this Brandon had another means of livelihood. Maybe sternman on one of the warring lobster boats. Jake gave himself a mental slap. Or any one of a dozen other part-time jobs. Hell, chasing bottom-feeders for the ATF had made him suspicious of everything and everybody. "Part of being the boss, huh?"

Kevin's brow clouded. "J.T.'s still the boss at Meagher Enterprises. You been in town for months and we've barely talked. Nora wants to see you."

"Nora's too good for the likes of you. You're a lucky man." Jake meant it. He'd need more than luck to find *the one*. Long hours and hard days when you could trust nobody and they didn't trust you made anything but short-term hook-ups next to impossible.

Kevin grinned. "Don't I know it! Come for supper soon. We'll boil some bugs." He sucked down the last of his beer.

Lobster and he didn't get along, heresy for a native Mainer. He'd rather spend his evenings alone, but maybe he'd become too much of a hermit. He'd take a steak to Kevin's, sell it as surf and turf. "I'd like that. Just say when."

The bartender, in tight shorts and a tank top that displayed her considerable assets, including a tattooed red rose in the middle of her cleavage, sashayed over. Ava Warren slid away the departed man's beer and swiped the polished-wood bar with a rag. A tattoo of a gold chain braceleted her right wrist. "You want a draft, Jake honey? Or *something stronger*?"

Ava could make a sexual innuendo out of a license plate number. In high school, she'd played it fast and loose. Looked like she still did. She'd be a definite source of gossip, even twelve-year-old gossip. He'd rather have Lani's memories, but he'd take info where he could get it. "A draft'll do me, Ava."

As soon as the bartender set down two mugs, he reached for his wallet.

"Put this on my tab, Ava," Kevin said. "It's not every day I can get caught up with another member of the state Class C championship baseball team."

Giving Jake the once-over, Ava pouted her lips. She poked at her spiky hair. A wonder her fingers didn't come away bloody. "Looks like *you* still keep in shape, Jake honey."

"I try." Jake tilted up the beer mug. Was she hitting on him or slamming Kevin?

Not one to give up, she smiled seductively. "You

two like some popcorn? It's fresh—" she stared with lowered lashes at Jake "—and *hot*."

Kevin gulped some beer and wiped his mouth, clearly covering a grin. "Um, popcorn. Yeah. Sure thing, Ava."

Jake bit the inside of his lower lip. Both of them had seen Ava in action plenty of times.

She swished toward the popcorn machine. Scroll designs twined around her upper back and disappeared into her tank top.

"Hear Ava's going through her second divorce. Maybe third." Kevin chuckled. "Didn't you date her back in high school?"

"The senior prom. Once was enough. She was hot then." But when she'd heaved up the rum and Cokes she downed behind the gym, he'd cooled faster than getting dunked in the bay.

"Hot, yeah, but Gail Cameron was the hot one. Me and Lani, you and Gail. Remember?"

How could Jake forget that summer a few years later? He nodded but said nothing as he rubbed his scar. Kevin hadn't changed in one way. Always did speak his mind without thinking. He was running for a seat in Congress, like his dad had years ago. How was that candor working for him in a political campaign?

They sipped their beers in silence for a few moments before Kevin spoke again, rattling on about working in his dad's company. He puffed out his chest, putting his shirt buttons at risk, as he wound down. "Big responsibility. I supervise job sites and my sister manages the office. Except now I'm out two, three times a week campaigning around most of the southern half of the state. What about you? You take leave from the government or quit?"

"On leave." He might return to duty after his undercover assignment here. And he might not. Hard to go back after what happened. "Life on board Uncle Joe's boat suits me while I fix up Gram's house. Gives me time to visit with Mom."

"You getting much done on the house?"

"Fixed the steps to the porch. Still working on removing the old plaster in the living room. My brother paid for half the new roof, so that helps." He'd built up solid savings and investments from his job. He'd accept some money from Hank to make him feel part of the deal, but the family man couldn't afford to fork over much more.

They drank in silence as laughter erupted over a dart game across the room. Ava deposited a basket brimming with hot popcorn in front of them. The steamy butter-and-salt scent made Jake's mouth water. "Guess I'm hungry after all."

He snared a handful. Kevin scooped up a bigger one.

When Kevin had downed his second beer and most of the popcorn, he said, "Gotta go. Nora'll be looking for me. I got a fundraiser tonight in Portland."

Jake pulled out a five for Ava, to keep on her good side while he avoided hooking up with her. Besides, he had another female messing with his mind. He should stay away from Lani, but shit, he'd keep tabs on her, push her to remember.

Outside the dark bar, he blinked in the sun, still high in the late afternoon. Plenty of time to pull out old laths in Gram's living room and grill a burger on deck. "You seen Lani?"

"Not yet. She and Nora get together, but not when

I'm around. They've stayed in touch over the years. I haven't seen her since... you know." Kevin gave a shudder. "I went to the hospital when they allowed visitors. You ever see a burn victim? Damned horrific."

"Yeah." Jake had gone too, but she'd lain there in a drugged sleep. Since then he'd seen other burn victims. Horrific didn't begin to describe the result of flames on flesh. He suspected what had happened next wouldn't reflect well on Kevin. "You broke up with her then?"

"I couldn't face Lani like that." He brightened. "Nora says surgery fixed her up. Hardly any scars."

"Modern reconstructive surgery can work miracles." No surgery could bring back the ones who didn't make it. Like Gail. And his partner. The memory triggered a spasm in his thigh.

"Wonder how long all that repair took."

"Good question." Jake slapped him on the back. "You can ask Lani when you see her."

Kevin bobbled his keys, nearly dropped them. "Are you nuts? I'd sooner kiss a live lobster than ask her that. She'd take off two layers of my hide."

"A definite possibility." And he'd deserve it.

Kevin climbed into the truck cab. He scratched his chin. "Guess she's great looking again. Both twins were back then, for damn sure. But Gail was the hot one. Whooee, man, it wouldn't have taken much for me to trade twins."

*Gail was the hot one.* Kevin had said it twice. Jake would ask what the hell that meant, but he'd be talking to the truck's exhaust.

\*\*\*\*

Driving north on the East Road at night gave Lani the creeps. Especially after painting over that ghastly burnt offering.

She and Nora had finished painting the upper cabinets. She would tackle the rest tomorrow. Then she'd spent more hours immersed the news coverage of the fire and neglected to think about the house's empty refrigerator—except for yogurt and milk. Tomorrow morning the supermarket in Bayport would stock her up for the rest of the week. For tonight she'd dine at the Eastward Inn in the village.

Coming here was the right move, though dangerous. The whole business hadn't left her thoughts all day. That and Jake Wescott. A blast from the past.

He had to see him soon. He had to know she wasn't giving up. Not now. She'd made some calls, but she needed Jake and his ATF creds to really dig. He wouldn't leave her thoughts, but she shouldn't read anything into his interest and concern. Only kindness and the ease of old friendship. Nothing more. Guys wanted beauty and perfection, not scars and attitude.

She stuffed her ambivalence into a box and shoved it deep. She should concentrate on her driving, on the challenge of the two-lane blacktop ringing the peninsula. The half moon cast light but the road was still too dark. And lonely. No other cars. Driveways shrouded in trees and bushes concealing the few houses on her left.

By Birch Brook Farm and farther down the peninsula, the East Road veered inland, so the farmland stretched toward the bay, but here, the road bordered the water. Beyond the narrow right-hand shoulder the earth fell away to ocean waves crashing on the rocks. She loved that daytime view, a major tourist draw. Now she saw only the reflective metal of the guardrail.

Headlights appeared in her rearview mirror. The

other vehicle closed the distance between them in a matter of seconds. The high beams stabbed through the car's rear window, the glare making it harder to see.

Lani blinked and frowned. She adjusted her rear-view mirror.

Sitting up that high, the vehicle must be some kind of truck. It rode close enough to swallow her rear bumper. Speeding, tailgating, not dimming high beams. Probably kids out for a joy ride.

The road's blind curves made passing impossible. That impatient driver might go for it anyway. On her side, nowhere to pull over, no scenic turnout. All she could do was drive. Whoever the jerk was had made this short journey dangerous. Her heart raced and her hands slicked the steering wheel. She wiped each palm in turn on her pants legs.

A yellow warning sign appeared ahead for a sharp curve. The familiar nearly V-shaped turn locals called the Devil's Elbow jutted outward to a sheer cliff. Bad enough in daylight but much more hazardous at night. Gripping the wheel so tightly her hands cramped, she leaned forward to peer into the darkness.

A hard jolt knocked her forward.

The seat belt caught and jerked her hard. Kept her head from hitting the steering wheel. The car swerved across the yellow line. The guard rail seemed to reach for her. She wrenched her car back into her lane. Her pulse pounded and blood roared in her ears.

This was no joy rider. That ramming was deliberate. "You idiot!"

When she glanced into her side mirror, the truck's high beams blinded her. But why was someone attacking her? And who would do such a thing? No time to wonder now.

The headlights behind her veered to the left.

*Thank God. He's going to pass.*

As the bigger vehicle overtook her, it lurched right. The truck rammed her. The force jerked her hands from the wheel and slammed the car to the side.

Lani stomped on the brakes. The tires howled as they ground on the blacktop. Momentum careened the car sideways. Toward the guard rail and the wave-battered granite below the Devil's Elbow.

The bottom dropped out of her stomach.

Chapter Four

JAKE RUBBED THE back of his neck. Driving to Birch Brook Farm this time of night was probably a butt-stupid thing to do. The arson investigator had reached a hasty conclusion based on too little evidence that the fire was accidental. Lani'd pulled her sister out of that damn barn. She must've seen something. Maybe someone. He had to question her some more. She'd probably had counseling years ago, but not now, not after returning to the scene of the crime. He winced at the phrase. Hell, maybe he'd talk her into hypnosis.

And it wouldn't hurt to make sure she was okay after discovering that smoking animal in her kitchen.

The half moon's beam poured like a ribbon of milk across the island-dotted ocean. Fucking poetic. That's what the coast of Maine did to him. Or was it thinking about Lani? How proud and determined this grown-up Lani was. The zing when he thought of her made denial impossible. But was it her he wanted or a ghost? Complicated and impossible.

The more he thought about her, the more he felt he owed her the truth about the night of the fire. Once he explained, maybe his conscience would be clearer. Yeah, right. She could already be in danger. He wanted her to remember, but what if someone else feared she would? Pain stabbed him like somebody'd dumped roofing nails in his gut.

31

A dark pickup whipped around the turn and careened toward Jake. Its high halogen beams blinded him. Dirt and mud covered most of the truck. The truck, more massive than his vehicle, straddled the middle yellow lines, occupying the whole road.

Jake let loose a string of expletives that seared the air. He nearly wrenched his vehicle into the hillside to avoid a collision. By the time he braked to a stop, the truck had vanished around the next turn. Damn, if only he could've seen the license number. He inhaled and blew out a harsh breath as he steered back onto the road.

He slowed at the next curve. Lights pierced the sky from a skewed angle. Headlights. And they weren't moving.

His beams slid across a white sedan at the apex of the sharp turn. Its driver-side tires hung a foot above the rocky ground. Shit, the vehicle had skidded partway over the edge. He lowered his window for a better look. The only thing holding it was the guard rail. Above the rumble of waves, straining metal shrieked.

He stopped the SUV. Was that the car from Birch Brook Farm?

*Lani?*

His heart rate lurched into high gear. He steered to the side and punched on the emergency flashers. As soon as he got out, the driver's door opened a crack.

The sedan rocked. Tilted even higher. The metal guard rail groaned and snapped.

"Don't move!" he shouted. "You'll send it over."

A head appeared in the driver's side window. "Help me."

Her terrified call stabbed him in the gut. His pulse clattered. "Lani, are you hurt?"

"Jake," she said with shaky relief. "I'm okay. Help me get out. The guard rail… it's going."

Gut tight, heart thumping against his chest wall, he'd do her no good this way. He tamped down emotion and assessed the situation. The driver airbag hadn't deployed because of the sideways skid. And she was right. One guard-rail support had popped from the rocky soil and another was bent. More weight or another shake of the vehicle would hurry the job.

He knew the rocks that lay below. If the car went over, Lani would die.

He returned to his vehicle. No towing gear, but he'd stowed a mooring line in back. The engine lacked enough power to pull the car to safety but could steady it. He ran over with the rope.

"Hold still until I give you the word. Then open the door and jump out fast."

She eyed the rope and seemed to realize what he planned. She wasted no breath or time on questions. "I got it."

Confidence instead of terror in her voice reassured him. He looped one end of the rope around the raised front wheel and tied it securely.

Unwinding the coil as he went, he returned to the SUV. He maneuvered the rear end toward the other vehicle and set the emergency brake. Pulled the rope through the trailer hitch until it was taut. His fingers flew to tie a bowline. A hard tug on the free end would release the knot.

When she jumped, he'd have to move fast or his ride might take a dive into the briny with hers. He had to take the chance.

He jumped in, put it in first gear, and released the

emergency brake. Kept his foot poised on the gas pedal in case the car started to go and watched her in his side mirror. "Car's anchored. Jump *now!*"

She shoved open the door, a hard task at that angle. Pushing herself upward, she widened the space with her shoulders.

Then she hung suspended, only her torso out, for long moments.

The car rocked and wobbled.

The rail shrieked in protest.

The taut line groaned.

Jake nudged the gas pedal before force could drag the truck.

"I'm stuck," she gasped. "Door's heavy."

Another rail support sprang free with a loud pop like a gunshot.

He was powerless to help her. Could only keep the line taut and wait. And pray. Those nails still in his gut jabbed him again and again. "Hurry! It's going."

She heaved at the door. Dived out head first. Landed in a heap beneath the tilted car.

The railing broke and tumbled over the cliff. Rocks and soil slid after it. The sedan skidded sideways a few feet. Rocked. Threatened to right itself. It could fall and crush her.

Lani lay still.

Jake's chest squeezed. Maybe the fall knocked her unconscious? He killed the engine, released the knot. Dashed to her. The stiff muscle in his thigh pulled but he pushed on. "Get up! *Move!*"

Sucking in deep breaths, she scrambled to her feet.

He slung an arm around her. Together they staggered away from the cliff and the teetering vehicle.

He looked back as the car rolled over the cliff.

The tow rope followed, whipping back and forth like a live snake. The first impact, as loud as a crate of C-4, killed the headlights. Steel scraped and slammed against rocks. Glass shattered with the impact.

The busted-up vehicle hit the water with a tsunami splash. Then all was silent except the waves churning against the rocks.

Still trembling, Lani clung to him. He wrapped his arms around her and held on. Waited for his heart rate to slow and for the tight pain in his gut to ease.

Feeling her against him, she felt athletic and strong, and her lemony scent—shampoo—reassured him. "You okay? Anything broken?"

"I'm fine. Just pissed as hell." With unsteady steps, she trudged to the cliff and peered over the edge.

He joined her. The moonlight showed only roiling water. "Careful. The edge is unstable."

She stepped back gingerly, sighing. "My poor car. Totaled."

"Did that speeding pickup have something to do with this?"

"Of course it was that asshole. You think I have a death wish?" She laid a palm on her cheek in mock dismay.

Her sarcasm ought to grate like sandpaper on sunburn, but in-your-face beat woe-is-me any day. "Chill. I was just asking."

"Sorry. I'm sniping at you when I should be thanking you for saving my life." She huffed out a breath and hugged herself.

He squatted down to distance himself from the temptation to hold her again. And to ease his leg. He poked through the stones at his feet and picked up one of the railing's bolts, now bent and useless. "After he went around the curve, he nearly hit me head on."

Her brows winged upward. "Can you identify the truck?"

Standing, Jake cursed himself inwardly. "Wish I could. Guy'd been in a mud run or a swamp. Front and back, both license plates were unreadable. His lights blinded me." Some trained federal agent. He didn't know the make or color either other than dark. He heaved the mangled bolt into the ocean. Should be the pickup's driver. "Could've been an accident. You sure he wasn't out-of-control drunk?"

"*That* was no accident." She angled her chin. Sharper than ever, her eyes blazed. "He might've been drinking, but what he did was deliberate. He bumped me once just before the turn. Then he smashed me sideways at the sharpest point in the curve. But why?"

The likely answer weaved like smoke through him, into every crevice, whispering dread. What the hell could he do? Protecting Lani would be a 24/7 job. Not a job he'd risk. To find answers in the cold case, he needed time, and he couldn't tell her he was eyes and ears on something else for the task force.

He took her elbow and headed for his SUV. "I'm afraid your arrival has awakened Dragon Harbor's live fire-breathing dragon."

She shook him off and stepped back, muscles taut and ready for flight. "The gossip network works fast. I arrived a week ago and started printing out the news stories in the library like you did. I've read them all. You're right to be suspicious. I phoned the Maine State Fire Marshal's office to obtain the final report but a prissy-voiced clerk said I need to file an official request." She huffed her disgust at the delay. "I did a timeline of the fire marshal's statements, of when the information came out. The fire was on August 8. Barely two weeks later, they declared it accidental. A mere two weeks!"

"Maybe the cause was obvious. Happens sometimes."

"Sometimes but not *that* time. The arson guy relied on the local firefighters' impressions. Shoddy investigating if you ask me." She kicked stones with her sneaker toe. "You know as well as I do Dragon Harbor firefighters are volunteers and barely trained. And they never explained the beam that fell on—" She folded her lips between her teeth.

Jake tucked his hands in his back pockets. "Okay, okay, I do see enough to warrant looking into the matter."

"So you'll let me help you?"

"I thought we'd covered that."

"Not by half. Especially now I've read more." Her eyes widened in sudden realization. "You said my 'arrival' awakened the dragon, not my research. What are you getting at?"

He shook his head. "Answer this first. You said you didn't remember. Nothing at all of the fire?"

"Not much. I remember mostly *before* the fire. Then coming out on the porch and seeing flames shooting out of the barn. After that, nothing."

"Tonight was a deliberate attempt to run you off the road. Think about it," he said. "Who would want to eliminate you?"

Lani's stomach sank. His question ignited what she'd tried to deny, squeezing her lungs so her breath burned in her throat. The burnt cat and the dollhouse. What if it wasn't bored teens? "You think the fire was no accident, but *arson*? And Gail's death was—" She couldn't utter the word.

"Murder," he supplied, his voice rough. "In the state of Maine, if an arson fire results in a death, that's considered murder." The moonlight shone on his face. He was studying her.

Shivers raced across her skin. "But I don't *know* anything. I don't know if I saw anyone. I don't remember."

"Yet," he said. "But you might. I doubt these attacks have anything to do with your library printouts."

She wobbled. Fatigue clawed at her. She was too frazzled to play verbal ping-pong.

"You should sit down. I'll call the cops." He led her to the SUV, opened the passenger door, and eased her to the seat. He touched a finger to her cheek. "You're bleeding."

"What?" When she reached up, blood dripped from her hand.

He cradled her hands in his big, warm ones. Turning them showed flayed flesh on her palms. Blood welled around the gravel and sand embedded in deeper gouges. "The blood on your cheek came from this."

Lani stared at her palms. "I must've scraped my hands when I fell from the car. They don't hurt."

"They will. Like hell. And soon. The cops can meet us at the hospital emergency room. I'll call 911 on the way." Taking out his phone, he closed her door.

Her mind reeled from his questions and the pickup's attack. Jake had saved her life. *Oh, Gail, what the hell happened that night?* Pressure built in her chest enough to explode.

He revved the engine and then peeled up the East Road toward town.

Her palms began to sting. Far more agonizing were the questions piercing her heart.

\*\*\*\*

Last night at the emergency room, Nora had been on duty and helped patch her up, clucking soothing nonsense as Lani fumed about the hit and run. The next morning, Nora helped her dress and changed her bandages. Then Nora drove her to the police station for an appointment with the police chief.

The police occupied part of a renovated brick fish-packing plant that also housed the fire department and the town offices. Forced to wait in the reception area, she could barely sit still. If not for her injury, she'd be popping her knuckles. Her sister used to rag on her about that nervous habit and she used to tease Gail about twisting her hair. Throat stinging at the memory, she tried not to fidget.

This morning she'd gone over the old newspaper stories again, but found nothing new. Only the final report was public information, not the evidence or tests done by the investigator. Lani couldn't even obtain the name of the investigator. She wanted his notes, not just his reports.

She listened to the static-filled calls of officers at the central reception desk. A cat up a tree, a fender-bender, a domestic dispute. Not major crime like the robberies and murders in major cities. The chief, a sergeant, and three patrol officers. A small force for a safe town— except for her cold case. And her hit-and-run. Maybe they'd found the truck.

A few minutes later, the chief sent for her.

"Sorry to keep you waitin', dear." Norman Galt's Down-East accent turned the Maine courtesy into *deah*. One of the deep creases in his chiseled face winked into a dimple as he smiled. "I was on the phone with M.C.U. That's the state police Major Crimes Unit. Doesn't pay to cut 'em short."

"I understand." She took the straight chair by his worn wooden desk. Rich coffee aroma rose from the mug in his hand. On it were the words, *#1 Grampy*. File cabinets and crowded shelves spoke of mountains of red tape, but certificates and photos on the walls showed his dedication. He offered coffee but she refused. Too painful to hold a cup.

"How're you doing today?"

"Not too bad." Her palms stung like hell and every muscle in her body ached like she'd been beaten with a mallet. A prescription allowed her to sleep through the night—without nightmares—but today she was sticking to ibuprofen. She needed to stay sharp.

"Devil's Elbow." He shook his head. "You were lucky to make it out of that car."

"Lucky Jake happened along." While Galt rattled on about the dangers of coastal roads, she nodded politely.

Warmth suffused her as she recalled how Jake had saved her life. His embrace meant nothing. He was only being kind. That he'd stuck by her at the hospital also meant nothing. Like any man, he couldn't be counted on long-term. She did need his help. What if someone really did cause Gail's death? And what if they were coming after her now? The questions chased circles in her belly like the nausea she'd felt last night seeing her hands leaking blood.

40

She noticed Galt had paused. "About my car, have they towed it out of the water?"

"Ayuh. Quite a chore too. A crane hauled it off the rocks at low tide this morning." He smoothed his graying hair with one hand. He then reached to a shelf behind his desk for a sealed plastic bag. "Got this out. Probably ruined."

"Thanks." She accepted her soggy canvas handbag with careful fingers. She had some cash at the house but the bag contained her driver's license, credit cards, and checkbook. At least the plastic would be usable. "Did you get samples of the truck's paint from my car?"

"Car's all stove up. Totaled, I'd say. But we didn't find any foreign paint."

She gaped at him. "How can that be? He hit me twice."

He shook his head. "Possible the rocks scraped it off. You sure you don't know the color? Or the make?"

"Just a dark pickup. A huge one." She sighed, but brightened when an idea struck her. "The truck should have dents, maybe white paint from my car."

"I have my sergeant checking into it." He folded his hands on the desk, and his skeptical gaze flickered to her before he looked away. "You insist the driver hit you on purpose?"

A pang at his skepticism stabbed her chest. She steadied her voice. "He hit me twice. His action was deliberate. Maybe the same person who burned that poor little cat."

"Seems doubtful. What's the connection?"

She twisted in her seat and crossed her legs. "Could be something to do with the fire that killed my sister and injured me."

A frown furrowed the chief's forehead. "I was an officer back then. First one on the scene along with the fire department. Terrible tragedy. This town hasn't had such a deadly fire since. Investigator had a hard time with that one, although in the end he pegged it an accident. Tough case for Frank Tyson. He retired afterward."

Ah, she remembered an investigator questioning her, but while she was drugged and grieving. And now she had the name that wasn't in the clippings. *Tyson.* "I'm sure you were in the loop. Do you have copies of the reports?"

Galt straightened, his expression cool, blank. "The fire marshal kept this office apprised of progress, but I have no reports."

Lani scooted forward on her chair. She had to make him understand. "I have reason to suspect the fire wasn't an accident. Arson would mean my sister was murdered. Maybe someone's afraid I'll find the truth. The flaming dollhouse and the burnt cat were warnings. Now someone has tried to kill me."

"The cat thing's a right nasty business, I grant you. But I can't see the crash your way. Both you and Jake Wescott saw an out-of-control pickup on that curve. Maybe that driver caused you to skid off the road and then your car rolled over the cliff. My department will try to find the truck and determine what happened."

His tone of voice said he doubted her story. Heat crawled up her neck. She'd curl her hands into fists if they didn't hurt so damn much. "*I* know what happened was *no* accident."

"Maybe somebody's threatening you. Maybe not. I'll give the fire marshal's office a call. See what they say. I doubt they'll see matters any different than I do. You'd be wise to lock your doors from now on and let us handle it."

She went still. Her pulse rattled. "Is that a warning?"

He flattened his palms on the desk. "Take it that way if it'll keep you out of trouble."

"Maybe a deliberate attack on me will get the fire investigators' attention." It sure as hell didn't have Galt's.

He shook his head, smoothed his mustache. "Too nebulous. They'd jump in if you had *real* evidence. As I understand it, you don't remember much of anything about the fire."

What she remembered and what she'd dreamed in the haze of pain swirled in her mind like soured cotton candy. She raised her chin. "That *was* true."

His eyebrows shot north. "I'd like to know if you remember something, anything at all."

"Not your case, is it, Chief Galt? It's the state fire marshal's office I should tell."

Chapter Five

WHEN LANI DIDN'T see Jake's blue SUV in the drive of his grandmother's house, her shoulders drooped. The walk from the police station was less than a mile, but her sore body felt like she'd just hiked the Knife Edge of Mount Katahdin. Backwards. But, whoo hoo, here came the man as if she'd conjured him. Maybe she was psychic. Then again, a psychic would have prevented the fire or run into the barn in time to save Gail. She rubbed her chest with the back of one hand.

"Hey, Lani," Jake called as he exited the vehicle. "You come to make fun of my amateur carpentry?"

He looked good in well-worn jeans and a blue oxford shirt that matched his eyes. No harm in looking. She'd looked often enough when they were younger.

"I didn't, but thanks for the warning. I need someone to do repairs at the farm, but I'll cross your name off my list."

They climbed the three porch steps, weathered and sagging from generations of running children. He opened the door and waved her inside. "For now, I'm doing mostly demolition. My specialty."

The sun-washed scent of his cotton shirt and a faint trace of spicy aftershave caught her off guard. Shaking off the impact, she filed past him into the bungalow's living room. Piles of jagged plaster and lath, a sledge hammer and power tools, and black trash bags filled to bursting lay about.

"Whoa, has Dragon Harbor had a tornado I don't know about?"

He laughed, the first time she'd heard his rich voice in full force. He used to laugh all the time. They all did.

"Told you. Demolition. Too much of the lath and plaster is mouse-eaten and mildewed from roof leaks. All of it has to go. Hank had the roof done so all's dry now. New drywall is next. A learning experience."

"So's driving my car off a cliff. Don't think I want to give either one a try. Kudos to you for having the guts. The farmhouse doesn't need nearly as much."

He gestured for her to follow him toward the kitchen. "We can sit on the back porch. I haven't messed it up too bad. I want to talk to you anyway."

"You said last night you were headed to the farm. Because you wanted to talk to me?"

He didn't answer her, but stopped in the kitchen to snatch a couple of colas from the ancient fridge.

She shook her head and held up her bandaged hands. "I'll pass unless you have a straw. Or maybe you want to hold the can up to my mouth."

The lines around his eyes tightened in embarrassment. He gave her a crooked grin. "My bad. I wasn't thinking. No straws, and I wouldn't trust me not to spill soda on you."

Scattered around the screened porch were a padded wicker loveseat, some Adirondack chairs, a stack of packing boxes, and a bench.

Gesturing for her to take the loveseat, he paced, regarding her with enough intensity to see through her bones. "Just wanted to make sure you were all right."

"Lucky for me you tried. I wouldn't be sitting here

otherwise. You'd think after all these years, I'd be over my fire phobia. Post-traumatic stress."

He shifted one shoulder in an offhand shrug. "PTSD's a hard thing to shake. Even with counseling."

"I've had plenty of that, believe me." She stopped there. More, like descriptions of her nightmares, would be TMI. She looked out over a freshly mowed backyard with overgrown shrubbery—lilac bushes, a row of rhododendrons, others she didn't recognize. The scent of late lilacs drifted on the light breeze.

"There's another reason I wanted to talk to you," he said. "Something you don't know about the night of the fire. Something I've regretted every day since."

The pain on his face made the breath clog in her chest. She forced herself to inhale slowly. Keeping her sore hands still in her lap took effort. "Regret. About what?"

He swigged down some of his soda and closed the distance between them. The force of his emotion reached out to her like the heat of his body. He dropped into the seat beside her as if he could no longer stand and rubbed his left thigh.

His aquamarine eyes bored into hers. "Gail was different that night. Edgy and jittery, like she wanted me to leave. We'd been having problems."

"Like what?"

"Broken dates. Rants about how she felt smothered. We used to have great talks, about everything—college, sports, our dreams. But for weeks before the fire, she was quiet a lot. Not sad, just distant. Other times she was almost manic."

"I noticed her moods too," Lani said. "Dreamy. And sometimes giddy. Or bitter. Gail was always moody but this was more. I called her on it, but she wouldn't open up."

"And there's something else you should know. Gail didn't dump me that night. *I* broke up with *her*." He drove fingers through his hair.

Lani shook her head. Jake had no reason to lie about it. "What? Because of the moods?"

He stared out the screening as if seeing a replay of that night. "I asked about another guy. She shrugged off the question. She called earlier and broke our date. Said she wanted a quiet evening. Another in a string of lame excuses. I went over anyway. Never got past the driveway. Told her if she didn't want me around, we were done. I didn't need the hassle."

"She came inside saying she'd dumped *you*." Gail had also called him boring. It was nuts. He'd always made Lani laugh, was fun to be with. "And then?"

"I drove around in the truck—used to be Dad's—for a long time. An hour or more. Ended up at Todd Hokkanen's house, his parents' place on Ridge Road. The guys had a poker game going. I played cards about twenty minutes or a half hour before we heard the sirens."

She dragged her eyes from his tortured ones while she got her mind around this new reality. "So what's your regret?" Although she could guess.

He shifted in his seat, rubbed his thigh. "Don't you see? If I hadn't left her that night, she might still be alive. And you—"

"Wouldn't have been burned. We've been through this. Spare me the pity party, Wescott. I should've saved her but I was too late."

"I should've made an effort to get at what was going

on with her."

"What *was* going on with Gail? I don't know either."

Jake's cheeks flushed red and as he swallowed, his Adam's-apple jumped a mile. "There's something you don't know. Gail had sex with someone that night."

She must look like she'd been socked with a fresh-caught halibut. Working with wily teenagers had taught her most people didn't lie well. She watched him for signs of dissembling. "With you?"

"Not me. Sure as hell not after that argument. The report says apparently consensual sex, not forced. Traces of condom lubricant but not enough DNA to trace. Dammit, there *was* another guy. She lied. *Son of a bitch.*" He shot his gaze upward, blinking, as if fighting for control.

He'd been a victim of the arson too. The fire had snuffed out that carefree guy. A sad note among many. She sank back against the wicker. "That explains my vague memory of someone—the investigator—asking me about Gail having sex."

"He asked me too, but I told him we had an argument and I left."

"I'll bet what's left of Birch Brook Farm that fire was no accident. The guy she had sex with started the fire. Did he kill her and use the fire to cover up his crime?"

In the backyard, a seagull landed on the gas grill. It gazed around with its beady eyes as if waiting for Jake's response to her statement. In the neighbor's yard, a dog barked, and the gull took off.

Jake pondered his next words carefully. He didn't want Lani haring off into more danger than she already had. "Let's not leap over the Grand Canyon to that conclusion. But I've found enough discrepancies that I believe the case should be reopened. Looks like the fire investigator started out thinking arson was a possibility. Why the final report turned a one-eighty to accidental fire, I'd like to know."

"I was going to Augusta to file a request for the investigator's report but—" As if realization struck, she held up her bandaged hands and sat up straighter, her gaze alight with hope. "Wait. Sounds like you actually have reports *and* notes."

"Some of the case files, yeah. Departmental courtesy. I'm waiting for the rest." He placed a hand on her forearm. Gingerly, taking care not to hurt her. He felt her tense before relaxing a fraction. "Be careful, Lani. The truck last night could be an accident but—"

"I told you; it was no accident." She heaved a long sigh. "Okay, if I want your cooperation, I need to level. There was another incident three days before the burnt cat. First I went along with the police chief's conclusion it was teenagers, but no more."

"Incident? Not an overt attack, you mean."

"More along the line of threat. I woke up to find a doll house burning on the front lawn—a big homemade, wooden one, the size of a dog house. The officer who came suggested bored teenagers. Everyone local knows about the Cameron fire, he said, but he'd look into it. Chief Galt knows about both dirty tricks but apparently the officer who came Friday didn't."

"Damn, both seem like twisted teen pranks, cruel ones. But damned sophomoric for a believable threat." He scraped knuckles along his jaw.

"If not kids, maybe calculated to look like pranks,

but created to scare me. Someone sees me as the weak link. The surviving sister, emotionally fragile, easily frightened."

He shook his head. "Frightened, yeah, and you should be. But if I the woman I see now is the same Lani Cameron I used to know, not easily frightened *away*."

She smiled. "My apologies to your mom, who ruled a tight ship, but the current D Harbor librarian's volunteers could give lessons to social networking sites. As soon as I followed your lead with the old news stories, word spread faster than 4G around the peninsula."

"Delinquents, maybe." He had his doubts. "But not the ramming on Devil's Elbow."

"Exactly." She tilted her head, her smile waning to something more serious. "I did some other research online. Found a news story in a New Hampshire paper. An ATF agent was killed and another wounded in the leg during a search of a suspected arms smuggling dump. The wounded agent was Jacob Wescott. Fixing this house is only one reason you're here. Recovery's the other."

"You're right, but that's no secret." He clasped her hand and placed it gently on his left thigh, on the hard ridge of scar tissue. "I have scars, Lani. Just where you don't see. I lost a friend in that explosion. I don't want to worry about *you* too."

"I'm already in this. Like you said, they can scare me, but they can't scare me away. Together is more efficient. Safer, and we can help each other. I'm good at research. Case in point, I'm waiting for a call back from two of the reporters. We both need answers, to know if what we suspect is true."

He slugged down the rest of his cola. Watching her,

he ran his tongue around his teeth. He set his empty can on the floor beside the wicker seat. "No, I won't have you help me investigate. I can do my own research or hire somebody." He clamped his mouth into a tight line and drew a deep breath. "I told you I'd share anything I find out. What you can do is work with me to try to remember."

She huffed. "What is that supposed to mean?"

"You said you had counseling. What about hypnosis?"

Lani shot off the wicker seat, wincing at the pull in muscles that had to be sore as hell. "Hypnosis, what a joke! I tried hypnotherapy a couple times, for the nightmares. The damn therapist couldn't take me under. I stayed just as alert as I am now." She stalked into the house.

"There must be a way." He followed her into the shambles of the living room.

She stopped and rounded on him. "And that was my plan. To find the facts of what happened that night. What do they say? The truth shall set you free?'

"Lani… come on."

"But no, I'm supposed to sit with my bandaged hands in my lap? Not gonna happen. I can't wait for you to—" she made air quotes with her bandaged hands "—share. When they find my cold, dead body by the side of the road, see how that hits your conscience."

He laughed, but without humor. "Whoa, you play dirty."

She marched out the door. "If you change your mind, you know where I am. Then I'll be happy to *share* with you what I find out—from *my* sources."

Chapter Six

JAKE HAD SPOILED her dramatic exit by insisting he drive her home, but the next morning, Lani was ready to charge ahead. She had coffee ready when Nora arrived.

A short denim skirt seemed easier to manage than capris throughout the day, topped by a camisole and tee-shirt. Dressed and her hair brushed, she felt better, alert after forgoing the heavy-duty meds last night. No nightmare for a change either, she realized as they descended the stairs.

Nora poured the coffee and they sat at the kitchen table. The rich French roast aroma blended with her fresh-scrubbed scent. She sighed over her steaming mug even as she tsked her disapproval. "You should've waited for me to make the coffee. Better yet, I should've brought coffee."

"I can't just sit around. I've done the invalid thing. No more. I'm okay." She had too much to do and no time to waste. Looking at the scabs as Nora dabbed antiseptic ointment on her palms, Lani figured she was healed enough to drive.

Nora finished taping the gauze. "Not too bad. Scabbed over nicely. You won't need bandages in a couple of days. But I'm worried about you out here all by yourself. If your suspicions are right and someone killed Gail, the danger won't end with that hit and run.

You could stay with us until Jake finds answers. The boys would love having you there."

*Really. Not all the boys, definitely not Kevin.* "I'm fine and I'll stay here. No problem. I love your sons, but I need to be here to organize the work on the place."

"Can't that wait a few days?"

It could, but she took a different tack to respond to Nora's real concern. "And with the police looking into the hit and run, no one will try anything. It'd be too obvious." Not that she really believed Galt and his little staff were doing much. She summoned a confident smile.

Nora held up her hands in defeat. "If you change your mind, the spare room is yours." She snapped her fingers. "I almost forgot. Tomorrow's Thursday. I can't make it in the morning. Dentist appointments for both my little guys. I could stop by later?"

Later wouldn't work, not if she achieved what she wanted today. "If you leave me some bandages and stuff, I can do it myself. By tomorrow, I should be self-sufficient."

Nora looked dubious but agreed. They chatted a few minutes more—about the upcoming town festival—as they finished their coffee.

She stood and deposited their mugs in the sink. "Got to get back to the boys. Mom's there for a bit. She'll take over when I go to work. Kevin has a campaign something tonight."

"I appreciate the help, Nore." Lani popped up. "Can you give me a ride into the village?"

"Again?" Her friend's eyes narrowed as she arranged bandages, tape, and the antiseptic ointment on the table. She hooked her medical kit over her shoulder. "Not the police station. What are you up to?"

"Only a little more research at the library. I have the old fire investigator's name. An Internet search ought to come up with his address." She shrugged into the hoodie on the back of her chair.

"God, Lani, you're going to end up with more trouble."

"Trouble, yes, but not for me."

"Why don't you just stay here and take it easy?"

"Not gonna happen. I owe it to my twin to find answers." *And fast, before another attack.* Ignoring the twinges in her chest, Lani collected her tote bag and slung it on her shoulder. "Now are you going to give me a ride or do I have to call Bayport Taxi, which would cost me at least forty-five dollars—one way?"

Her friend's gaze softened even as she sighed. "When have I ever won an argument with you?" She shook a finger in admonition. "But I'm watching you lock this house up tight."

Gingerly, with her forefinger and thumb, Lani fished out her keys and held them up. "Ready to lock up, Mommy."

\*\*\*\*

Lani's research took longer than expected. She found three obituaries for a Frank Tyson, but none of them had worked for the state in any capacity, let alone arson investigation. A cement company in Bridgton was headed by Frank Tyson, but he was forty-five, too young. Finally typing into the search engine in quotes *Maine retired arson investigator Frank Tyson* uncovered a small news article. Two years before, Tyson, of Oak Mills, spoke on fire safety to his granddaughter's fifth grade class. Then an online phone directory supplied his number and address.

She tucked her legal pad and pen in her big bag and left the library. After a shrimp salad plate—easier to manage than a sandwich—at the Cuppa-'n-Suppa, she picked up a ready-made salad and a frozen dinner at the general store. She stowed them the thermal bag she'd brought in her tote.

Finally she set out to rent a car. Buoyed by her success, she didn't mind the half-mile hike up the East Road beyond the village. Her muscles didn't feel as tight today, but by the time she arrived, the sun beating down beaded sweat on her brow.

The owner of Buddy's Garage and Bait Shop stepped from beneath the sedan on his lift and ambled toward her. Two other men in the garage's tilting wooden building continued working amid the whine of power tools. Buddy wiped his grease-covered hands with an equally filthy rag, then tucked the cloth into a pocket in his coveralls.

Affable as always, he ambled toward her, his narrow face crinkled in a smile. "Heard about your car. Rotten luck. Some jackass run you off the road, folks're sayin'."

"Something like that, Buddy."

His eyes lit up with the prospect of work. "Need some body work, do you?"

"I wish. Nope, the car was totaled."

"Well then, you must need some wheels to tide you over. I got just the thing. Cheap."

Twenty minutes later, Lani was the proud renter of a battered lime-green coupe. Thank God for automatic transmissions, she thought, as she headed south toward the farm. Steering on the curving road aggravated her still-tender hands but not as much as shifting gears would have.

She concentrated on the beauty around her—sun glinting diamonds on the bay, pine-tree-dotted islands beyond the shore—and not the sheer drop on the far side of the narrow road. A big black pickup sped toward her, high on oversize tires, and her heart began to pound.

The driver gave a wave out his open window as he passed. Just another Mainer being neighborly. She blew out a breath and waved back. The guy probably wondered about her hand, wearing what must look like a white mitten. Not your normal June attire.

"I got this. No prob," she said to the VW.

Up ahead loomed the Devil's Elbow.

Her heart tried to jump into her throat, and she swallowed hard. Forcing herself not to grip the wheel too tightly, she slowed to negotiate the sharp turn. No monster truck bore down on her. No cliff edge tried to drag her over. Only the severed guard rail dangling over the waves crashing onto the rocks.

And then she'd made it past and the road turned more inland, toward the farm.

After eating her nuked turkey dinner, she vowed to shop for real food now that she wasn't dependent on anyone for transportation.

Armed with the legal pad on which she'd written Frank Tyson's information, she keyed his number in her cell phone.

When he picked up, she said, "Mr. Tyson, this is Lani Cameron."

A harsh intake of breath. "What do you want?"

\*\*\*\*

Lani suppressed a smug attitude as she sat in the passenger seat of Jake's SUV. They headed up the East Road from the farm in what locals called a "thick-o'fog," typical of June's fluky weather.

Jake showing up this afternoon as she was leaving was no coincidence. She'd kept her research away from the nosy library volunteer's gaze, but Buddy outed her on the car rental. When the garage owner clucked over her driving with sore hands, she'd said something like, "Not far, only to Oak Mills." If Jake figured out her plan, she wasn't turning away the result she wanted in the first place. Don't look in a gift horse's mouth or something like that.

"Bad move to set out alone like this. Dangerous." He looked straight ahead, at the road, not at her.

He looked sexy as hell in khakis and a black French-terry shirt. Brown hairs curling above the V-neck invited touching. A scar on his face she hadn't noticed before. His hands held the steering wheel lightly, regardless of the irritation in his voice. He had broad hands, calloused and sun-darkened, like his sinewy forearms.

She went on the offensive. "I could've driven just fine. I drove the rental car home last night."

He reached for her left hand and turned it palm up. His blue gaze was direct and unflinching. "You're still bandaged. Driving could open the wounds."

She snatched away her hand. "But it didn't."

"So now you're stubborn *and* independent. You wanted my help the other day."

The rich timbre of his voice tripped her pulse. She sniffed with what she hoped conveyed disdain. "I don't want charity. You refused, unless I'm dreaming. Oh, I guess not. Here you are."

"Word's around you remember things you didn't before. If that truck's love-tap was an arsonist's first attempt to kill you, I'd hate to see the encore. Why go see Frank Tyson?"

"You have files. I don't. The police chief mentioned the other day the investigator was retired. I researched Tyson like I did you and found he lived less than an hour away. I talked him into seeing me. The fire marshal's office won't provide more than the final report—and apparently neither will you—but I thought Tyson might have personal notes."

When he didn't respond, she went on. "Stupid of me to object to you driving. Thanks for coming. I need your savvy about fires and interrogation."

On a slow grin, he tipped his head toward her hands. "Must be hard to admit you can't do everything. Give up some of your independence."

She sniffed. "Only temporary."

The DHPD had no leads on the hit-and-run. Eliminating a few lead-footed fishermen and teens with dark-colored trucks was the extent of the progress. She, on the other hand, had a lead. Maybe Tyson's notes would provide a clue. Anxiety and hope bubbled inside her.

\*\*\*\*

When the scene of Lani's near disaster loomed ahead, Jake cast a sideways glance at her.

Mouth compressed and shoulders tight, she stared through the mist at the severed guardrail of the Devil's Elbow as if daring it to intimidate her. As the SUV took the sharp curve and passed the site, she exhaled.

"Nerve-racking, driving this yesterday?"

"Wasn't bad. Like getting on a horse after falling."

"Atta girl."

She glared at him, but with teasing in her hazel eyes. *"Girl?"*

"*Atta woman* doesn't resonate." When she started to object, he added, "No more than *atta man*. But I stand corrected. *Woman. All* woman."

Color rose in her cheeks and she turned to look out the passenger window.

The bravado and longing in her defenses tightened his chest. He had to admit he wanted the truth almost as much as she did. And she roused all his protective instincts when he should take a U-turn. No one should trust him for protection. If the retired investigator had nothing new, maybe he could persuade Lani to quit.

Right. And the harbor's rock dragon was a living sea monster.

The road took them through D Harbor with its antique Cape Cod and Federal-period houses. Outside the village, private roads led to houses hidden in stands of spruce, birch, and hackmatack. The verdant fields of a farm rolled down to the bay. Cattle grazed in one and a woman on a tractor was mowing the first hay crop in another. When he'd worked as sternman on his uncle's lobster boat, he admired those same fields from the water. Good to see some things hadn't changed since those days.

He slanted a glance toward Lani. Getting her talking might open up other topics. "You said your mom was on a cruise. What about your dad?"

"In his office, I suppose." She hunched a shoulder in a gesture of nonchalance. "My parents are divorced. They've both remarried."

A rift with her dad? He wondered, but she didn't seem interested in expanding. "I'm sorry to hear that."

She turned toward him, her expression softened. "It's okay, mostly. But your dad died years ago, when you were just a kid. It must've been hard, losing him like that."

The first sympathetic thing she'd said. "Thanks. I guess you never knew him. The boat was swamped by a freak wave. Neither he nor his sternman had a chance."

"How's your mom? Is she still in Portland?" She turned away as if embarrassed to indulge in small talk.

His fingers tightened on the wheel. "She retired a while ago, bought a little house in Bayport. But now she's at Pine View Rest."

"My God, Jake, I'm so sorry. What… happened?"

Her empathetic tone cracked open his defenses about Grace. Lani'd known her in much better times. "When she started forgetting things, neither of us—Hank and me—realized what the decline meant. We were clueless idiots. Gradually she lost it. Stopped seeing her friends. Drove through traffic lights, wandered the East Road. Got lost in Bayport."

"Dementia. Alzheimer's?"

"Early onset. And meds for acid reflux weakened her bones. After she broke her hip in November, my brother took care of things. She couldn't really participate in physical therapy so she's in a wheelchair."

"A third reason you're back in Maine. Her care is up to you now? Where's Hank?"

"He manages a boat yard in Portland. Has a wife and son. We see each other more now I'm here."

She pressed her tongue to her upper lip and then turned away. Was she thinking about what he'd told her or was he reading too much into her silence? Lani could have a sharp tongue but when people were hurting, she was always kind.

"Before that summer," she said, "you were majoring

in architecture. The ATF, you joined because of the fire, because of Gail."

At her interest, a pleasant buzz curled along his nape. "No denying it. I changed my major to criminal justice."

"Your leg scar, that's from a serious wound. Has your injury ended your ATF career?"

"PT helped. I'm okay. Stiffens up some but the muscle's getting better all the time." Now if only his internal scars could be healed by physical therapy and stretching.

After a moment, she said quietly, "I had a lot of therapy too."

The anguish in her voice shook him. "Your burns were pretty bad."

She tucked her bandaged hands beneath her arms. "Severe, yes, on the side of my face, my back, and shoulder. The Massachusetts General Hospital Burn Center kept me for months. I was wild with pain and grief for Gail. Medication put me out of it through the surgeries. I don't remember much of that time."

Reconstruction must've taken its toll. Maybe too much. "At the time, I heard burning debris fell on you from the loft."

She nodded, lifting a hand to touch her facial scar. "Fixing this scar would've skewed in my hairline, so I let it go. I'm lucky to have my hair. Apparently I covered my head with a wet towel before I charged into the barn."

"You pulled Gail out." A damned brave and foolhardy move, but it was her sister. He got it.

"Too late. Getting knocked out by a beam, she inhaled too much smoke." The pain in her voice reached into his chest and twisted sharply.

When they stopped at the traffic light marking the head of the peninsula, she said, "Go left, then Route 23 to Oak Mills."

When they were headed that direction, he said, "I'm surprised Tyson agreed to see you."

Her eyes brightened. "He didn't, not at first. When I threatened to park in his driveway until he talked to me, he gave in. He said he kept his personal notes. Exactly my hope."

The route took them away from the coastal fog and into clear skies. The narrow two-lane road climbed tree-covered hills and dipped into a valley where a lake gleamed blue in the sun like stretched plastic.

"We're early. Tyson's place is closer than I thought." He pulled over at a public boat-launch ramp and stopped the vehicle. Three trucks with boat trailers sat in parking places, the owners out buzzing around on the lake.

He walked around to open her door, but Ms. Independence had managed in spite of her bandaged hands. The clean air smelled of wet sand and algae.

He stood by her side at the lake's edge. Silvery minnows darted in the clear shallows. Squeals of delight rippled from the public beach farther down the shore. "So what's this about you starting to remember?"

On a sigh of resignation, she turned to look at him. "I let the police chief think I remembered something. If what we learn from Tyson jogs my memory, maybe I *will* have something new. Then they'll have to reopen the case. Maybe I saw something. Or someone."

He touched her nose, pinked by the sun. "You're poking your pretty nose in where it could get bitten off."

A blush crept up her golden-tanned cheeks. Didn't

she know she was hot? Gail flaunted her looks and used them. But not Lani. Was it the fire that had taken away her self-confidence?

She huffed and twitched her shoulders. "Dammit, Jake, finding some shred of evidence to get the case re-opened is worth the risk."

He wanted to look away from the pain and longing in her eyes, but forced himself to hold her gaze. Odd, but when he looked at her, he no longer saw Gail's face. There was too much shared pain between them for anything more than friendship, no matter how drawn to her he was.

But he couldn't help himself. He lifted her chin and brushed a quick kiss on her mouth.

Or he meant to be quick, but the trust in her eyes and the warmth of her lips and her lemony scent clouded his brain. And when her mouth clung to his, instead of pulling away, he wrapped her in his arms. Her taste went from sweet and warm to zinging shock waves of heat through his system. Not dragging her down on the ground and going for more took all his will power.

When at last they separated, her eyes were at half-mast and her lips were plumped from his kiss. He backed away. "I shouldn't have done that. I can't—"

"No big deal, Wescott. A kiss." She dismissed it with an insouciant wave. But her cheeks flushed almost as red as her tee-shirt. "You must be deprived. Just shut up and take me to Tyson's." She sashayed back to the SUV.

"Yes, ma'am." Back in the driver's seat—but only literally—he turned the key and steered back onto the rural road. He'd almost blown it back there. Sensations rocketed through him. The yearning of a man who'd been out in the cold for too long and had just found hearth and home. Was it Lani he wanted? Or was he remembering Gail?

Dangerous. He had to stash those confusing feelings where they couldn't pop out at him.

She rattled the paper with Tyson's directions. "We should be almost there. It's a cedar-shingled Cape."

A few moments later, she leaned forward, peering ahead. "I smell smoke."

He caught a hint of it. No surprise she was hypersensitive to fire. "Probably someone burning brush."

Eyes wide with dread, she'd gone as pale as the paper she held. She pointed ahead. "I see Tyson's mailbox up ahead, the red one shaped like a fire truck."

Jake smelled charred wood but musty and sour and mingled with an acrid tang. He knew that odor better than she did and it wasn't from burning brush. He braced for the worst as he turned into the gravel drive by the rural mailbox. Yellow police tape blocked the drive. He cut the engine and stared.

"Oh, God!" She pressed her bandaged hands to her mouth. "I talked to Tyson only last night."

Two water-soaked walls and a brick chimney were all that remained of the house. A broken picture frame hung askew on soot-blackened stripes of wallpaper. A few blackened posts marked the location of the attached barn.

"He could've gotten out. Maybe he's all right." But his ATF sixth sense told him otherwise.

They left the vehicle and stood at the tape barrier. Tendrils of smoke curled from smoldering embers in the granite-block foundation and that of the attached barn.

Up close, the flat-out stink stung his nose and eyes.

"No, no, please, God, no," Lani whispered. "It can't be."

Blue lights flashed behind them. He turned to see two black sheriff's department cruisers pull in behind his ride.

Chapter Seven

BY THE TIME Lani and Jake made it to Birch Brook Farm, night had fallen. She was exhausted, mentally and physically, and her hands were bleeding.

The deputies had been watching for anyone who came to the scene. One escorted them to the sheriff's office, where a state arson investigator questioned them. Frank Tyson died in the fire. The investigator revealed no other details, but the implication of arson was clear. Also clear was that Lani and Jake were under the microscope. Jake carried no official ID with him, so his claim to be an agent on leave merely roused smirks. No worries, he told her. He'd clear things up later with the fire marshal's office.

While they waited for pizza delivery, she sat at the table and Jake cleaned and re-bandaged her palms. Part of his ATF training, he told her. He dumped the old bandages in the trash and washed his hands in the kitchen sink. Over his shoulder he said, "You can't blame yourself for Tyson's death."

She stared at her hands, palms up in her lap. The healing scabs stung and itched. An ache throbbed in her chest but the rest of her was numb. "He must've had something important in his notes. If I hadn't phoned him—"

"Don't guilt yourself." He sat at the table with a beer from the refrigerator. "Whoever set the fire is the murderer."

An icy finger trailed down her spine. "Don't you think I know that?"

"Who knew you were going to see Tyson today?"

"No one. I didn't mention him, only Oak Mills as my destination. I told Nora. Steve Quimby. I saw him in the general store. Buddy, of course."

"Half the town, once Buddy got to the Wheelhouse. The killer knew exactly where Tyson lived, drew the logical conclusion. You—we—might not need to do more. This fire is tied to the old fire. No question in my mind." He sipped his beer, looking too in charge. Too settled in her kitchen. "Re-opening the investigation was our goal, remember? That could take a while, so I intend to continue. He's killed again, so there's no time to waste. You're in danger. Is there anything you haven't already told me about the night of the fire?"

Grief dragged at her. On a deep sigh, she surged to her feet, unable to remain still. "I guess the part about Gail going out to the barn."

A muscle in his jaw tightened and his mouth thinned under her gaze. He set down his half empty Sam Adams bottle. "Give me what went down and when." He withdrew a spiral notepad from his back pocket and reached for a pen in the jar she kept on the sideboard. With a boyish grin, he shrugged in apology. Or by way of explanation. "Old habit."

"I don't remember much, although bits and pieces are popping up in my head like ghosts. The shrink described my lost memory as repressed because of the traumatic event, not amnesia."

"I've had arson and bombing cases with the same outcome for the victims. Plays havoc with an investigation. Sometimes people remember later. Sometimes they never do."

"You know that, yet you keep pushing me to remember. What if I never remember? What if I do, and nothing I saw or heard is any help? What then?"

"Whatever, we'll deal. I know it's painful, but anything might help."

Painful? Wrenching. Increased nightmares. Most of the time, she could keep grief for Gail sealed in a back corner of her heart and soul. But forcing herself to think about it unlocked the cage so all that pain came roaring out as raw bleeding wounds. *But if I want answers—*

"I *have* to try," she said finally. "Being in this house brought back some of the evening. Where should I start? With when my parents left for the Blueberry Head Resort?"

"Sounds good. Shoot."

She linked the tips of her fingers on the table's cool surface and closed her eyes to picture her sister. Rich brown curls like their mother, hazel eyes like their father, but unless she looked at old photos, Gail's features were becoming harder to conjure separate from her own mature and scarred ones.

Anguish pegged her dead center, a thump in the chest. But she remembered Gail being in a snit. Could picture her movements and gestures. She opened her eyes.

She crossed to the kitchen counter, leaning against it for support. "Mom and Dad left around seven, a hospital fundraiser banquet. Around seven-thirty I went into the living room to watch TV. Gail was upstairs until you arrived." Her throat turned to sand and her breath hitched. She blinked back tears.

Jake crossed to her. He laid a hand on her shoulder. She didn't expect his touch to make a difference, but his warmth seeped into her and loosened the tension tightening her muscles.

"Take it slow, Lani," he said. "Go on when you're ready."

"I'm okay." She drew a deep breath. "You two were in the driveway. I heard your voices but not your words. I could tell you were arguing, but I turned up the TV volume. Gail hated anyone eavesdropping."

"I stayed only about twenty minutes," he said. "Then what?"

"After she slammed in and dropped the bomb that she'd dumped you, Nora phoned. Neither of us had a car, so we were stuck at home. We were gabbing, playing Alanis Morissette CDs. Loud, I guess. Too loud for Gail. After about an hour, she ran out to the barn with some magazines. Said she was going there to read in peace."

"Ten o'clock." His gaze rose to the ceiling, as if he was calculating the time frame. "How long was she out there before you saw the fire?"

She lowered her head. When she looked up, tears blurred her vision but she willed them away. "Twenty minutes, maybe forty. No longer. I smelled smoke, so I cut off the music and went onto the porch. I had the cordless phone in my hand. No cell phone service on the peninsula back then. I remember seeing the flames. I yelled to Nora to call for help."

He started to reach for her.

The last thing she wanted was sympathy, especially from Jake. His presence uncovered that insecure girl bookworm who always lurked beneath the surface. She had to force herself to be mature and not react with defensive snark. She held up a hand and shook her head.

"Lani, you've got guts. Going over all this is hard enough for me, and I didn't see the fire until it was out. What then?"

"A wall of red. Nothing more."

He swigged down the last of his beer and closed the distance between them. The skin on his face looked stretched tight with emotion. He propped his arms on either side of her. His eyes bored into hers. "If I'd stayed, that bastard wouldn't have had the chance to start the fire."

He'd ditched when the relationship hit the rocks, but that meant his leaving wasn't desertion. Even knowing the truth, it appeared he felt responsible, guilty.

Being so close to him made her skin prickle. She gave a wild shake of her head. "Allow me to repeat your own words—not your fault. You couldn't have known. I loved my sister but she was a flirt and impetuous. Worse. She cheated on you big-time. Then she pushed you into breaking up with her."

"Maybe." His gaze swept over her face. He caressed her hair absently, almost as if he didn't know he was doing so.

If her hands hadn't been a damn mess, she'd have grabbed his collar and pulled him closer. "I have to keep looking for answers for Gail. And for my peace of mind." She jabbed a finger at her scar. "You feel responsible. I feel responsible. Guilt makes no sense but there it is."

His warm breath, yeasty with beer, puffed against her face. He gripped her shoulders, his big hands gentle and warm through her thin tee. "Failing Gail—and you—isn't the only time I've screwed up. The explosion you read about in New Hampshire, I couldn't protect the agent who died there either. I hate the danger you're in, but you're right. We have to keep going."

The anguish in his voice drilled her chest. Too ironic that he warned her against himself. He was removing from the equation the very thing she feared—having to rely on a man. She hated relying on anyone, but the cold North Atlantic tide was rising over her head. Almost did for real the other night.

Wounded palms out, she laid her hands on his chest.

His heartbeat thudded into her very bones and made her want to melt into his arms. She tried not to think about the feel of his arms around her at the lake. Or of the kiss. She'd kissed him back, absorbing his strength and his sun-warmed scent. Honorable and dedicated, tortured and sexy, he made her feel all squishy and liquid and needy. More compelling than sex was another need. A dangerous need that would lead to hurt and heartache.

She met his gaze. "Failure at protecting? Jake, that's a load of crap. You're a natural protector. Didn't you come with me today in spite of yourself? But never mind. I don't want protecting. I want the truth. I want your experience, your expertise. You can help me question our old friends, the people Gail worked for—"

She stopped, thrown off balance by the blazing blue heat in his eyes. He wanted to kiss her. And God help her, she wanted him to.

He lowered his head and rocked his mouth over hers.

The first time he'd kissed her had startled her. This time every cell in her body thrummed and heated. His rough fingers glided up her throat, sparking wildfires in their wake. He wedged her into him and she felt him stir to life against her belly. She kissed him back, absorbing his strength and his scent. His tongue caressed hers, testing and enticing, making her senses reel and her center tingle.

"Aw, shit... Gail."

His murmur against her mouth hit her like a slap. Sharp, stinging, scorching hot coals jolted through her. She shoved away from him, stumbling toward the hall.

She heard his rasp of breath behind her but didn't turn around. She couldn't bear to look at him yet.

"Dammit, I didn't—"

A knock at the mud-room door announced the pizza's arrival, and he strode away.

Weak at the knees, tingling from his embrace, she returned to the table and sank onto a chair. It wasn't her he wanted. He saw Gail in her. He still wanted Gail.

She would not be a stand-in for the woman he really wanted.

**\*\*\*\***

Shifting from foot to foot in the mud room, Jake felt as if he'd stuck his finger—no, his whole body—in an electric socket. He stared at the pizza carton in his hands but saw only Lani's face, ashen and blank with shock. And now he'd hurt her, when all he meant to do was... What had he meant, saying Gail's name?

He cared for Lani, wanted her, but maybe he confused his feelings for her with his past feelings for her twin. Desire for her and surprise she seemed to feel the same for him. Growing respect for her determination and protective urges he thought he'd quashed for good. A growing fear she needed protecting from a murderer. For damn sure, his emotions were too jumbled to sort out now. When he could delay facing her no longer, he entered the kitchen. He had to say something, had to fix this.

Lani sat slumped at the table, her eyes cast down. Her slim shoulders heaved with furious breaths.

He set the pizza on the table and thrust fingers through his hair. He wanted to punch the wall, the pizza, something. "Lani, I'm sorry. I didn't mean to say that. I don't know why I did."

She turned away, hiding her bandaged hands under her arms and hugging herself.

"I was kissing *you*, not Gail. It was about what went on with her." He thought.

"Maybe." She pushed to her feet and turned toward the hallway. "Take the pizza and go. I'm not hungry anymore."

"This situation has us all churned up," he gritted out. "The hit and run. The fire investigator's death. True confessions. Chalk it up to emotional overload. But you need to eat. I'm not leaving until you do. Pizza's getting cold. Where are the plates?"

With tight motions, she stalked to the cabinet. China clattered and she deposited blue-flowered plates on the table. "Another beer?"

He saw the wince as she handled the china. "Let me. You sit." After delivering bottles, two glasses, and a basket of napkins, he sat opposite her.

They ate the spicy pie in silence, tense and awkward at first, then companionable as they settled into their food. His gaze slid to the dollop of pizza sauce at the corner of her mouth. His mouth watered as her pink tongue flicked out to lick it away. He lowered his eyes to his plate. Two slices remained in the box by the time their appetites were sated. One kind of appetite, anyway. The only one likely to be sated anytime soon. Hell of a thing.

"What?" Lani cocked her head and shot him a wary gaze. Still suspicious. He couldn't blame her.

Temporizing, he rose and poured a glass of water. Enough beer. "Just realized the true confessions are one sided—mine. You know my history. What about you? After you recovered."

Her eyes flashed. "No need to tiptoe around me, Jake. *I'm* not afraid to speak *my* mind."

"No kidding. Tell all then."

Her lips curved in an oddly shy smile. "I needed a couple years of therapy and skin grafts before I felt recovered and presentable enough to face the world."

Pain flitted across her features. Picking apart a discarded pizza crust, she appeared to shake off the emotion. "I took online college courses at first, then finished up at UNH. For the last six years, I've taught special education students in a Concord middle school."

He could see how Lani could coax challenged kids to stick up for themselves and to achieve. "Why special ed?"

"It started with kids I saw in the burn center. One girl in particular who'd been burned over most of her body. A candle started a curtain fire that spread to her baby crib. Roni was five when I met her—back for more skin grafts—and so eager to read she memorized every book I read to her. She could barely hold a book because most of her fingers were gone." Her mouth thinned and she blinked rapidly before continuing.

"As I took courses, I did internships in schools. The kids asked about my scars matter-of-factly. They accepted me as one of them. I guess I was. I knew the challenges they faced in everyday life and I wanted to give them skills to make it easier."

"Did you ever see Roni again?"

Tears welled but didn't fall. "Once more. When she was nine. She read two stories to me. She was so proud. But by then she was hunched over like an old woman and in constant pain. They couldn't do enough skin grafts to keep up with her bone growth. She couldn't walk and her breathing was shallow." Her voice rasped with emotion. "Finally her heart gave out. I went to her funeral. She was ten."

He swallowed. "I'm so sorry." Trite, but he couldn't think of anything to say that wasn't.

"Yeah, me too." She stood and reached for the plates.

He started to take them from her but she waved him off, so he sat and nursed his beer.

Holding the plates by the tips of her fingers, she dumped the pizza dregs in the trash. Then she ran water on the plates in the old-style slate sink, likely original to the farm, like the one in his gram's house.

She'd taken her tragedy and turned it outward to give to others. After his partner was killed and his leg damaged, he'd been too self-absorbed to think of anyone else. Past time he did.

He took his glass to the sink and leaned against the counter beside her. "I've been thinking. Rather than give you my conclusions, I'll share the entire file from the fire marshal."

When she turned toward him, excitement smoothed her brow. "Won't that file have the information we want? Didn't Tyson grill everyone back then?"

"The news clippings you showed me implied his investigation didn't go much beyond conducting initial interviews, like the one with you."

"One of the reporters called me back. That's what he said. No follow-up. Tyson sure never came back to see me after that one time. Maybe Gail's friends didn't tell him about the other guy. Maybe they didn't want to say anything back then. Sometimes kids are scared, afraid they'll get in trouble. Her best friends might know about her new lover."

"Or they might remember something new about that night."

Lani blinked as if startled. "I remembered something new just now. Gail's watch. She kept looking at her watch when she came in after your argument."

The same memory flooded him. "She kept an eye on the time while she was outside with me. Damn! She was pushing me away so she could meet this guy in the barn."

"They had sex. Then maybe they argued?"

"Another argument after me? She sure was in the mood." He patted her arm.

The touch of her soft skin soothed the beast prowling inside him but hiked up his blood pressure. Wanting Lani was complicated but undeniable. She might slug him, but he started to pull her into his arms.

She slid away, breathless. "No, Jake. I can't do this I need to be focused, in control. I'll take you up on the case files and work with you, but that's all."

****

Jake left his ride in Tyson's driveway, where he and Lani had parked yesterday. The overcast skies suited the pall over this destroyed house where the old man had settled into retirement.

Pulling up his windbreaker collar against the light rain, he ducked under the now sagging yellow police barrier and ambled toward the blackened ruins of the attached barn. The smoke and chemical stench had dissipated some. Not enough.

Starting with the first tragic fire, that smell had become a permanent part of his olfactory makeup. His senses had refined with experience and study so now he could discern individual odors—insulation and mold and wood and a dozen other elements. But no matter how many burned-out hulks he experienced, he never could get past the most overpowering smell, the stench of death.

He turned as he heard the crunch of tires on gravel as a vehicle pulled in behind his. Not the deputy sheriff's cruiser this time, but Sergeant Paul Robichaud. The arson investigator unfolded his tall, lanky body from the state sedan. The yellow slicker he shrugged on did little to brighten the gray day.

Yesterday Robichaud had phoned that Jake's credentials had cleared him of suspicion. The state fire marshal's office would get a copy of the entire Cameron file to him as soon as someone could make copies. Most of it was paper, not digital. Then, strangely, Robichaud had called back later to ask Jake to meet him today at the Tyson place. Odd place to meet to hand over the report.

"Robichaud," Jake said by way of greeting.

"Thanks for coming." The investigator bent to cross beneath the tape. The two shook hands. "Got that report for you, but I want to show you something in the barn."

"Good. So that was the point of origin?"

"The barn, yes. Black smoke and some of the burn looks like gasoline, but there are some anomalies. We put a rush on the tests."

Their shoes swished through the grass and crunched

on cinders as they crossed the lawn. They picked their way around fallen beams into the remnants of the attached barn. The fresh scent of rain mingled with the ashes and chemicals in a morbid stew.

"At first it looked like Tyson tripped over the gas can and got knocked out as the fire started," Robichaud said.

Like the Cameron fire. The conclusion in Tyson's report. It'd be interesting if what was left in this barn matched that conclusion.

The other man indicated the corner where a charred lawn tractor stood. Black greasy smears leaped high on the two walls and across the floor.

"I hear a *but*?" Jake said. He grasped the problem but wanted the other man's take.

The investigator nodded. "There were two gas cans, two different brands, sizes. And you see the size of the flash."

"More like an explosion than a fire spreading gradually from spilled gasoline." Jake's scalp began to prickle. He'd seen that particular kind of explosion before. That particular kind of flash pattern. "What did your GC tests tell you?"

Robichaud scratched his head. "Don't get much in the way of sophistication with arson in these parts. Folks use gasoline or some other accelerant easily purchased in hardware stores. Most arson is for insurance or to cover some other crime."

"I suspect this one's related to another crime." Jake would press the issue, but it looked like the investigator needed to do this in his own time.

"Remains to be seen. Fire seems to have been set with matches and gasoline. Maybe one can was Tyson's and the arsonist brought another. But then he wanted to trigger a big bang. Lab did more than one gas chromatography test. Came up with cyclonite."

*Better known as C-4.*

Chapter Eight

NORA TAPED A gauze pad on Lani's left palm. "You can probably go without bandages after today. Your scrapes have nearly healed."

Lani gave her a warm smile. Nora's patio was the perfect spot on a sunny morning. "Great. I don't mind not being able to do dishes, but the pile's attracting flies."

"No dishwasher? Heck, I'd buy paper plates. No washing dishes for this gal if I had injured hands. Not my fave chore in any case."

Lani knocked the back of her other hand on her forehead. "Well, duh. Not very eco-friendly but temporary. I'll add them to my shopping list."

"Speaking of shopping, I need a new dress and maybe so will you. Kevin's dad and his campaign manager arranged a big fundraiser for him at the Blueberry Head Resort the Saturday after the Fourth. You and Jake can come together." As Nora shaded her eyes from the sun, her wide grin showed her dimples.

Lani had no interest in furthering Kevin's political ambitions, but she'd attend. For Nora. She'd donate a minimum. "I'll be up for shopping as soon as my hands heal a bit more."

She lifted her face from the Meaghers' faux-glass patio table to the clear blue sky. A breeze had blown the rain clouds out to sea. Sunlight danced off the water in the swimming pool and the remaining puddles on the

Once Burned

flagstones around it. Gary and Sam splashed each other from inflated polka-dot dinosaurs.

"Thanks for the invitation and the hairdo. Cooler this way." Lani patted the French braid that barely tickled her neck.

"My pleasure. I'm grateful for your company. Kevin's off in West Paris speaking to some civic club or other. I've forgotten which one." Nora poured them both more coffee and added a splash of cream to Lani's. A sly look narrowed her eyes. "I thought maybe you'd bring Jake along this morning."

Lani knew that look. "Forget it. No matchmaking. Not Jake. That's over the top, even for you." She put on a scowl, hoping Nora wouldn't perceive her ambivalence.

Nora chuckled. Then her eyes widened. "Wait. I just remembered something." She dashed inside.

Lani stretched out her legs and sipped her coffee. Jake and her? Twice Jake had kissed her. Twice she'd let him, had participated with enthusiasm. But no. The wall between them was too high and too wide. Unfortunately she couldn't kid herself about the attraction. He roused emotions she'd never thought to feel.

When he let down his guard, the pain and determination in his eyes squeezed her heart. And he was more. Still funny and kind. Protective. That, she didn't want, although, dammit, she probably needed protection. And steady, unswerving. That, she liked. She needed his expertise. And he didn't back down from her mouth.

She felt her cheeks heat as she caught the double meaning. But she wasn't Gail, so it didn't matter.

"Here's today's *Portland Press Herald*. I forgot about this until just now." Nora tossed the front section on the table and pointed to a story below the fold.

Lani couldn't miss the headline—*Retired Fire Investigator Dies in Blaze*.

"It was on the eleven-o'clock news last night too." Nora looked over Lani's shoulder.

Popping her knuckles, Lani skimmed the initial reporting of the fire and the efforts to douse it and stopped to read when she came to the reporter's interview with the investigator.

*State Fire Investigator Sergeant Paul Robichaud said the fire was set deliberately, but would divulge no details on the accelerant or other evidence. The home owner, Frank Tyson, a retired state fire investigator, died at the scene. Arson means the perpetrator will be charged with murder. When asked if Tyson might have had enemies, Robichaud replied, "Who doesn't?"*

The piece continued with background on Tyson and his long career. His daughter had been contacted. Toward the end, Lani saw her own name. And Jake's. The story mentioned them as "persons of interest" who had shown up at the scene of the fire. She read on.

*Lani Cameron's sister died twelve years ago in a barn fire in Dragon Harbor. Frank Tyson was the investigator on that case and declared it accidental after a brief investigation. When asked if Ms. Cameron was a suspect in this fire, Robichaud said, "We're looking into all possibilities."*

Lani's pulse pounded in her ears. Nora's coffee sat greasy in her stomach. Had Jake seen the paper? She had to know what he thought.

A frown creased Nora's round face. "What does *'persons of interest'* mean?"

"It means *suspects*." Lani already knew that. Now

the whole state knew.

She slapped the paper back on the table. "Thanks for the coffee, Nore. I have to go."

\*\*\*\*

Jake set down his mug and his cream-cheese-smeared everything-bagel from Cuppa-'n-Suppa on the plastic table beside him in the *Amy Jo*'s cockpit. Propping his bare feet on the stern rail, he inhaled the sea air. Glistening at low tide, the flats reeked of rotting fish and old mud, but even that aspect of the harbor smelled sweet. On such a bright summer day, in contrast to the recent rain, drizzle, and fog, the recreational boaters had sped out early past Dragon Rocks. Only the fishing boats rested at their moorings.

All was peaceful except for a great black-backed gull perched atop a nearby piling. The bird eyed his bagel.

"Don't even think about it, bub."

He read the fire story in the *Press Herald* for the third time. Halfway through, he tossed the paper. Damn, he was worrying too much about Lani. He wasn't supposed to worry about her. She didn't *want* him to worry about her.

*You're a natural protector.*

She wasn't the first to voice that accusation. Maria Soriano had said something like that. And look where it got him. She was dead. Because of his lack of protection.

He wasn't protective. He just preferred having control over… certain situations. Being damned lousy at the job equaled no protection. So he was out of that mode. Finito.

Especially this time. *Not this woman. She could die.* When he failed her, it'd kill him too.

He'd counted on avoiding working with her, protecting her—except for one problem. Robichaud's news nuked his resolve to avoid working with her into oblivion. Jake had no choice in the matter. The prospect scraped his insides raw. Explaining it to Lani would be no fun.

The seagull swooped down with a swish of wings and made off with half the bagel in its yellow beak.

"You can have it, you thief. My appetite's gone."

\*\*\*\*

"Fifth slip down to the left. The *Amy Jo*," the harbormaster said, with a tip of his cap, khaki with the black dragon logo on the brim. "Can't miss her."

Lani glanced at the brass nametag pinned to his green work shirt—Ed Pascal. "Thanks, Mr. Pascal. I see it, a sort of lobster boat."

"That'd be the one, Ms. Cameron. And make it Ed."

She couldn't place him. At least ten years older than her, unless his sun-leathered skin aged him. Maybe someone's older brother. "I used to spend my summers here when I was a kid. Should I remember you?"

His smile dug creases around his small eyes. "Not a bit. Been here less'n two years. But I know who you are. This town has plenty o' flapping mouths."

Lani laughed. "You got that right." She counted on those flapping mouths—and the owners' memories.

Rows of lobster and other working boats tied to floating mooring balls rocked in tandem with the tide and wind. She smiled. They were like a flock of synchronized seabirds.

*Amy Jo*, she mused as she neared Jake's boat slip. A lover? None of her business if he named his boat for a woman. An older lobster boat, about thirty feet, with the typical round bottom, small forward wheelhouse, and open cockpit aft. And a For Sale sign. Interesting.

Hauling the front section of the *Sunday Telegram* from beneath her arm, she sidled down the narrow plank walkway. She'd been helpless for too long after the fire. No more. With someone trying to harm her, she had to be strong, at the same time eliciting Jake's take on the fire story.

"Ahoy, Jake. I found something you have to see." She waited, pulse dancing as she listened for noises below. Conversations from a dozen other boats floated across the water.

A moment later, he appeared in the companionway, a towel draped around his neck. His damp hair rioted in its natural curl. Golden brown hair dusted the smooth contours of his chest. His torso was bare, lightly tanned, and just as mouthwatering as she'd suspected. Seeing him framed in the companionway stopped her breath. The sight took her back to days when the group would swim off the dock at Birch Brook Farm. She'd worn dark shades then so she could ogle Jake without him—or Gail—knowing.

"Hey, Lani. Come aboard. I'll be right with you."

She nodded dumbly as she stepped onto the deck, almost forgetting the reason she'd come. Until she saw sections of the identical newspaper strewn on the deck.

"You already know," she blurted when she heard his firm step on the cockpit deck.

"The fire article, yeah." He set down a tray laden with a thermal carafe, two orange mugs, and a pint container of milk. "Coffee?"

She shook her head. "If I get any more wound, I'll need an anchor." She flopped into a deck chair and waited as he poured the steaming brew into a chipped ceramic mug. The rich aroma filled her senses.

A black polo shirt covered his chest and shoulders. Just as well. Cargo shorts hung low on his lean hips. Just below the hem, she could see the tip of a nasty red scar amid the same burnished hair. He'd combed his unruly hair into submission, she observed with regret.

"So are you wound up about being a person of interest?" he said.

"You mean *suspect*, don't you? Seeing it in the newspaper really bugs me."

He wagged his head as he tipped up his mug. "Whatever the arson investigator intended, mentioning you as a person of interest might take the heat off."

"What do you mean?"

"If you're a suspect, any accusations you make are dubious. No matter what you think you remember. The arsonist might back off."

"*Might*. But if that's true, I can put up with grilling by the fire investigator."

For want of something to do, she took him up on the coffee offer. Never mind that her nerves were already jangling like circus bells. And she hadn't slept.

With efficient movements he poured coffee, then glanced up, waiting.

Milk, she told him. Their fingers brushed as he handed her the hot mug, and his fresh-washed scent came to her over the salt tang of the harbor. Surely she could ignore her senseless attraction. Did he feel the same sizzle? Or was he thinking of Gail? Outgoing, fun-loving Gail had been the popular twin, the one the guys flocked around. Not Lani, with her nose in a book and her one-line zingers.

Was Jake still in love with Gail after all these years? The question still hung like a poisonous spider between them. Whatever the truth, she couldn't let herself depend on him. She couldn't count on anyone but herself.

She noticed him leaning back in his deck chair. Left ankle on his right knee, he sipped his coffee and gazed at her with an expression she couldn't read. Waiting for her to explain her presence, maybe. She averted her gaze from his startling blue one.

"I was at Nora's. She showed me the fire story. Then I stopped at the general store to pick up my own copy and came here." She fidgeted, unsure.

He stared at her hard, as if seeing inside her. "What else? Something else has happened. Not the news article. Give."

His intense scrutiny eddied heat through her veins. The deck chair squeaked in protest at her squirming like a guilty suspect under interrogation. "Well…"

"Out with it."

She sighed. "Okay. You might as well know. Someone tried to break in last night."

"Dammit, Lani, you're way out of the village. Remote. That old house isn't safe."

"Tried, I said. Tried. Didn't get in. I stopped him. Them. Whatever." She managed a shrug to demonstrate her lack of concern. "No biggie."

"Bull. You're scared, and you have every right to be." One eyebrow inched up a fraction. "You stopped them. Exactly how?"

She grinned. "Granddad's shotgun. I fired a shot out the upstairs bedroom window. They ran away." She wouldn't mention she'd sat up the rest of the night with the weapon in her lap. She'd have crashed this morning except for gallons of coffee.

He swore softly between gritted teeth. He scraped the fingers of both hands through his hair. "I don't suppose you called the cops."

His tone was neutral, but she caught the accusation loud and clear. She huffed. "Like Galt would care. He'd ignore it like the other threats."

"Maybe. But threats need to be on record. I'll take care of it."

Her first reaction was to blurt something snarky like *who died and put you in charge.* Because she didn't want to be dismissed by the police chief again, she said, "Go for it." Maybe Galt would listen to Jake as a second party, an ATF agent.

An outboard roared down the middle of the harbor past the No Wake Zone sign. Pascal yelled at them. A bunch of teenagers. They laughed. They so didn't care. She remembered those days. Before the fire.

She stood. "Well. Thanks. I'll see you later."

Jake set down his mug and rose from the deck chair. He took her hands gently in his.

His hands were warm on her skin and his clear blue eyes mesmerizing. The masculine smell of soap and aftershave nearly had her burying her nose in his neck. She swallowed.

"Don't go. After Robichaud verified my ATF credentials, he gave me a copy of the old arson report and all the other files. And there's been a development in the Tyson fire. The fire marshal isn't sharing that or our actual status with the media."

"A development? What?"

The speedboat's wake rocked the *Amy Jo*, sending Lani stumbling toward the side rail.

He caught her to him. "Steady. Don't want you taking a dive. Especially at low tide. Harbor's supposedly clean but who knows what's in the mud."

At his embrace, every cell in her body danced the cha-cha-cha. She swallowed and backed away. "Way to brighten my morning a little more, hot shot. What new development?"

"Voices carry over the water. What do you say we take the boat out to Ragged Rocks? Seals should be sunning for another few hours before the tide's too high."

Chapter Nine

JAKE HELD HIS breath when Lani paused, studying him. He could almost see her skeptical brain turning over his offer. Was she questioning his motivation? She should question his sanity.

"Sure," she finally said. "Why not."

"Great!" He released her and set to getting ready to motor out.

He let out his breath slowly as he cast off the bow line. She was so wary of him, he wouldn't have been surprised if she'd run away. Except she was too determined to get answers.

He hadn't lied. Taking her out on the boat seemed the safest location for sharing his tale. But when he'd held her hand, the pull of attraction was powerful. She was brave and yet so vulnerable he wanted to tuck her in his pocket. He couldn't seem to resist her. Stupid. No future in it. She sure as hell didn't encourage him. But her eyes did darken and flicker with heat.

As he released the stern line, two men back by the harbor office shed caught his eye. The harbormaster was talking to the workman named Brandon who'd spoken to Kevin at the Wheelhouse. The two men were staring at the *Amy Jo* but then turned away, still in conversation.

Jake's gut clenched. Ed Pascal had probably heard about the Cameron fire and this latest arson. A man with his finger on the pulse, the harbormaster. Jake had seen

Brandon around the village a few times since the Wheelhouse. A little younger than Pascal, he had an amiable enough face, not hostile or furtive. If that meant anything at all.

Brandon sucked the life out of the cigarette hanging from his mouth, threw it down, and jogged up the hill. Pascal ambled down the dock toward the rowdy teenagers' boat slip.

Maybe Brandon had nothing to do with the fire. Either fire. Maybe the two men had been ogling the beautiful woman on his boat. Wouldn't hurt to ask Donovan to add Brandon to background checks he'd requested. Pascal was already on the list.

A few minutes later, he guided the *Amy Jo* slowly past Dragon Rocks, no dragon now, at low tide only a hazardous line of rocks. A double-crested cormorant, its black wings outspread to dry, perched atop one outcrop.

Once past the lighthouse on the point, he opened the throttle and plowed through the water, wrinkled in the freshening breeze. Careful to steer around the string of lime-green lobster buoys ahead, he inhaled the clean salt air and eyed the woman standing beside him.

In a blue-and-white striped tee-shirt and navy pants that reached just below her knees, she looked ready for yachting, not an outing on an old stink-pot. Retrofitted but still a noisy old lobster boat. She could've sat beside him on one of the padded stools his uncle had added to the cockpit, but chose to stand off to the left. Away from him. The breeze blew a few escaped strands of hair around her face, softening her fierce demeanor. For the first time, she looked relaxed, even at peace, instead of defensive. Maybe being out on the water.

"What?" Shoulders squared, she glared.

"Chill. Just admiring your hair. Looks good that way."

"Oh. Thanks. Nora did the braid. Cooler off my neck." She returned her gaze to the open waters, where two schooners from the Rockland fleet sailed downwind into Penobscot Bay. Looked like the *Heritage* and the three-masted *Victory Chimes*, their white sails fat-cheeked in the brisk breeze.

He did like her hair. Liked the way pulling it back showed off her elegant neck, although he preferred it loose. Spread across his pillow, it'd—

*Don't even go there.* He was already losing the battle to maintain a distance between them. Not the way to adhere to his rule—he couldn't fail someone if he didn't get close. She might be able to blow off the attempted break-in, but he knew better. The scum meant business. He had to convince her to take more precautions.

In a half hour they arrived at Ragged Rocks, a mussel-encrusted black ridge that barely peeked above the waters at high tide. He spotted the bobbing orange-and-white regulatory marker above the submerged rocks but checked his chart and the depth finder anyway.

"Oh, look." Lani edged nearer, pointed with one hand and laid the other on his forearm. "There are the seals. They're so comical."

Almost every surface of the jagged outcropping had its temporary resident harbor seal, basking in the sun. The biggest males had the prime spots. Females and youngsters had to make do with narrow ledges or lumpier perches. Unafraid of the intruding humans or the boat, they fanned their flippers and stretched their necks.

His hand itched to cover Lani's. "They're so fat, you

wonder how they climb up on those rocks. They look like sausages."

She erupted in a rich low laugh. "Ick, I'll never eat a sausage again. The seals remind me of balloons. You know, those balloon animals some guy always makes at the county fair."

"I never saw a brown or gray balloon animal," he said.

"You are *so* literal." She turned on him, then blinked. "You're kidding. Right?"

When he air-chalked up a point, she laughed again, before she noticed her hand remained on his arm. She jerked it away.

Her reaction reminded him in a rush this was temporary. She was easy to talk to, understanding and not judgmental, and they still had that banter thing between them. Comfortable, but it meant nothing.

"Jake, either you lured me out here under false pretenses or you have secrets to share. And don't think I've forgotten about the case report. Get to it or take me back." Her protective thorns were back in place, judging from her wary gaze.

"Some of this isn't going to be easy to hear." When she nodded, he drew a breath before diving into it. "The Tyson fire was started with spilled gasoline and matches."

"Like the fire that killed Gail."

"Right, as far as it goes. This one was supposed to look like Tyson tripped on the mower or a gas can and knocked himself out as he hit the barn floor. An accidental fire. Except for two things."

"The matches, for one. How did they survive the fire?"

"Good call. Make that three exceptions. The remains of the matchbook fell between the floorboards into the dirt. Not unusual. Second, the wound on Tyson's head showed he was hit by a blunt instrument considerably smaller than a floor."

"Like a two-by-four?" She stepped closer, leaning on the console.

"Something like that. The weapon could've been burned up in the fire."

"You're saving the third as your secret weapon. Give, Wescott."

"You know anything about cyclonite, or C-4?"

A frown crimped her brow. "I've come across that in novels. Isn't C-4 a plastic explosive used by the military?"

He nodded, still trying to get his brain around this turn of events. "Military, yes, or in this case, bad guys who've stolen it."

"And that's how the investigator cleared me? Because someone used C-4?"

"They didn't really suspect you or me before. That news story was a little inaccurate. Chalk it up to bad reporting. But the C-4 drives this arson in a whole new direction."

"Holy crap. Looks like I woke up a bigger dragon than I thought." Seals forgotten, she sank onto a stool and waited, her summer glow paled to the color of a whelk shell.

"The Mexican drug cartel wars have been in the news the past few years," he began. "But what you probably don't know is that at least one of the cartel leaders, a drug kingpin nicknamed El Águila—"

"The Eagle." When he gaped, she added, "Spent a

summer semester in Mexico working with an NGO. Became pretty fluent in Spanish, more than my high school class had accomplished."

"You keep surprising me." He continued, "El Águila moved part of his operation to the Northeast to escape the violence and the stricter border control. He smuggles both ways—drugs like cocaine, heroin, and prescription painkillers into the U.S. and illegal weapons out."

"Like the C-4."

"That and rifles, machine guns, rocket launchers, to name a few." No point in mentioning the explosion in New Hampshire was C-4. "The ATF and DEA and some other alphabet agencies have formed Task Force Eagle to cooperate on the case. We think one of El Águila's men is using this coastline for the smuggling. Name of Hector Vargas. No description. It's probably an alias."

"Maine hires Guatemalans and other Central American workers for summer harvests but not in D Harbor. Dark-skinned or not, a Hispanic would find it hard to hide out here."

"Exactly what's making my job so hard," he said. "We suspect a local must be working with Vargas. Only a local would know all the coves and islands and inlets, as well as places to store the weapons until they move them offshore."

His gaze tangled with hers for a long moment. The idling motor's rumble and the sea's wash battled with his thudding heart as he waited for her to reach the conclusion he had. She wrapped her hand around his forearm and her fingers held on tight. "Then Gail's murderer, and Tyson's, could be the same. And he's somehow gotten involved in the gun smuggling."

He let out a long breath. "His career in crime didn't

stop with one arson-murder. Or this time he hired a pro with connections to the source."

She kept her thoughts to herself but left her hand on his arm. He figured she needed time to absorb the enormity of what she'd just learned. They watched the lounging seals until another craft came roaring up behind them. He turned to see the power boat casting up twin walls of water as it plowed through the sea.

"Jake?" She stared at the other boat.

"Damn idiot. He could ram us if he doesn't turn. Hold on to the safety grips." He spun the wheel, veering the boat to starboard.

As rapidly as the intruder had zoomed toward them, it turned and zoomed away again. The giant wake nearly swamped the old lobster boat's stern. Seals plopped into the roiling water.

The turbulence rocked the *Amy Jo* like a Nor'easter.

He wrapped an arm around her, pulling her against his body as he throttled forward to feed power to the diesels below. Hell, like the other night with the truck, he didn't get the boat name or registration number. Except this time he would remember the hull's conformation and the red paint job zig-zagged by silver lightning bolts.

When the *Amy Jo* reached calmer water, Lani still stood in his embrace. He savored the bump of her hip at the boat's movement, the swell of her breast against his side, the lemony scent of her hair.

A moment later, she must've come out of her shock because she stepped aside. "What the hell was that turkey doing?"

His jaw cramped. "Maybe a warning. For me this time." Before she could respond, he went on. "The arsonist must believe you saw him or know something that connects him to the fire. Why do you suppose he waited until now to attack you?"

She dragged her gaze away from the seals, now clambering back up on the rocks. The pain had returned to her eyes, dulling their amber luster. "I'm not sure he did wait."

"What do you mean?"

"There were a couple incidents I've wondered about. Years ago, not long after the fire. Mom came into my hospital room to find a strange man near my bed. He said he was a doctor ,but I was the wrong patient. He left in a hurry. When she described the man, the nurse said they had no such doctor."

"Can you describe the fake doctor?"

She shook her head. "I never saw him. I was sleeping. Mostly that's what I did those days. Meds kept me out."

He wanted to pull her back into his arms and leach the hurt out of her and into himself. Impossible. "You said a couple times."

"Yes, about eight years ago in Boston. An accident or I could've imagined it. Someone on the subway platform pushed me as the train was arriving, but a woman pulled me back from the edge in time."

"And nothing more until now?"

"No. You think he decided I really didn't remember?"

"Maybe. You were far away and had put the fire behind you. He figured he was safe."

"But now I've come back to Dragon Harbor."

"And you've spread it around that you're starting to remember." He shook his head at her rashness. "Staying out of town in a house with old-fashioned flimsy locks isn't safe."

She backed up and crossed her arms. "Where do you expect me to go? The Eastward Inn? Like I could afford that on a teacher's salary." She rolled her eyes.

She'd gone exactly where he wanted her. "Then get new locks. Talk to Mike Spear at the marina tomorrow. I'll install the suckers." He could see the brain cells sizzling as she considered that one. She couldn't be so stubborn she didn't see the need for safety.

"Mike's on my list of people to interview," she said. "Gail used to babysit for his son. Two birds with one lock."

"*Three* locks. Front, kitchen, and garage entrance." And he'd nail the windows shut if necessary.

"You're a royal pain in the ass, Wescott."

"My mission in life, honey. And stay locked up, or soon you may find more than some guy you can scare off with a shotgun. This killer probably has plenty more C-4."

Chapter Ten

BRUSHING MIST DROPLETS from her nose, Lani entered the Tidewater Marina store the next morning. The tang of salt and a hint of ozone hung in the damp air. The old salts in the Cuppa-'n-Suppa had called yesterday's brilliant day a weather breeder. Looked like they were right.

She still reeled from Jake's revelations. Everything was turned upside down, herself included. Who in D Harbor would know how to buy explosives from a Mexican cartel? If a professional set the Tyson fire, he might not be local. But who would hire—? Oh, wait, answer: someone who would murder and set a fire to cover it up, but who wanted no connection to a second arson-murder. Maybe his tangled web would be his undoing.

When they'd returned to the dock, Jake suggested a cookout on the deck, but she demurred. Hard enough to resist her attraction to the man without candlelight and wine. Not that having him come to the house to install locks this evening was much better. But it gave her more time to shore up her defenses.

She meandered along the aisles until she spotted Mike Spear. He was waiting on a lobsterman who needed rope, but who seemed more inclined to complain about careless yachters "from away." He claimed propellers had cut his trap lines.

Mike was a big man with a thick crew cut and a square jaw. He looked to be in his late thirties, maybe early forties. Twelve years ago he'd have been only a few years older than Gail and her, almost a peer. Gail might've confided in him or his wife.

While she waited, she wandered down another aisle in the Tidewater Marina. Roofing nails, light bulbs, and wood stain filled shelves across from depth gauges, boat hooks, and life jackets. In a peninsula village without a hardware store, a marina had to fill the gap to stay afloat.

Plucking a deadbolt assembly from the wall display of doorknobs and locks, she sagged. Replacing the locks on the farmhouse doors meant replacing history. Modernizing the place somehow desecrated its memories, its integrity. But Jake was right. She needed solid, secure locks. Whoever bought the place would change more than the locks.

"Can I help you find something?"

At the deep, mellow voice, thick with Down-East intonation, she looked up to see the man she'd come to talk to.

Mike's gaze skimmed her scar before meeting hers. A wide grin crinkled his brown eyes at the corners and transformed his rugged features from harsh to handsome and charming.

She smiled back as she explained what she needed.

"You're in the right place," he said. "Got the best locks on the market." He cocked his head and winked. "Unless you want to go high tech. You'd need a locksmith in that case."

"What you have is fine."

"*Finest kind* is what I have." He chuckled at his application of the old Maine expression and picked up a brass-finish deadbolt. "This LokMan's a jimmy-proof vertical bolt, double cylinder."

Lani didn't know what all that meant but accepted it. The price wasn't too bad. "Is this your best?"

"One of 'em. Miss Ida Hallowell bought this one. She told me she wanted a jimmy-proof lock because it'd keep out her no-good nephew Jimmy. Although she's ninety plus, she's still sharp. I think she was puttin' me on."

A laugh bubbled up in spite of her serious purpose. He showed her more locks, interspersing anecdotes with their descriptions. His ebullience relaxed her taut nerves.

After she chose new door handles and deadbolts, she introduced herself. "You probably don't remember me, but my sister Gail used to babysit your son in the summers."

Mike Spear's smile fell as if she'd slugged him between the eyes with one of the locks. "I remember Gail."

She waited for the inevitable sympathetic clucking but it never came. "My memory the night of the fire is really spotty. I want to understand what happened."

"Terrible tragedy." He turned, no more the jovial salesman. All business, he carried her choices to a counter.

*Thanks for the compassion and sympathy, you insensitive toad.* Okay. Lani could be all business too, *her* business. "Mike, did Gail ever mention to you or your wife anything about troubles with a guy she was seeing?"

He padlocked his gaze to her purchases as he entered them in the cash register. "Don't think so. Mostly we talked about Josh, what time me and Patty'd be back, stuff like that. No time to jaw about anything else."

"Maybe your wife would know?"

"Doubt she'd remember anything. They didn't talk much."

"Maybe I'll go talk to Patty. She works at the hair salon, right?"

"She's pretty busy. Be better if I ask her later," he said, his jaw tight enough to crack walnuts. "You want me to?"

*Do I want? We're only talking murder here, jerko.* The retort was on the tip of her tongue, but he didn't know it was murder. She hoped. She manufactured a smile. "Sure. That'd be great. I'll check back with you in a couple days."

After bagging her purchases, he vanished down an aisle so fast the New England Patriots ought to sign him up as a running back.

Outside in her rental car, she stared through the misted windshield at the glass double-doors. Maybe Mike was uncomfortable with emotional stuff. The strong silent type unless he was selling you something.

But psychology courses and years of working with evasive kids told her no. When she mentioned Gail, he went from Chatty Carl to Silent Sam like a door slamming. He wouldn't meet her gaze and hustled her out of the store.

Mike Spear said he knew nothing. She didn't buy it. He was lying. She started the engine and backed out. No better time to find Patty at the Color and Curl.

****

"Appreciate your time, Otis. I've enjoyed our chat." Jake shook the man's gnarled hand.

"Glad to help," the old man said. "Shame about your

102

ma. Too young to have that Old Timer's disease." He shook his head in sorrow.

"Absolutely." Jake thanked him and picked up the bill for their pie and coffee. He left a tip on the yellow laminate counter. After paying at the cash register, he left the Cuppa-'n-Suppa.

Outside he zipped his windbreaker against the chilling fog that had crept in during the night. Mist hung in the air, clinging to anything and anyone. Droplets beaded his face and hair before he took the three steps to his SUV.

He didn't care. He'd finally hit on a way other than the Wheelhouse to dig up local dirt.

Otis, an old pal of his granddad's, and a bunch of cronies met every Tuesday and Friday at the diner for coffee and reminiscing. Afterward in good weather they hung around the harbor. They knew local routines better than he did and might spot someone or something he hadn't. If there was anyone suspicious in town or in the harbor, Otis would let him know.

Background checks on the harbormaster and some of the lobstermen turned up zip. Too soon to have anything on Brandon. Jake was heading up the peninsula, heater on against the damp, when his phone trilled.

"Hey, you all right?" Hank said. "What's this I saw in the *Telegram* about you and Lani Cameron? Another damsel in distress?"

Jake shrugged to convey nonchalance even though he knew his brother couldn't see him. "Seems our interests intersect. No big deal."

"Ri-ight. Bet she's filled out some since her teens. Still… um, spirited? Or did that fire change her?"

Change her? The fire had changed them both. That

night had turned him in directions he'd never have taken otherwise. But Lani? The fire had tempered her like steel. He grinned, picturing her hands propped on the sweet curve of her hips and the sparks shooting from her eyes. "Still holds her own."

Thomas chuckled. "How's Ma?"

"Saw her yesterday afternoon. Took her some of the tea she favors. Seemed to perk her up some." The brothers talked a few minutes about Hank's son and his wife's return.

As soon as Jake disconnected, his cell rang again.

This time it was his task-force contact. "Status report, Wescott? Or are you still partying on that yacht of yours?"

"You should do stand-up, Donovan." Jake pictured the club audience snoring in their martinis. "Briefed Lani Cameron. She's scared but on board. Going to her house tonight to plan strategy. I want to keep her out of it as much as possible."

"Won't work. She's the key to drawing out Vargas and his local partner."

"Afraid you'd say that." Lani would never agree to fade into the wallpaper anyway. He was stuck watching over her. His gut clenched at the thought. For more than one reason. "What've you got on your end?"

"Zip. We might as well have our UC guy carry a neon sign announcing he's a Fed after Vargas killed Ruiz. They're not biting. But some of the weapons have been moved into Maine. You might see some action on your end."

Not likely. But Jake made hopeful murmurs. He resisted telling Donovan about his dad's old buddies keeping watch. Unorthodox didn't fly with the Feds. "I should have something here in a few days. Progress on the old arson case might lead somewhere for us. I need you to do another background check."

"Shoot."

Jake gave him what he knew on Kevin Meagher before ending the conversation.

When he reached Route One, he turned right toward the county seat. Originally a limestone and fishing town, Bayport had morphed in recent years to an arts and tourist destination. Good in some ways, bad in others. Dismay pursed his mouth as he passed the chain restaurants and big-box stores that had displaced local, unique ones.

He pulled into the paved parking lot of Meagher Enterprises. Now here was one business that continued to thrive. Beyond the new brick office building spread an array of outbuildings. Not too shabby, as old Otis would say. Earth moving, foundations, industrial developments—Meagher did it all.

Kevin had invited him to stop by this morning. Jake intended to find out more about his old buddy's interest in Gail. If he'd followed up on that interest, Jake wanted to know.

Inside the office building, Tammy Meagher, a younger and slimmer version of her brother, greeted him from her desk. "Kevin's about finished with a meeting. Have a seat."

"Place looks great," he said, taking a leather-padded wooden chair beside a blue loveseat.

Tammy wrinkled her nose and beamed a smile. "Except for this ugly gray carpet. Gotta have one that can withstand muddy boots." She returned to her computer.

He perused an *Architectural Digest* while he waited.

But he couldn't concentrate on the beautiful houses for beautiful people. Houses he'd once dreamed of building. In spite of the reason he'd gone into law enforcement, the work suited him.

His thoughts drifted to earlier that morning. Down at the far end of the docks, he'd spotted the red speedboat, silver lightning bolts on the side. When he described the reckless attack to the harbormaster, Ed Pascal said the boat belonged to a Boston family who came only weekends. No one should've been out in it midweek. Sometimes people were careless and left the keys under the seat. He promised to check into the matter, saying it was probably kids goofing around.

Too coincidental. Little fucking chance of finding out who actually drove that racy boat.

After that he noticed Lani's VW at Tidewater Marina. Safe enough if she took her new locks home and stayed there afterward. Not likely. Fear for what might happen if he couldn't protect her dumped more sharp implements in his gut.

"Hey, Jake. Glad you could make it."

Jake looked up to see Kevin marching toward him, grinning his campaign-trail toothiest.

"Wouldn't have missed it, buddy." He swept his arm in a broad gesture. "Damned impressive. I remember that little house the company used to be in."

"Tore that old eyesore down when we built this." He ushered Jake down a hall. "Let me give you the tour."

Jake made appreciative noises as Kevin showed him the conference room and other offices. He introduced him to draftsmen using computers to draw plans. A completed plan cranked from a blueprint-sized printer. When they left the bookkeeper's office, J.T. was striding down the hall.

What had been salt-and-pepper hair was now silver to match his gray eyes. Unlike his son, he'd maintained his trim waistline and angular features. J.T. pumped his hand as if he was running for office instead of his son and Jake had a hundred votes in his pocket. "Good to see you. Kevin said you might drop by."

"Thanks. Good to see you too, sir. Been a long time." Jake jerked a nod at Kevin. "You must be proud of your son. I hear he's doing well in the polls. After November, we'll be addressing him as Mr. Congressman."

Kevin's wide countenance lit up. "Mr. Congressman. Has a nice ring."

J.T.'s brows lowered, nearly hiding his deep-set eyes. "Won't happen if the boy doesn't hustle more." He turned to his son. "You have a speech scheduled tonight?"

Color bloomed on Kevin's cheeks. He shifted his feet. "Not tonight. Got one tomorrow night in Brunswick though."

J.T. wagged his head. "When I ran for Congress, I was out every night on the stump."

Some things never changed. Jake felt his friend's discomfiture in his own heated face. He saw Kevin's compressed mouth and wondered if he was biting back the rejoinder that J.T. had lost that election.

Whatever Kevin accomplished would never be good enough for J.T. His older brother by two years, John Thayne Meagher, Junior, had died in a car accident a few years after college. He'd been the golden boy, the son J.T. set his hopes on to succeed him in the business and in politics. Not Kevin.

"You have to chase those votes," the older man continued. "Mainers don't care so much about the TV ads. The personal touch. That's the ticket." He elbowed Jake and laughed. "The ticket. Get it?"

Jake nodded but couldn't laugh even when Kevin did.

When J.T. strode off to meet his client, Kevin said, "Don't mind Dad. He's raised so much money for me, he gets all worked up."

Jake had nothing diplomatic to say to that, but he wondered which one this campaign was more important to, father or son. He followed Kevin outside for a look at the new excavator in the one of the outbuildings. He zipped his windbreaker. Spider webs of mist hung in the air, dampening his face and hair.

After the tour, Kevin accompanied him to the parking lot.

"Something I need to know about Gail Cameron," Jake said.

Kevin's mouth twisted as if he'd bitten into a sour apple. "Heard you and Lani were asking around. Hope it doesn't bring more trouble."

"Me too." Jake didn't intend this to be an interrogation. He kept his expression mild, non-threatening. "You said the other day Gail was the hot sister. What did you mean by that?"

Kevin barked a laugh that held no mirth. He waved at the air. "Oh, man, you ought to know. You were going with her."

Jake didn't comment. Merely waited. People often felt the need to fill the silence.

Kevin heaved a sigh. Color crept up his cheeks again. "What's that saying? Don't speak ill of the dead?

But if you insist, here it is. Gail got around that summer, if you get my meaning."

Kevin's revelation drove a battering ram square in Jake's solar plexus. *Got around?* Gail was having sex with other guys? Not just one?

Beeps sounded at Kevin's waist. He glanced down at the number displayed on his cell phone. He let it go to voice mail. "I'm due at a job site now. Thanks for coming."

Jake swallowed the churning mix of emotions that burned his chest and clamped a hand on Kevin's arm before he could hurry off. "Sex with other guys. You mean while we were going together that summer?"

Kevin's gaze dropped but he nodded.

"I need to know who Gail was with. It's important."

"I'm not sure. Talk to some of the guys." Kevin stared pointedly at his arm. "I gotta go."

Jake lifted his hand. "No offense meant."

"No problemo." Kevin swiped mist from his nose and trotted away.

Muttering every expletive he knew, Jake stayed put by the SUV's open door. Was he the only one who didn't know Gail was sleeping around? Did Lani know? Man, it'd be a long time before he could see the whole picture in this jigsaw of the past.

He watched Kevin drive away in a company SUV. Next time he saw his old buddy, old pal, he had another question for him. Like why when Kevin suggested asking "the guys" about Gail, he didn't deny his own involvement with her.

Chapter Eleven

LANI APPLIED MASCARA and a light blush. The only makeup she ever wore. Lipstick occasionally. Should she? Forget it. He'd get the wrong idea.

She smoothed her hands down her grass-green V-neck tee and, in true neurotic fashion, hoped her jeans didn't make her butt look big. Tough. That was as good as it got. Why was she bothering? Jake was coming over tonight, yes, but only to replace her door locks and so they could share their lists of people to interview. She'd make coffee, just to be hospitable.

No date. Just work. She looked at her watch. Seven. He'd be here any minute. Her heart gave an extra hard thump against her sternum in case she wasn't paying attention.

She glared at herself in the mirror. *I'm a grown woman, not some starry-eyed teenager.* She could control her hormones. Even if he did heat up her daydreams. Was it his sexy good looks or his innate kindness or the way he didn't back down from her smart mouth? All of the above. She heaved a sigh of frustration.

When she heard a knock, she ran the brush through her hair and dashed down the stairs.

"Hey," Jake said when she opened the door.

The sight of him in a charcoal tee-shirt that clung to every muscle and soft, worn jeans that clung to his lean hips rippled warmth from her neck downward regardless of the cool night. "Hey, yourself."

He carried a zippered sports bag into the kitchen.

She planted her hands on her hips. "I hope you're not planning to spend the night."

Flames ignited in his eyes. One side of his mouth hiked up. The playful grin shot a jolt of longing into her chest—for the boy who used to be. "I might. If I was invited. Fog's pretty thick out there."

Heat rushed to her cheeks. Dammit, she never blushed. Maybe he'd attribute the color to makeup. "In your dreams, Wescott. What's with the bag?"

He shook it. Metal clanked against metal. "Tools, Cameron. You did buy those new locks we talked about?"

"I may be stubborn but I'm not stupid." She stepped aside and gestured at the plastic packages on the table.

Dropping the bag with a thunk on the table, he snatched her hand and turned up the palm. The scabbed-over sores were dry and healing. "Hey, looking good. No bandages. Pain?"

The feel of his big, rough hands on hers fizzed electricity across her arms. With great effort, she shrugged. "Not enough to mention."

When she tried to tug her hand away, he captured the other one and held her fast. The heat in his eyes nailed her feet to the floor. "Jake."

He grinned. "Lani. And you'd know pain, I expect."

She knew, all right. Intimately. The stinging aftermath of surgeries and skin transplants. The ache of treatments and physical therapy on her shoulder. And the ever-present pain of losing her sister.

She remembered his leg wound. "You know pain

too. Sometime you'll have to tell me about that leg."

"Sometime. But you'll have new scars to add to your collection."

"In case you haven't noticed, I don't have a collection. Only the one."

"Two. This one." He sleeked his big hand over the top of her head and around to the scar surgery hadn't eradicated. A murmur of pleasure rumbled in his chest.

"Jake, don't—"

"And the bigger scar inside." He lowered his hand and pressed his fingers against her upper chest where her heart was tripping over itself.

*Does he know about the other scar? No, he can't possibly.*

She saw he intended to kiss her. She tore herself away from his gaze and turned her back. Only then did she realize he'd released her hands moments ago. "We agreed not to do this."

She heard the rasp of a zipper and the rattle of tools behind her. So he was getting to work. She sucked in a breath but wasn't sure if she felt relief or disappointment.

"*You* agreed. Said you needed to focus. I made lame excuses. But we have this attraction. Don't try to deny it."

She rounded on him. "I'm not denying it, just *focusing* on what has to be done."

"Big whoop. As a reasonably intelligent adult, I can *focus* on more than one thing at a time. And you can't? I heard women were big on multi-tasking."

*What?* He turned the tables without breaking a sweat. Was having a smart mouth contagious?

"And… I bring blueberry pie." He held up a square box from Donna's Garden Stand.

"Blueberry," she whispered, in spite of herself. Her favorite flavor. How did he know?

"Box is a little dented from being in the bag." His little-boy grin made her breath catch. "When we were kids, Donna used to sell pie by the slice, like pizza."

Her mouth watered. "I remember."

"Mom would send us boys on our bikes to buy vegetables. She'd always give us enough money for a slice of pie—apple or blueberry or chocolate. If we were lucky, the filling would still be warm. Hank usually didn't let me tag along, but he made sure I went with him to Donna's. I could always talk her into adding a scoop of ice cream."

In spite of herself, she smiled, picturing Jake as the mischievous little brother who always worked being cute to his advantage. He'd learned his flirting skills early.

He picked up the tool bag and the locks and ambled into the hallway. A left took him toward the front door.

Just because he brought her food and just because he dazzled her with a smile, she couldn't allow anything to come of whatever was zinging between them. His sensitivity and flashes of humor were cracking her defenses. She wanted him but didn't see any way but to protect herself beyond her usual defenses. And it wasn't her he wanted anyway.

Men didn't stay when the going got tough. Especially with her.

\*\*\*\*

Jake squinted in the dim light over the back door leading to the attached barn, now a garage. He pushed up from his crouching position and dropped the screwdriver in his bag. Done. The last of the three rusty antique locks replaced. He checked both—door handle and deadbolt.

Keys worked. He flipped the deadbolt. Secure. Window latches were better than he'd thought. And at least on the first floor, some worker bee doing maintenance had painted some of them shut. Damn secure.

Unless her slimeball attacker broke the glass. Or knew how to pick locks. She was too isolated out here. He shook his head as he made the trek down the long back hallway.

His thoughts detoured at the smell of coffee brewing. "Woman, you read my mind," he said as he entered the kitchen. "Caffeine to keep me awake while we talk suspects."

"And blueberry pie. Thank you for this." Smiling, she slid wedges onto two plates and set them on a wooden tray painted with pale blue flowers.

He followed her to the living room. Always liked its comfortable feel. Only outlines remained of an array of family pictures on the wall. The wallpaper's bright colors had faded, but the welcome lingered.

When they were settled on opposite ends of the cushy sofa, Lani poured the coffee.

He forked in a mouthful. Buttery crust and sweet wild Maine berries. Perfect. Just as he remembered. A look at Lani stopped him in mid-chew.

Apparently she loved Donna's pies as much as he did. More. Eyes closed. Beatific curve of lips as she chewed. Fierce hums of delight from her throat coursed heat through him. Blueberry goo dribbled from one corner of her mouth. She lapped it up with her tongue and caught him staring.

Sparks shot from her eyes. "What? Pie on my face?"

He cleared his throat. "Nice to see a beautiful woman enjoying her food. That's all."

Eyeing him with suspicion, she set down her now empty plate. Did she think he was making fun of her? There was that uncertainty about herself again. Or distrust of him. Whichever, he liked that high color in her cheeks even if it was temper.

"Hey, no big deal. Just enjoying the pie, enjoying your, um, pleasure, having fun. You have heard of fun?"

Her mouth compressed and her shoulders shook. Lines fanned out from her eyes and a sputter like a broken faucet erupted into a rolling gust of laughter.

Whew, he'd been worried she might toss the pie at him or toss him out on his ass.

No dainty feminine titter, her hearty laugh was way sexier. The mirth that lighted her hazel eyes let the real woman come out to play. The only reason he didn't pull her into his arms was the certainty it would shatter the light mood.

When her mirth trailed off in a raspy chuckle, she collapsed against the sofa cushion. "Oh, Jake, you're right. I needed a little fun."

So did he, he realized, chuckling with her. "Honey, you need more than a little, but that laugh'll do for starters. Good for the soul. Like Donna's pie."

She laughed again as she lifted a spiral-bound notebook from the table and opened it.

He scooted closer to her and waited for her to call him on it. When she said nothing, he unzipped the folio pad he'd carried in the gym bag. "Looks like we're open for business."

"I have only a few names on my list."

"I'll make a copy of the fire report for you. Got a few names from that. I'll take your names and get started right away."

She propped her hands on her hips and glared at him. "Excuse me. *You'll* get started? I'm not sitting on my butt eating bonbons while you do your federal agent thing. We can divvy up the interviews, share information."

Jake's jaw clenched. He knew she wouldn't stay out of trouble. He pressed an index finger to her lips. "I meant I need your list so I can have my ATF contact start checking backgrounds. We agreed to do this together. But I won't let you go out alone."

Because of the C-4's probable connection to the Mexican cartel, Holt Donovan would be doubly thorough and quick with whatever he needed.

As if removing a dead insect, she lifted his finger with her forefinger and thumb. Way to squash a guy's ego. And his libido.

She narrowed her eyes. "I doubt my sister's girlfriends are dangerous. I'm having lunch with two of them tomorrow."

"You wouldn't be with them every minute."

"They won't tell me *anything* if you're with me. Guaranteed."

The set of her chin said he wouldn't win that argument. "Okay. But don't go off on your own on any other interviews. You're not The Closer. Even Brenda takes detectives with her."

She grinned at the analogy with that old series, then turned serious. "I know damned well how dangerous what I'm doing is, Jake. I'll be careful."

He crossed mental fingers she meant it.

They spent the next few minutes dividing up who would talk with whom. Jake took the guys they hung out with, including Kevin, although he was keeping that to himself for now. One he wondered about was Steve Quimby, who'd arrived at the poker game as the fire trucks had screamed down the peninsula. To keep Lani out of too much trouble, he made sure she'd see mostly Gail's friends and Ava Warren. Gail had waited tables with Ava at the Eastward Inn that summer.

"I talked to Mike Spear this morning." She outlined her encounter with the marina store manager. "I didn't trust he'd actually ask his wife, so I went to see Patti. Nothing, just as he said. Patti couldn't remember Gail ever talking about guys."

He noted her suspicions. "You had good instincts there. Doesn't mean Spear isn't keeping something from you." He was afraid he knew Spear's secret about Gail, but he'd wait for a check on the man before he warned Lani off a second chat. Or he'd talk to Spear.

She glanced over her list. "Some other old friends don't live here anymore. Some were summer people. None of them can be the one threatening me." Her expression brightened, putting the gold glow back in her eyes. "It can't be a person no longer in Dragon Harbor."

"Good point, but he could've hired someone. There could be more than one person."

"Oh, great." She rolled her eyes. "Thanks, Mr. Ray O'Sunshine. *Two* killers."

"This is serious shit. Don't let down your guard. My guy'll do checks on absentees as well as locals."

"On Kevin too?" She glared at his open zipper pad, then stood and marched back to the kitchen with their plates.

He followed in her wake. "You don't miss much. Yes, Kevin too."

She plunked the plates into the sink with a clatter of

china. "You didn't mention him. Why's his name on your list?"

He really didn't want to tell her. Temporizing, he tucked her hair behind one ear. "I can't keep from wanting to touch you."

She leaned into his caress for a split second before her ire won out. Her brows drew together, crinkling the tender skin above her nose. He enjoyed rattling her. "Jake."

Shit, she wouldn't be deterred. He lowered his hand but only to her shoulder. "I don't know where he was that night. Not with you apparently."

"You're right. He had to accompany his father to the hospital fundraiser. His mother had just had a chemotherapy treatment for her breast cancer. She wasn't in shape to go. John Junior stayed with her. Figures Kevin would prefer to party. An opportunity to glad-hand, show how much they cared about sick people." She huffed out a breath.

Her snarky tone had him asking, "You doubt J.T. cared?"

"Politicians. Who knows?" Her jaw worked and her tone turned thoughtful. "That was the last night we were happy."

"Who's *we*?"

"Take your pick." Her jab was tempered by the hurt in her eyes. "One look at me in the hospital with all the tubes and IVs and bandages turned Kevin pale as snow. Then it was adios, adieu, and ciao, baby. He added some bull about giving me space before he peeled out of the room like his shoes were jet powered. I wonder how he treated his mom a year later when she lay dying."

Hearing her tell it made Kevin's actions worse.

Appalling. Jake didn't know what to say. He slipped an arm around her shoulders. Felt the shiver of her nerves under his hand, but she let him draw her closer and then leaned into his embrace.

She gave him a tremulous smile. "When you came a couple days later, you didn't run from the Phantomette. You stayed. You talked to me about getting lost on Boston streets, about being back at college. Even left me a funny get-well card."

"You faker. I thought you were asleep or so drugged you didn't know I was there."

"After Kevin, I wasn't taking chances."

He started to say that Kevin had been young but couldn't cut the guy slack on this one. "A lot of people can't deal with people's injuries. Especially people they care about."

"Like my father." She pressed fingers to her mouth as if she hadn't meant to speak the thought.

His pulse jumped. "You said your parents divorced. What happened?"

Her shoulders twitched in what she probably intended as a shrug of nonchalance but beneath his hands felt like anger. "He couldn't handle it. All of it. Gail's death. Seeing her in my face, even with bandages and scars. My surgeries, the long recovery. My parents fought constantly. He finally left."

Jake brushed a kiss on her forehead. "Maybe it wasn't you or your recovery. Maybe your parents had their own problems."

She shook her head with vehemence. "They fought about Mom having no time for him. She was either at the hospital with me or tending me at home. Don't get me wrong. I don't blame myself. Dad wimped out."

"I'm sorry."

"No big deal. I'm over it." She leaned her head against him, giving him a solid whiff of her hair, her flowery shampoo.

"Honey, no one gets over parents' divorce, like I won't get over my dad's death. You get used to it and move ahead one step at a time."

"How did you get to be so wise? Or is that wiseass?"

"Can't resist, can you? Neither can I—" He curled a finger in a strand and tugged so she'd look up. He made sure she was looking at him. "Lani."

Another tug on her hair brought her mouth to his. He settled his lips over hers, testing, until she parted to let him in. She tasted of blueberries and coffee. Defiance and courage and a burning spirit that blazed brighter than any fire. She answered his demands with equal hunger, drinking him in as if parched. She wrapped her arms around him and pressed against him.

Lifting her onto the counter, he shuddered. She wanted him as much as he wanted her. He savored the feel, the scent, the taste of her. His feelings for her went beyond sex. How could he ask her to trust him to keep her safe? His heart raced and he made himself back off.

"You have your moves, don't you, Wescott?" Her voice was husky.

"So do you, Cameron. Objections?"

"I don't know what you want. *Who* you want." The turbulence in her expressive eyes told of her warring emotions, her fears.

"I don't know why I said Gail's name that time, but it's you I want." He couldn't explain it to himself, so why should she believe him or trust him? Shit.

She stared at him, as if wanting to believe, wanting

to incinerate her doubts. Then she looped her arms around his neck and tangled her tongue with his. Wrapped her long, sexy legs around him and ground against him where he strained against his fly.

When he slid his hand beneath her sweater and trailed his fingers over the smooth skin of her belly, she shifted to give him better access.

"So soft," he growled. "You feel like cream."

Unsnapping the front closure of her bra, he stroked the silken curves and budded nipples, moaned into her mouth at the feel of that exquisite flesh. His body thrummed. A rush swept through his blood, strong and deep, nothing like the slam-bam hook-ups that were his norm. Physical release but empty and unsatisfying. Only once had he ever felt like this. With Gail—a driving need, a burning to possess. In the darkened barn…

But holding Lani obliterated his thoughts. She tangled his circuits, cracked his shell, and made him long for completion. With her. Blanking out the world, he let the warmth and the feel of her fill his senses. Reality dissolved into feverish sensations and a rush of furnace heat that left them both gasping for breath when he finally pulled away.

"I hope you're not going to say you have to focus." She scooted from the counter and twisted around to fix her bra. She pushed a hand through her hair.

"Not me." His chest heaved with the effort not to carry her to the sofa and continue what they'd begun. He could have her naked in sixty seconds. But with her, he wanted to take things slow. He needed her to be sure. Of herself. Of him. "Just didn't want to exceed the speed limit."

"Cryptic but a lame excuse. I'm used to guys

kicking me to the curb. If you don't want me, just say so."

Before she could step away, he swung her around, clamping her against his arousal. He rotated his pelvis and thrust against her. "Lani, Lani, Lani, does that feel like I don't want you?"

She didn't answer but tightened her mouth.

"I want you so bad I can barely breathe. I'll be up front. I can't offer long term. You should have time to consider if you want me under that circumstance. Or not." He kissed her, hard and quick, then rested his forehead against hers. "Besides, I don't have any protection."

She sputtered a laugh and he let her slip free.

Later on the drive to the harbor, what he'd learned about her tonight wouldn't leave him alone. So Kevin left. Kevin was a freaking idiot. He should lose the damn election. And her dad left. He was no longer *Dad*. She called him her *father*, acknowledging only that he sired her. Remote and dispassionate words. Dispassionate wasn't how she felt. About either man.

Their defections were responsible for the thicker wall. The reason she didn't trust anyone but herself. So she wouldn't count on him either.

He should be glad. Relieved. So why did a little voice inside him insist he wanted to be worthy of being counted on?

Chapter Twelve

LANI PRETENDED TO admire the Eastward Inn's glorious view but her mind kept drifting.

Banishing the fog, the sun had steam-cleaned the morning. The clear light had lured three local artists to the inn's lawn where they were painting the gleaming white lighthouse on its windswept island. She smiled at the seagulls crowding behind a circling boat for the choicest bits of stinking old bait the lobsterman tossed out.

For contrast, the dining room boasted cream linen and burgundy carpets that matched stripes in the wallpaper and the fragrance of fresh flowers and baking bread. Classy and elegant, like the inn's prices.

Inviting Gail's old friends to lunch here better pay off. Give her some direction. Some of their crowd had been summer residents like the Camerons. But her thoughts couldn't stay on these two locals, either.

*Jake.*

Last night he'd kissed her and caressed her until her bones heated and melted like wax. Good thing he lifted her to the counter or there'd have been a Lani-sized puddle on the scuffed old tile. If he hadn't kissed her mind blank, she'd have hit him with both barrels about his up-front offer of sex with no strings and no future.

And her impulsiveness would've been a mistake.

She said she was used to guys dumping her. But

since the last sad affair, she hadn't gone with anyone in two years. Jake would leave her, but at least he didn't try to bull her or bulldoze her. He was honest about his intent.

She couldn't be cool about sex. Never could. When his work here ended, so would their time together. With Jake, the heartbreak afterward would be worth it. If she had the nerve. He not only didn't dislike her sass, he encouraged her and teased her about it. He made her laugh. He made her feel beautiful and desirable.

As long as she could banish the niggling doubt it wasn't her he kissed and caressed.

She looked up to see the hostess escorting Gail's friends to her table.

Heather Nadeau was a small, plump woman with a mass of blond hair clasped at her nape. Chic in a slim navy sheath, Becca Allen stopped at a table to speak to a middle-aged couple. She smoothed her glossy dark bob as she hurried to catch up to Heather.

Lani stood and greeted them. "It's wonderful to see you. I'm so glad you could come."

"Sorry about the detour. The Huppers are clients in my investment firm." Becca air-kissed Lani's cheek. "So nice of you to get me out of the office."

"Yes, thanks, Lani." Looking frazzled, Heather said, "I appreciate a lunch out that doesn't involve meals packaged with toys. And I don't have to hurry back. Mom has the girls."

Lani tried not to react from their obvious scrutiny. They must wonder at the reason for the lunch date, but they were also looking her over for more signs of burn scars. *Sorry. The one is all you get to see.*

She ordered a bottle of sauvignon blanc for the table.

Alcohol might encourage the others to dish on Gail's secrets. After ordering their meals—three orders of crab cakes, the inn's specialty—they sipped and chatted about Becca's office mates and her divorce, Heather's pictures of her twins, and Lani's work with handicapped kids.

Halfway through their meals and their second glasses of wine, Lani began. "You may have heard I'm trying to get the state fire marshal's office to re-investigate the fire."

Heather made clucking noises. "Nothing new has come up, has it?"

Lani's stomach clenched but she kept her features neutral. The local paper had called the attack on her an accident. No point in telling these women what really happened. "Nothing definite. I invited you here today because I need to ask you some things about Gail."

Becca bristled. "What could we possibly tell you that you don't already know about your twin sister?"

Lani smiled. "We went to different colleges. I had my own friends. We were close but didn't share everything." Beneath the table, she popped her knuckles. "For instance, the guy she was cheating on Jake with."

Heather paled. She and Becca exchanged a glance. They knew something.

Lani's pulse leaped like a mackerel at dangled bait.

Heather set down her wineglass and dabbed her lips with her napkin. "I don't see how that would help."

"You never know." The scenario she'd worked out ought to prick their consciences. "At the time, the fire investigator concluded the blaze was an accident—gasoline spilled near the oil lamp. But more and more, the cause looks like arson. Suppose after Jake left, Gail met this other guy in the barn. And suppose they had a fight and he hit her and knocked her unconscious. Then he started the fire to cover his butt. That makes him a murderer."

Becca blanched whiter than the tablecloth. She guzzled half her wine. *"Murderer?"*

"When someone dies in an arson fire, the crime is arson-murder. Don't you want the authorities to catch your old friend Gail's murderer?"

Heather and Becca exchanged a look. Becca nodded slowly.

"You'd better pour yourself more wine," Heather said, her round cheeks pink from the alcohol. Or something else. "You won't like what you're going to hear. I'll join you."

Becca held out her glass. "Me too."

****

A great black-backed seagull landed on the other end of Jake's picnic table. Cocking its head to one side, it lasered one red eye at his clam basket.

Great black-backs were scarcer than herring gulls. Looked like the same gull that had stolen his bagel. Nah. Just his imagination. The overlapping cases making him paranoid.

"What is it with you guys and my food? Shoo." He picked up a pebble from the ground and heaved it in the general direction of the would-be thief.

The gull shook its feathers as if to say, "Can't you do better than that?"

A volley of pebbles sent it squawking into the air, a blur of black and white against the smattering of cotton-balls in the blue. The fiend landed on the next table, kept its eye on Jake.

On the fresh salt air, aromas of fried seafood drifted

from the restaurants that ringed the landing, including the red wagon where he'd purchased his lunch. Hell of a forest of masts beyond the Bayport public landing. Dozens more than in tiny Dragon Harbor's anchorage. Jake polished off the crispy fries that accompanied the fried clams.

After he'd left Lani last night, he worked on his laptop doing reports and sending Donovan what he knew on the people from his and Lani's lists. Background checks would take time but he'd done his part.

Earlier this morning he'd found Steve Quimby at ABC Building Supplies, where his old buddy designed kitchens and baths. Reluctant at first, Steve finally consented to talk to him but not at work. Here on the landing during his lunch break.

Hearing stones crunch under heavy shoes, he turned to see Steve striding from the parking lot toward him. He carried a bag from the lunch wagon. Tall enough to play center for the Celtics, he towered over Jake's six-two. He shook Jake's hand with a massive paw.

"Thanks for coming, Steve. Good to see you," Jake said, gesturing for him to sit.

"Yeah, good to see you too." A familiar, diffident grin softened Steve's face as he folded his long body onto the picnic bench. Broad-shouldered and powerful-looking, he had the kind of crookedly agreeable looks women seemed to like. Looks that might've attracted Gail.

Jake allowed time for Steve to inhale his two burgers and for them to get caught up.

"It's a good job," Steve said. "Every room's a puzzle. I have to take the pieces the owners want and fit them into a workable arrangement. I bet the ATF solves puzzles too."

"Definitely, sometimes dangerous ones. I've got a puzzle going now," Jake said. The analogy made a convenient segue. "You remember the fire that killed Gail Cameron."

Steve blinked and then nodded. "A long time ago, man."

"Twelve years." He paused for emphasis. "You ever hook up with Gail?"

His broad forehead creased and he squinted as the sun came from behind a cloud. "Wasn't she your girl?"

"Seems she had a few guys on the side. You weren't one of them?"

"Me? No way." Steve huffed a sigh. "Look, she hit on me a couple times when I danced with her at parties, but I didn't take her up on it. Why are you asking me?"

"I'd like to eliminate you from my list."

"Your list? What the hell's going on?"

Jake worked up a minimal smile. He'd expected this reaction. "That fire might not have been an accident. Lani Cameron and I want the state fire marshal to re-open the investigation, prove the cause—accident or arson. If someone set the fire, we want justice. That's all."

"That's all? That's a hell of a lot. Arson, you say. Bad business."

"So you'll answer some questions?"

Steve chewed that over with the last of his lunch. "Shoot."

"I want to get clear where everyone stands. Where everyone was that night."

"You know where I was. Playing poker at Todd's until two, three in the morning."

Jake nodded. "True enough. So you do remember that night."

"Some. I remember the fire trucks and the sirens blasting by the end of Ridge Road on their way down the East Road."

"As I recall, you were late. Got there after me. We played several hands before you came. Awhile later the trucks blew by. At least the other guys and I remember it that way." Keeping his voice even, he smiled to mitigate the implicit accusation.

"Hey, I had nothing to do with that fire. Why would I?" Steve crumpled his sandwich wrappings into a tight ball.

"Not saying you did. Investigator never asked you back then for an alibi because you were at the game. You mind telling me where you were between seven thirty and ten fifteen?"

"If the guys remember that much, they—and you— ought to remember I lost big time that night. I was drinking pretty heavy before and during. I dunno where I was before Todd's. Too long ago to remember." He swung his legs over the picnic bench and rose to his considerable height. "I gotta get back to work."

So Jake wouldn't have to stare straight up into the sun to face the man, he rose to his feet. He held out a business card. Maybe the official ATF logo would provide encouragement. "I'd appreciate it if you'd try to recall. You can reach me on my cell."

Steve took the card, pocketed it. "No guarantees."

The black-back landed lightly on the end of the table.

Watching his friend hoof it across the parking lot, Jake said to the bird, "How much you want to bet Steve won't make that call? He remembers all right. Remembers the sirens. Remembers the game. Five to one he remembers where he was *before* the game."

The quiet, shy teen Steve had been would've fallen for flirty Gail like a lightning-struck spruce. He seemed easygoing but any man might snap if pushed hard enough by a gorgeous female. If he had a temper and Gail dumped him, he could've swatted her like a fly without breaking a sweat. And started the blaze as a cover-up.

Made sense that was the way events went down, whoever committed that crime.

Steve was a possible. And Kevin. His outbursts on the baseball diamond when calls went against him were legendary. And Kevin admitted he'd had a thing for Gail. If only the backgrounders on both these guys would come through.

Jake reached for the last of his clams to find only tartar sauce. The last succulent clam was disappearing down the gull's gullet.

**\*\*\*\***

*Not just one guy but a stream of them.*

Good thing Lani was already seated because her knees couldn't hold her. Her head ached, and not from the wine, as she stared at the four names she'd written. The only ones Becca and Heather were sure of. How many more? Jake hadn't explained why Kevin was on his list. That Kevin could've been one didn't bear considering.

Finally Gail's moodiness that summer made more sense. She'd always been fun-loving, but that summer she went overboard with the dancing and flirting and skimpy outfits. Then she'd mope and lie around in her room for hours. Mom had sighed about her being so temperamental. But more was going on than anyone in the family suspected.

Jake had commented on the moods, but he didn't have any more of a clue than she did that Gail was sleeping around with more than the one guy. How was Lani going to tell him? The crab cakes she'd eaten regenerated their claws and raked her stomach.

"Are you all right, Lani?" Heather patted her hand.

"Yeah. I'm trying to wrap my head around this side of my sister." She picked up her wine glass and set it down again. Enough alcohol. She needed a clear head.

"I thought you knew." Becca pushed the lettuce garnish around with her fork. "I warned her she was on the edge of a cliff. STDs, AIDS, pregnancy. A girl has to protect herself. She just shrugged me off. Said I didn't understand."

"Is there more? Do you know *why* she was hitting on every male in Dragon Harbor?"

Heather leaned forward, elbows on the table, the crème brulée she'd ordered for dessert forgotten. "What do you know about her illness that spring?"

****

After the final blow, Lani didn't know quite how she managed the drive home, her mind and heart roiling with Gail's secrets. Secrets Gail kept to herself. Secrets that explained her moods. Secrets that drove her to act out her pain and desolation in self-destructive and manic fury. *Why, oh why didn't she confide in me?*

Her tires sprayed gravel as she screeched into the farm driveway. She barely made it out of the car. Overwhelming nausea doubled her over beside the forsythia, and she lost her lunch.

Chapter Thirteen

JAKE ARRIVED AT Birch Brook Farm the next afternoon with the complete file on the Cameron fire and a preliminary on the Tyson one for Lani. After his meeting with Steve, he would made copies in Bayport.

He had put her off to give himself more time alone to study them with a professional eye—and, he hoped, a dispassionate eye. Besides, being with her distracted him too much. He wanted to miss nothing significant.

One particular item stood out. The condom lubricant was unusual, from a specific brand sold in pricey sex shops. No drugstore variety. Had to come from Portland or Boston. Whoever purchased those boutique condoms had long since disposed of the evidence, but if he narrowed down the suspect list, knowing the condom source might prove useful for intimidation purposes.

He'd climbed the porch steps and was automatically rubbing his thigh muscles when he spied a note on the door.

*J, too nice to stay inside. Follow the path behind the house to the dock.*

She signed it with a smiley-face drawing except with an oversize *O* for the mouth.

Jake chuckled in spite of his concern as he pocketed the note. He made his way along the grassy path. Damned foolish. She had no idea about security. Alone on the dock. A neon sign inviting the killer. *Come and get me.* Headline—*Summer Resident Dies in Accidental Drowning.*

"Fuck." He cranked up his stroll to a jog.

He wound past the disused paddock, across the wooden bridge spanning the brook, and through a stand of white pines, where his sneakers scuffed up their scent. The run loosened the kinks in his thigh and soaked the back of his tee-shirt.

The path opened to a spectacular panorama—rolling seas and a smattering of spruce-dotted islands—he only peripherally registered as he searched. There was Lani, perched on a boulder. He whooshed out a breath before he called her name.

She turned, her smile brightening his day more than the sun. She'd pulled her hair into a ponytail. Above the scoop neck of her pink cropped top matching her shorts, he glimpsed the tattoo but not enough to decipher its design.

When he approached the dock, she beckoned him to join her on the shore. "Walk out on the dock at your own risk."

The wooden structure extended a dozen or so feet from where a set of matching steps descended. Water splashed up through gaps that had once been boards, and one side sagged where a rotten piling had given way. Unless a bad guy swam in, he wasn't going to sneak up on Lani from that dock. One less threat to worry about. But only one.

Seeing her face tilted up in greeting defused his fear-fired temper. Too tempting to pass up. He planted a quick kiss on her lips. The memory of being wrapped around each other in her kitchen hovered between them like heat waves rising from pavement.

Before he got carried away again, he settled onto the slab of rock beside her. "The dock one of the things to repair before selling the place?"

She shook her head. "I'll leave that to the buyer. Most people nowadays use aluminum or a synthetic that looks like wood. Something that won't rot."

"What are you having done?"

"Just got new locks. A hunky locksmith gave me a great price."

"Hunky, huh?" He grinned, winging a flat stone out over the water. It skipped twice before sinking. He wanted this camaraderie with her to go on without the downers of danger and secrets. But the light purple shadows beneath her eyes were a testament to the grief and worry keeping her from sleep.

He cupped her shoulders and turned her. "You've been hanging tough, but something upset you. What?"

Her eyes darkened. "About Gail. I don't know how to say this except straight out."

"About her multiple… lovers, you mean?" How much else she knew, he wasn't sure so he left it at that. His belly heaved whenever he thought about it. How must the news have affected Lani?

Her brows winged upward. "*That* was in the case report?"

He shook his head. "Gail's friends and lovers didn't tell the fire investigator or the prosecutor. But they're talking now. I've heard the stories. Like you have."

"First, by no stretch of the imagination can I call her sex partners *lovers*. What she was doing had nothing to do with love or desire."

The bitterness and pain in her voice stopped him from asking what she meant. For now. He accepted the folded paper she took from her pocket.

"Those four are the only names Becca and Heather knew for certain," she said. "There were others. Maybe even Kevin."

He read the names, all familiar. Two local—not Mike Spear or Steve Quimby. Two new ones to track down.

"That's not all." Her shoulders sagged, clearly with the weight of what she'd learned. She stared past him into the trees as if the answers lurked in the chickadees' chatter. "Her other secret explains her moods that summer."

"That secret *was* in the report." Jake ached for her. "According to what your parents told Tyson, she had an abortion that spring. A guy at college. He had an alibi that night."

"That's what I found out from Gail's friends. The abortion, I mean." She pressed a hand to her chest as if her heart hurt. Her mouth trembled but no tears welled. Sheer will power. Did this tough cookie ever let anyone see her cry? Or did she let herself cry at all? Somehow her fight for control made her seem more vulnerable.

"The infection she had must've been caused by the abortion," she continued after a moment. "Mom said mono was the reason she dropped some of her classes."

"A white lie to protect Gail's secret?"

"Guess she was ashamed. Or maybe it was the rest. I don't know."

"The *rest*?"

Damn, he still didn't have the whole picture. This mystery had more layers than Maine had rocks. "Okay, lob the other hand grenade."

"Heather said the infection left her sterile. Knowing

she could never have babies sent her into a tailspin. Every time she slept with a guy, she told her friends it didn't matter because she couldn't get pregnant. She wouldn't listen to them about STDs."

Damn, that sucked. No wonder she went into tailspin. "Depression. The reason for her moods and the frantic coupling." The wanton sex that had probably led to murder. And could again if he didn't nail the bastard. "Seems neither of us really knew her."

"All this surprised you too?" Lani said.

He jabbed a hand through his hair. "I had no clue. She made a big deal out of exclusivity between us." Rather than dwell on the myriad blows to his masculine pride, he switched the focus. "Everyone else knew what was going on but she didn't confide in you. That has to bite."

"Big time. She knew I wished I was hot and popular like her. It hurts she didn't feel she could share her pain with me, her twin. I screamed at her ghost when I got home, I admit. But sitting here thinking, I get it. Sort of. My folks were protecting me, protecting her. Maybe they thought I'd give her a hard time about it. Maybe I would've." She gave him a rueful but wobbly smile. "The usual sibling stuff."

So she didn't believe in herself as a woman because she'd felt overshadowed by the more outgoing Gail, but still hung in with her twin when things got rough. She didn't realize she was every bit as hot. Every bit as beautiful. More so—inside. Kind and caring. Genuine and loyal.

Lani extricated herself from Jake's embrace. In his arms, she felt warm and secure, but no way did she want to depend on him. "Thanks for making me feel better.

Don't think you can distract me from the case reports. Hand 'em over, buster."

"Not so fast, Quick Draw." He held the folder out of reach. "I had a chat with Steve Quimby today, remember?"

Resigned, she sat cross-legged and listened while he went over Steve's interview. Ol' Steve had been just as evasive as Mike Spear. The Eagle Task Force research found zip on them but both had murky alibis. Mike's depended on his wife and Steve claimed he didn't remember.

"Just great. And Kevin?" Crap, she shouldn't have asked. But she had to know.

"According to the report, lots of people saw him at the fundraiser party that night. But none of them at the crucial times. J.T. kept the car keys. Kevin didn't drive away, so he had to be there. I'll follow up on that."

"And the other? Kevin, with Gail?"

"I haven't gotten a straight answer out of him."

The thought sickened her. Her old boyfriend with her sister. Did Kevin have sex with both of them? But what possible motive could he have otherwise?

Her chest constricted as if fire seared her lungs. Bile crept up her throat from her still shaky stomach. Dragging in cleansing sea air, she forced herself to stop dwelling on all of that. She didn't want to throw up again. Not in front of Jake.

She turned to him. "You going to let me read those reports?"

He was studying her as if perceiving her inner torment, but he said only, "Sure. Here you go. But much about the fires themselves is professional jargon."

She skimmed the report. Arcane terminology like

fire triangle and gas chromatography had her head spinning.

When she looked up, Jake was watching a lobster boat idling beyond the dock. The lobsterman and his sternman, both clad in waterproof overalls, winched up a trap dripping with seaweed. The trap would reek of rotten bait and contain creatures with snapping claws—not unlike what this investigation was uncovering.

"I yield to your expertise. Explanation, please."

"The fire triangle is oxygen, heat, and a fuel source, or accelerant. Oxygen was plentiful in the open barn, with more openings to the upper story. Gasoline fires make black smoke, witnessed by the first firefighters to arrive. And they later found the gas can for the lawn tractor in the barn. Empty. No fingerprints."

"That's oxygen and the accelerant. And the heat source?"

"Matches and maybe also the oil lamp. But the accelerant's where things get tricky. Complete information about the evidence didn't make it into Tyson's report. He launched an investigation, sketchy as it was. Mostly he talked to the firefighters, your family, me, and a few of Gail's friends. He concluded that Gail started the fire by accident when she tried to light the oil lamp and knocked over the gas can."

"What about the evidence?"

He held up a hand. "You'll see. The state fire marshal at the time was satisfied, but he may not have seen all the notes. The heat source was a book of matches. Light one and set it near gasoline-soaked bales of hay and there's a hell of a fire damned fast. But not before the arsonist can split."

"But doesn't the matchbook burn up in the fire?"

"There's usually something, even minute, to nail down the fire's origin, like at the Tyson fire. The burn pattern tells the investigator where the fire started, where to look. In the old fire, the burn patterns on the remaining timbers showed that the fire started in more than one place. Someone splashed gasoline around on three hay bales and the wall. The base of the matchbook remained as well."

"What about the fire that killed Tyson? The same method, except for the C-4?"

"Close, but more in line with premeditation. The heat source was one of the most common used by arsonists—a lit cigarette attached to a book of matches by a thin wire. The cigarette gives the arsonist more time to escape before the fire explodes."

She brightened. "What about DNA on the cigarette?"

"Report says there was none. Another sign this guy knew what he was doing. Probably lit the cigarette without touching it to his mouth. Also, he came prepared with his own gasoline and knew how to make the fire spread faster—the C-4. What we don't know is how he enticed Tyson out to the barn."

The possibilities were too much to absorb. "Professional or pyromaniac?"

"Not necessarily either, but someone with experience. He's done it before."

"You think the same person started both fires."

"Maybe. Hard to say. If that's true, he learned more about fire starting in the past twelve years. Pyromaniacs don't usually commit murder. The fire's the goal. And sometimes the fire fighting and publicity. Deaths if they occur are a secondary outcome. But the C-4 connection to El Águila makes a firebug less of a possibility."

"Tyson's report obscured the truth."

"He didn't cover all the bases. Like asking the questions we're asking now. Those kids would've cracked and named names if he'd interviewed them more than once. Pushed them a little. Maybe he was in a hurry to get the report done fast and retire."

She managed a weak smile. "Then why was he killed? To implicate me?" If the killer wanted to keep her from questioning Tyson or throw suspicion her way, she was still responsible in some way for the man's death.

"Good question. I want to run all this new info by Robichaud before I start supposing." He pushed to his feet, stiffness cramping his leg before he evened out.

"Why not your smuggling task force?"

"This state guy is steady and logical. He'll see the holes if there are any. He has an understanding of Maine people the task force doesn't. Plus I like to keep in good with the fire marshal's office. They'll have this case before long. Then I'll call my task-force contact."

"Is there enough similarity to the old case?"

"I have no doubt the two fires are connected. If the first arsonist didn't start the Tyson fire, he instigated it. And is somehow involved in the smuggling operation."

The implications boggled her mind. "There could be more than one player."

"A distinct possibility. I'll mention it to Robichaud." He held out a hand. "You ready? You shouldn't be here alone. Our bad guy could sneak up on you from the woods."

She placed her hand in his big, wide-palmed one and let him tug her into his arms. His kiss tasted of the salty breeze. His steadiness made her feel way too needy, too elated to be with him. How could she hang onto her tough-chick routine?

She tunneled her hands in his thick, wavy hair before pulling away. "I thought I was discredited and out of danger." Well, if she didn't count the attempted break-in. But that was before the news story.

"Don't count on it. He's probably watching you just in case."

Her mouth flapped like a hauled lobster's tail. "Um, there's a man. I think he's been following me."

"What man?" His gaze and his voice sharpened.

She hiked a shoulder in an attempt at nonchalance. "I don't know. Ordinary looking. Middle aged, dark hair. I thought nothing of it. At first. Small town. You see the same people in the grocery store, at the post office, in the street." But now her stomach tightened at the idea someone was tailing her. The nausea that had emptied her earlier twisted her middle.

"Where'd you see him?" Anger radiated off Jake. He fisted his hands as if he'd like to pound the guy. The hyper-protective attitude both irritated and thrilled her.

"First time was after I talked to Mike Spear. The guy turned away when I came out of the store. Then he was hanging around outside the inn after my lunch with Gail's friends."

He scraped knuckles over his jaw. "You need a keeper."

He grabbed for her again but she danced out of reach.

"Maybe you should supply me with an assault rife so I'll be ready for him in case he sneaks up on me here." She struck a gun-toting pose, concealing her trembling.

"Honey, he'd whack you over the head and dump you in the water before you could turn around."

Chapter Fourteen

ALONG WITH INTERVIEWS, Jake split his time checking on Lani and making notes on the reports. Any one was a full-time job, especially keeping tabs on Lani, who resented his interference, as she called it.

He put her objections down to her anxiety about depending on anyone and thanked God she was still in one piece. Spending time with her cheered him—whatever mood she was in. Go figure. If that was a side benefit to making sure she was safe, so be it. He tried not to think about what could happen *if* and/or *when* he screwed up.

Last night on the phone, she'd admitted the banister needed repairs, ones requiring a carpenter. She hired a guy who couldn't start until mid July. A shaky banister was too dangerous to leave alone, Jake told her. He ought to be able to handle a simple shoring-up job like that. When she offered to steam lobsters, he made some dumb excuse about the meal.

So he arrived bearing tools and steaks for the grill. He insisted he needed to finish his notes and reports first and set up his laptop in the kitchen. While he worked, she painted walls and woodwork. They talked about everything from sports teams, which they agreed on, to politics, which they argued about. She fussed about his hovering but didn't shove him out the door, so he was good, if horny as hell.

"What do you have against lobster?" Lani asked later as she set dishes on the wicker table outside. The aroma of grilling beef enveloped the porch. "Around here that's heresy."

"Hey, a lot of lobstermen don't eat their catch." He flipped the steaks. When she cocked an eyebrow, he lifted one shoulder. "Something about the chewy texture turns me off."

"Good enough. Thanks for coming to fix the banister."

The steaks were ready, medium rare for both. He deposited them on the platter and carried them to the table where she'd already placed a vegetable salad and baked potatoes.

After they finished eating and carried the dishes inside, he headed up the stairs with his tool kit.

"Jake, one thing." She smiled sweetly from the foot of the stairs. "While you're up there, you can check under the beds and in the closets for boogey men."

Busted. "Your safety's not the only reason I'm here, Lani."

Her mouth quirked as if she didn't believe him. Huffing a laugh, she disappeared back to the kitchen.

****

Before he left, Jake made Lani swear to lock all the doors and set 911 on speed dial. Then, armed with a list of Gail's old gal pals, she hit the phone. Before she could punch in the first number on her list, her cell rang.

"Hello, sweetie. I was afraid I wouldn't get you."

"Mom!" Lani nearly leaped to her feet. "Where are you?"

"Santorini," Hope Cameron Nash's voice sounded relaxed and happy. Lani pictured her tanned, smiling

144

face.

"But it must be after midnight there. You party animal, you."

Her mom laughed, musical like Gail's and so unlike Lani's hoot. "Hardly. The hike along the cliffs exhausted me because we kept getting lost in all the winding lanes. But I can't sleep. Charlie's playing Texas Hold 'em with some other men in the ship's card room."

"Sounds like an awesome time."

Her mom expounded on the Aegean's gorgeous islands, the friendly Greeks, the wine, the overabundant food, and trying to hold the waistline with walks around the deck. "Enough about the cruise. How're you doing with the house?"

"I've gotten started with the painting." Lani described the colors she'd chosen and the new locks—to modernize, a little white lie. She didn't mention Jake or any of their—what would she call them?—challenges. "The dock is a loss. The kitchen's okay but I have work scheduled later this month to install a new toilet in the upstairs bathroom and fix the banister."

"It's your house, so do anything else you think will make the house saleable. Your father said you don't need to repay him for the costs."

Lani had no intention of taking Brody Cameron's guilt money. "The repairs aren't that costly. I'm okay. You have any other ideas?"

She made notes on her mother's suggestions while she gathered her thoughts. She'd tried calling her father but could reach only voice mail. If the tension between them prevented him from wanting to take her calls, that stung. She would have to work around that. Somehow. But she wanted to know if what Jake had suggested was true.

Not that his questioning was the first time the issue had come up. She'd always discounted any excusing of her father's desertion. Refused to listen, her standard routine. Playing tough had gotten her nowhere and hadn't protected her except in her imagination.

But returning to the farmhouse revived memories—good ones along with the horrific one. The faded blotches where pictures had hung reminded her of happy summers. The time her father took two full weeks off. He taught her to ride and cheered when she trotted the pony with the proper seat. Every room held memories and images she'd not thought of in years.

She swallowed over the hard lump in her throat. "Mom, I want to ask you something. About… my father. About the divorce."

From the silence, she imagined the older woman stiffening, bracing herself for round seventy-five. "What do you want to know?"

"What you tried to tell me before, about the reasons. He abandoned you… and me. But is there more?"

"Now?" Emotion clogged her mother's voice. "You want to know this *now*?"

"It's just, well, being here has me thinking." The long-held issues were a gray cloud swirling inside her. Like smoke, the emotions couldn't be controlled. "Mom?"

"When I get home, we'll have a long talk, but I'll tell you this much. He had trouble dealing with Gail's death and your burns. And yes, there's more. The fire and its aftermath only brought matters to a head." She sniffed, as if stifling tears. "Here's Charlie. He wants to say hi."

Lani liked her step-father, but she didn't want to talk to him. She wanted her mom to divulge the rest.

"Hey, baby girl," Charlie said. "I held my own with these card sharks, but you could've beaten them."

She managed a laugh and chatted for a few minutes before disconnecting. Sinking into the sofa cushions, she pressed her fingers to her burning eyes. Her stomach roiled like the onset of a flu bug.

She'd been wrong all these years. Her father's leaving was only partly about Gail's death and her own treatments. There was more behind the divorce. But what to do about it now?

After a couple of ibuprofen and a glass of water, she felt better. Ready to tackle Gail's old friends. By the time she finished, her cell-phone battery was drained and so was she.

One woman professed to know nothing about Gail and sex. Another hung up on her. But two more confirmed what the local women said. And she added two names to Gail's figurative bedpost. At ten o'clock, she sank into a hot tub to try to soak away the crawling, nauseating sensation of probing her sister's desperate last months.

Jake phoned twice, once from his Jeep to make sure she'd locked the doors and again for— She wasn't sure why, maybe just to say good night.

She'd thought she was too exhausted to dream, but the fire nightmare sneaked up on her in the wee hours. She sat up screaming, the image of her sister's body as real as if the blaze were still burning. If she'd seen the killer, wouldn't she have remembered by now? The notion he would snuff her out regardless had her wrapping herself in a blanket against the resulting chill.

\*\*\*\*

Afraid the nightmare would return if she fell asleep, Lani dragged herself out of bed at four. Coffee and a mad spurt of housecleaning cleared her head. Then she browsed the Internet for news. A headline leaped out at her like a neon sale ad—*Suspects Cleared in Arson Fire.*

The fire marshal's office issued a statement clearing Lani Cameron and Jake Wescott in connection to Frank Tyson's death. Jake had told her it was only a matter of time. The authorities couldn't keep the fiction going with the press without pursuing them as actual suspects.

She'd experienced no threats the past few days, either because Jake had hovered or the arsonist actually backed off due to Tuesday's *persons of interest* story. She shuddered to think what he'd do now.

At least the press would stop phoning her. So far she'd cut them off with "No comment." She closed her eyes briefly on a sigh of relief she wouldn't have to jump through that flaming hoop any longer. Wincing at her analogy, she read on.

No mention of other suspects. Nothing about the similarity to the old fire. Nothing about the C-4. They were keeping that information under wraps so the arsonist didn't know the connection had been made.

Today she intended to see Ava Warren. Maybe Gail had spilled something during a waitressing shift. Instead of waiting to see Ava at the Wheelhouse—where any number of busybodies could eavesdrop—she'd try to catch her this morning at home, a single-wide in a small development up the peninsula.

Soon Lani was dressed and armed with her notebook and cell, both in her big handbag. She locked and bolted the mudroom door before heading to the back.

The attached barn had been converted into a lawn equipment storage room and one-car garage. After having a local handyman haul away rotten lumber and fire hazards like near-empty paint cans, she began parking the rental VW inside. When she crowed to Jake about her self-protective move, he pointed out the outer garage door couldn't be locked.

She wanted to call him arrogant, but he was right. Still, the house was secure now. She closed the door with a firm push. A whisper of sound behind her had her turning to look. In the faint light of the small window, only the car and dust motes in the air were visible. Probably mice. Or a squirrel.

Jake's warnings spooked her. And anyway, she had a weapon—a can of pepper spray. He'd be proud of her.

*Take that, squirrels!* Grinning, she stepped down onto the crushed-stone floor of the small garage and fumbled for the deadbolt key. Jake was paranoid, but she had to admit he had good reason.

*Failing Gail—and you—isn't the only time I've screwed up.*

He'd hinted at something happening in that explosion several months ago, something that damaged more than his leg. He carried a heavy load of guilt, heavier than hers for not getting to Gail sooner. The more she learned, her own actions bore rethinking. She would wheedle his guilt out of him. He was quizzing *her* every other minute, wasn't he?

When he wasn't locking lips with her. Could she keep things light or would she fall for him? *Fall* for him? She was already hanging on by her fingernails halfway down the precipice. When he left, she'd hit bottom. So what. She'd survived hurt before.

Wagging her head, she clicked the deadbolt home and checked her watch. A night bartender like Ava should be up by ten thirty, so she was good to go. On the way, she'd call Jake.

The crunch of stones and a crackling noise behind her froze her in place. Chills brushed the back of her neck. *That* was no squirrel.

Before she could get her fingers around her pepper spray, pain exploded. It vibrated inside her like a giant tuning fork. She tried to move, to escape, but her muscles wouldn't work. She fell, hard, on her side.

"Gotcha."

The voice seemed to come from a long distance before everything faded away.

Chapter Fifteen

"THANKS, GENTLEMEN." JAKE stood and set his mug on the blue-and-white checked tablecloth.

"Sorry we wasn't much help," Sonny said. The oldest of his granddad's old friends, the octogenarian had the morose expression of a basset hound.

"Worth a try. But I enjoyed your stories about Grampa and my old man. They mean more than I can say. My brother will enjoy them too."

Otis stood and shook his hand. "If we think of anythin' else, I'll call you. Hope you find the answers you need."

"I appreciate that." Jake tossed down enough cash to cover everyone's bill and a tip.

Outside the Cuppa-'n-Suppa, he checked his watch. Ten fifteen. An hour's chat over two cups of java and a piece of lemon-meringue pie had added zero to what he already knew.

He might as well have finished cleaning up the rest of the plaster and lath debris at Gram's house. Next came the new walls. Piecing wallboard together in a room with more nooks and crannies than an English muffin would be cutting out and putting together a giant jigsaw puzzle. The more he considered the problem, hiring someone sounded better and better.

He should check in with Lani. She was way too blasé about safety.

No ringing. The call went directly to voice mail.
*What the hell.*

He could blame spotty service along the rural coast. But the connection worked when he called last night. She wouldn't turn off her phone. His gut knotted.

He hustled across the parking lot to the SUV. A U-turn nearly slammed him into a pickup piled with new lobster traps. Waving an apology to the cursing driver, he whipped out onto the main road. He nudged the speed-limit envelope until the Come-Again sign outside the village blurred past him.

He tried Lani's number again. Same deal. The knot in his gut bunched tighter. What was going on? Gunning the engine, he sped down the twisting road. When eons later the farmhouse came into view, he didn't exhale a sigh of relief. No sign of Lani or the VW.

Brakes squealed and stones sprayed as he slammed to a stop in the driveway. Shoving the gear shift into first, he flipped off the engine. Ignoring the vehicle's protesting shudder, he flew out the door and up the porch steps.

He pounded on the door. "Lani! Are you there?"

Nothing. Silence.

He tried the doorknob. Locked. Through a crack between the door and the frame he could see the deadbolt set. He checked the front door. Buttoned up as well.

He headed around the house. If she'd left in a friend's car, hers should be in the garage. That didn't explain why her phone was off. Dammit to hell, she should've called him if she went somewhere. She'd agreed to the precaution. Or maybe he dreamed that. She went her own way. Too much.

As he approached the attached barn, he heard a

vehicle farther down the road. Across the field he caught a glimpse of a tailgate as a truck disappeared around the turn. Must've come from the dirt track beyond the field. Too much like the truck that tried to deep-six Lani.

The garage had two old wooden doors that swung outward. He reached for one and stopped. The hum of a motor came from inside the building.

Lani's face, alive with intelligence and determination filled his mind. Adrenaline surged.

*Please, God, not Lani.*

He focused on the possibility she needed him and wrenched the heavy door open. A cloud of exhaust fumes engulfed him. Staggered, he coughed as he waved his arms at the attacking aura. His eyes burned but he managed to widen the opening.

"Lani, where… are… you?" he choked out.

He yanked up his tee-shirt and covered his mouth and nose. Pushed inside through the noxious fumes. He could barely see for his streaming eyes. Through the car window he spotted a form slumped in the driver's seat.

His throat tightened but he swallowed. He yanked the door open. Reached in and cut the engine. Grasped her shoulder and shook her. "Lani, it's Jake. Wake up, honey."

She didn't move but her chest rose and fell with shallow breaths.

*Alive!* His heart started again. He scooped her up. Pulled her out of the car. She was slim and fit, but with his gimpy leg, could he carry her?

Cold sweat misted his forehead. His breath caught as if giant pliers had clamped onto his chest. He couldn't fail her now. She could die of asphyxiation. No option. The miasma was clearing, but enough remained to make his head ache. He had to escape the fumes too.

He hoisted her up along his right side and slung her left arm around his neck. Her head lolled against his shoulder. Her sneakers scraped across the crushed stone as he trudged to the opening and fresh air.

The weakened muscle in his thigh screamed with the strain. He pushed onward to the field. Safely away from the fumes. Too damn far across the drive. He stumbled twice but caught himself, gritted his teeth, held onto her until he reached his goal. He sank to his knees and deposited her on the grass.

He opened his cell and punched in the emergency number. He inhaled a deep breath. Another. One more cleansing breath and he was able to speak when the dispatcher answered.

Then he smoothed back Lani's disheveled hair and kissed her forehead. Battery acid burned inside his chest. "Wake up. Talk to me. Please, honey. You have to be all right. I can't lose you."

No response. She lay still as a stone statue.

*Not breathing.*

His heart slammed up into his throat but he swallowed down the panic. She needed oxygen. Bad. CPR might not be enough but he had to try until the paramedics arrived with an oxygen mask. He held her nose with two fingers and bent his mouth to hers.

He hadn't been to church in years but he prayed with every breath he blew into her oxygen-starved lungs.

**\*\*\*\***

Jake downed the dregs of the worst coffee a vending machine had ever produced. The stuff even smelled bad, like road tar. He tossed the paper cup into the recycling basket. Air conditioning cooled but didn't remove the faint medicinal and lemon cleanser smells of the ICU beyond the open archway.

He'd waited for two hours but no one would tell him zip. Not even Nora. A small facility, Bayport Hospital sent the more complex cases to one of the larger hospitals in Portland or Bangor. The fact that Bayport kept Lani for treatment comforted him. But not much.

The ICU's hushed quiet, broken only by the hum of electronic monitors, was unnerving. He leaped to attention every time he heard a voice or a clatter. At squeaking footsteps on the tile floor, he turned to see the man he recognized as Lani's doctor.

"Mr. Wescott, sorry you had to wait so long." Kind-eyed and tall, Dr. Laurenz had enough gray at the temples to indicate experience. His shoes squeaked on the tile floor as he crossed the room.

Jake strode forward to meet the doctor. "Lani? Is she…?" He couldn't go on.

Laurenz held up a hand. "She's out of danger."

Jake sank onto an armchair. "Thank God." When he saw his hands were trembling, he gripped his knees. "What can you tell me?"

Laurenz tucked the clipboard he carried beneath one arm and took the adjacent chair. He loosened his tie, a blue one arrayed with Red Sox logos. "When I told Ms. Cameron you were in here wearing out the carpet, she asked me to give you the scoop." His warm voice and genial demeanor didn't relax Jake. He needed info.

"So she'll be all right?"

"She'd breathed the carbon monoxide for only a few minutes. Enough to render her unconscious but not long enough to cause brain damage. I believe she has you to thank for reaching her in time. The paramedics said you performed CPR. Also key to the good condition she's in now. We administered pure oxygen to cleanse her system. And now a drip with saline and electrolytes to correct the blood imbalances."

Jake scooted forward on his chair. "When can I see her?"

The doctor's smile conveyed his indulgence at Jake's impatience. "As soon as Police Chief Galt is finished interviewing her. We've moved her to a room. Twenty-five."

Jake hit the door. He tossed a thank-you over his shoulder.

He cursed the hospital's circuitous corridors. The damn building was laid out around a central courtyard so every patient room looked out on landscaping and seasonal blooms. But that consideration for patients forced him to slow down and look for the guide arrows.

When he finally arrived at Lani's closed door, he heard angry voices from inside the room. Correction—one angry voice.

*Lani.*

For the first time, he relaxed enough to smile. If she felt well enough to ream the police chief a new one, he wasn't worried about her recovery. Galt had already questioned him, so he knew what set her off. And the chief must be damned sorry.

A moment later, the door was jerked open and Galt emerged, looking dazed.

"Sliced you off at the knees with her tongue, did she?"

"I'd wait a few minutes before going in there if I was you." Galt tucked his notebook in his uniform back pocket. Settling his cap, he hustled off.

Braced, Jake knocked and pushed open the door.

Lani sat up, propped with pillows, a fluid drip in her left arm. Her near brush with death showed in the pallor beneath her tan.

"Jake. You're here."

The relief and welcome in her voice doused the fire his gut. "Hey."

"That Clouseau of Dragon Harbor suggested I did this to myself! Like I tried to off myself with the pepper spray first and turned on the engine when that didn't work." She jabbed an accusing finger at the doorway. "Get a damn clue!"

Her fury at Galt had her sputtering, but anguish dimmed her eyes. He couldn't let her wear herself down. Her desperation was worse than tears. Nothing he could say would help. Only some*thing* he could do.

He sat on the edge of the bed. Muttering soothing sounds at her continued rant, he wrapped his arms around her and pulled her against his chest. Beneath the hospital smells, he took in the familiar fragrance of her hair. He stroked the dark silk and held her, ignoring her squawks of objection. She made attempts at freeing herself, tough with a needle in one arm.

"Easy, Lani. You're safe. I have you." As he said the words, their double meaning stabbed him deep. No, they were just words. Words meant to soothe and calm.

Her right arm went around his waist until she clutched at him, knotting her fingers in the cotton of his polo and pressing her face to his neck. At first a couple of sucked-in breaths made him think she was crying, but she just held on.

Lani let Jake's embrace leach the fear and frustration from her. Venting unwieldy emotions with sarcasm didn't always make her feel better. Maybe because she'd had no one to hold her. He knew the right prescription when she didn't.

She took a deep breath. Okay, now she felt more together. She eased out of his arms and lay back on the pillows. His strong features were lined with concern. She shouldn't let herself lean on him so much. No matter how wanted and safe he made her feel. She wasn't Gail. She wasn't the girl he'd loved then and he didn't love *her* now.

"So Galt asked if you tried to commit suicide?" he asked.

She felt her eyebrows shoot upward. "Not you too?"

He held up a hand in defense, his blue eyes alight with humor. "Not for a nanosecond. Galt asked me the same thing. You're reckless. But suicidal? No way."

"What then?"

"My take is the killer—the arsonist or his hire—set this up to *look* like suicide."

"I told Galt I tried to use pepper spray, but he said the cops didn't find the can."

"The dirtbag is careful. His attacks could all be considered accidental or self-inflicted by someone who didn't know the truth."

"Careful and clever. Direct attacks but none that *appears* direct." She shuddered.

"But it means out in the open and in public you should be safe enough." He hiked up his right leg and made himself comfortable on the edge of the bed. Sunlight through the window flecked gold in his brown hair. "Pepper spray. How long you been carrying that?"

"Not long." No point in telling him she'd bought it the day before in Bayport. "For all the good my attempt at self-protection did."

"Doc said nothing about concussion. The guy didn't knock you out?"

"He knocked me out, all right, but not over the head." She described the attack, from entering the garage until she passed out.

"A stun gun, a powerful one, to put you out like that. Must've hurt like hell. Through your clothes so it didn't leave a mark. And he collected the barbs. Did you tell all this to Galt?"

"Yes, but he didn't comment. Close-mouthed lawman, I guess."

"So then he gathered up your bag and put it in the car with you," he went on, frowning. "He made one mistake though."

"There's a freaking news flash. I'm *alive*."

He grinned at her vehemence. "If he'd opened the car windows, the fumes would've affected you sooner and I might not have reached you in time."

"Why *did* you come?"

"You didn't answer your phone. Went right to voice mail."

She knocked the heel of her hand against her forehead. "Crap. I turned it off last night when I recharged. When I grabbed it this morning, I forgot to turn it back on."

Jake extracted his notebook from his back pocket. "Probably a good thing. While I waited around this afternoon, I figured out the time frame. I called before you went to the garage. If I'd reached you—"

"We'd have chatted and I've have gone my merry way to my death." Tears burned but she willed them away. She hadn't wept since she cried an ocean over her sister's death. Now was no time to let her emotions run wild.

"Where were you going?"

"To talk to Ava."

"She'll keep. You won't."

At the affection in his voice, she nearly teared up again. She linked her fingers with his. "Thank you for saving my life. I should've said that before."

"After Chief Galt's bombshell, you were otherwise occupied."

She huffed. "That man hasn't taken seriously any of the attacks on me. He refuses to believe—" She clutched his hand. "Wait. I just remembered. Galt was the first cop at the barn fire scene."

She saw the instant he understood. His expression hardened. "How do you know that?"

"He told me. In his office. Is it possible he was involved? *Is* involved?"

Jake's brows drew together in his analytical expression. He was nothing if not methodical in process. "The investigator's report must have that info. I just disregarded it. Galt was out on patrol. No reason to ask for his alibi. As a police officer, he'd have known about the fire-starting technique with the matches and cigarette used at Tyson's. But why?"

Bile stung her throat at what she was thinking. But it fit. "Maybe Norman Galt was Gail's secret lover that night."

A dark look—his cop look—shuttered his expression. "Gail was eighteen. He's what? Nearly fifty? Twelve years ago he'd have been thirty-eight or so. Not much younger than her dad. Or mine." He shook his head.

"She said something that night I didn't tell you."

"Because?"

She sighed. "I didn't want to hurt your feelings. At the time, it seemed inconsequential."

"Give."

"It was when she was storming around after claiming she broke up with you. She said something like she was glad to be rid of you because you were only a *'boring boy.'* Ouch."

He winced as he scribbled something. "Yeah, ouch. Sour grapes or her lover *could've* been older. How much older is the question. I'll have my contact do some more digging." He slipped the notebook back in his pocket.

"They're keeping me overnight for observation, but I can go home tomorrow."

"About that…" he began.

She sat back and freed her hand. "You want them to keep me in this antiseptic prison?"

Smiling, he shook his head. "You have to admit that even with new locks, your house isn't a fortress."

She stiffened. "I told you before I can't—"

"Afford a hotel. I know." Smiling, he squeezed her hand. "The *Amy Jo* has plenty of room. Room that includes privacy."

The heat in his eyes said privacy was an option. And reminded her how much she'd wanted him the other night—how much she still wanted him and liked him. He'd saved her life twice. With him she'd be safe from harm. But staying with him in the confines of the boat's cabin? Intimacy with this complicated man would shoot holes in what resistance she had left.

"You could stay at the farmhouse," she said. "Plenty of bedrooms. And privacy. Better yet, you could prowl

Susan Vaughan

around all night protecting me."

He ran his tongue around his teeth, clearly to hide his amusement. "Honey, protecting you is a 24/7 job."

"A job you didn't want to begin with." As if he needed reminding.

He wagged his head. "No more than you *wanted* me to protect you."

"You've saved my life yet again, Jake. And you say you're no good at protecting?"

"Just dumb luck. Doesn't make up for my failures." He paused, his expression suggesting a struggle with the idea he could fail again. "For now I see no alternative for either of us. Agreed?"

"Having me out there alone makes me bait. Wouldn't that help you catch our bad guy?"

He shook his head at her outrageous—yes, she admitted it was outrageous—proposal. "You'll still be front and center for interviews. *Live* bait is preferable to *dead* bait." He watched his words sink in. "So, agreed?"

"We seem to be stuck with each other."

"Whoa, who'd ever believe I could talk you into anything? But no 24/7 in a big old farmhouse. I need my sleep. If I have to protect you, I'd prefer an easier location. That farmhouse is too vulnerable."

"You installed new locks. I thought I was all set. What else?"

"One, too many rooms to monitor." He ticked off the reasons on his fingers. "Two, too isolated. The public landing has security lights. Two blocks from the police station. Three, when I go ashore, the harbormaster and any number of boaters are there if you call for help."

He gathered up her hand again and kissed the healed palm. She nearly sighed at the gentle caress of his lips.

162

"And four," he said, his voice low and his words precise, "the killer has set two fires already. That we know of. No reason he wouldn't start another to eliminate his last possible witness. Even if she never remembers anything. The dry wood in that old farmhouse would burn like a matchbook."

Eyes wide open, she smelled the smoke, felt the heat, heard the roar and snap of flames. She never wanted to experience that terror again. Her throat closed and her whole body shook.

Chapter Sixteen

LATE THE NEXT morning, Jake picked up Lani at the hospital and drove her to the farm, where Norman Galt waited for them beside the garage, the scene of the crime. She requested the appointment so she could show the chief of police how the attack had happened. And quiz the man about Gail.

Jake hustled around to her, but she slid out before he could reach the door. She was still shaky and weak from the carbon monoxide. Pale but determined. All he could do was stand by in the light fog, thinning under the sun's rays.

The big man stroked his mustache and hitched up his gun belt as they joined him. Although shaded by the brim of his DHPD cap, his unsmiling face held a skeptical look. "Glad to see you're up and about, Ms. Cameron. I won't take too much of your time."

"I'm fine, Chief." She kept a firm grip on the garage door handle. "Showing you what happened yesterday is important."

"My sergeant and another officer went over this place for evidence. Like I told you, we found nothing to suggest anyone was here but you." His mouth thinned as he glanced at Jake. "And then Wescott. You can see the drag marks when he pulled you out."

She flashed Jake a small smile before turning back to Galt. "Nevertheless, I'll walk you through what happened."

Jake observed as she entered the small garage, her sneakers scuffing the stones. No noxious odors greeted them, only earthy and slightly musty smells mingled with traces of motor oil and gasoline. The rental VW sat on their right. A shelf on the left wall held clippers and other small garden tools.

Lani narrated her actions as she went through yesterday's events. Locking the door, hearing rustling but thinking it a squirrel. Hearing a new noise, worrying and readying her pepper spray. Then excruciating pain and nothing. "I never saw anything but a blur of movement in the shadows, so I have no description. You didn't find anything in the car? No fingerprints?"

"Only yours. A few hairs, long and dark, like yours. No alien fibers. My sergeant talked to Buddy. The car was detailed before you rented it, wiped down from stem to stern. If there was an attacker, he wore gloves."

"*If*, Chief?" Jake said, stepping closer to Lani, who looked shaky. She waved him off. "I saw a truck pull out of the woods and speed away."

Galt shrugged, scratched his nape. "Can't prove a connection. No tracks through the field or anywhere else. You got no tag number. Lots of trucks around. Could've been some guy clammin'. Low tide at the time."

Jake had seen the truck before realizing Lani was in trouble, so he hadn't paid attention. But he *did* return yesterday afternoon to go over the scene. He couldn't refute what the chief said, even about the mystery truck. Walking the old woods road yielded nothing. Countless tire tracks, all old in the rocky soil. Beer cans, cigarette butts, none fresh.

The assailant could've walked across the field or

under cover of the pines and birches between the field and the shore, the same path Jake took the other day to join her. The same path Gail's lover might have taken to join her twelve years ago.

He barely heard Lani arguing a point with the chief. A new suspicion turned him toward the pines. What if Gail's lover, her killer, hadn't arrived by car? He could've come by boat. But twelve years after the event would make sorting that out near impossible.

"You warned me about stirring up trouble by asking questions," Lani said, and Jake shook himself back to attention. "Now when trouble pops up to whack me good, you refuse to believe me."

"Didn't say I didn't believe you," Galt's deep voice lost its smooth finish as he strode out of the garage, increasingly stuffy as the sun heated its old-style tin roof. "But there's no evidence to follow. I'll keep my people on the case. Still, all this questioning riles folks."

Lani followed him, stride for stride, skirted him, and pinned him with her gaze. "You're already *riled*, so I'll ask you. Did you know my sister back then?"

Galt blinked, backed up a step as if remembering the lecture she delivered yesterday. Jake ran his tongue around his teeth and studied his shoes.

"I remember you twins." The police chief's expression shuttered into cop blankness. "Hard to miss two girls so identical, but that's all. Never spoke to either of you that I recall. Had my own troubles that year. Went through a rough time with my divorce."

****

"What do you think about Galt's answer?" Lani asked later in Jake's SUV. After the unsatisfying meeting with Galt, she'd packed a bag and they were

166

driving to the harbor.

"He didn't much like your question," Jake said. "Hard to know how much his divorce colored his response. What do you want to do?"

She relaxed against the headrest. "No one has mentioned ever seeing my sister with Galt. No whisper about him. Only my suspicion because he keeps warning me away. I'd like to look into the possibility."

"Galt's background check came back. Honorable service record in the Navy, then came home to join the DHPD. Been divorced twice."

She sat up straighter. "Wonder if he was sleeping around."

"My thoughts exactly. My old guys at the cafe might have a line on that."

Lani had another idea, but the library would have to wait until another day.

\*\*\*\*

Jake stared out the porthole at the wispy clouds netting the gibbous moon and listened for sounds from the other berth beyond the canvas curtain.

He'd smothered a chuckle as Lani stowed away essentials for what she called her "protective custody" on the *Amy Jo*. For supper they ate the general store's potato salad and chicken thighs he grilled on deck.

Fatigue was one of the fallouts from carbon monoxide inhalation, the doctor had said, so no surprise when she fell asleep in her deck chair. He bundled her below and into her berth before crawling into his. A little early for him, but he needed to assure himself she was all right.

He heard the shuffle and slide of cloth as she changed from her shorts and tee and slid between the sheets. Was she wearing her bra and panties? Or a silky nightgown? Or only her skin wrapped in the sheet and thermal blanket?

The remembered feel of her breast in his hand stoked his yearning to see her, all of her, and had his hands itching. Images scrolled through his imagination in an erotic video presentation. Heated to simmer, he tossed off his sheet and adjusted his boxers to accommodate his hardening body.

He held his breath as he listened, feeling like a voyeur. But hell, it was his boat. Sort of. More rustling as she settled. A murmur or two. Then silence. He exhaled. Tried to relax. No go.

Having her so near, hearing her sighs, catching her scent, he hadn't been able to fall asleep even counting the pings of the halyard against the neighboring sloop's mast.

That was earlier.

Now after midnight the groan of the old boat and the slosh of water still kept him awake. An occasional gull squawk punctuated the quiet. He flopped around on his pillow. A breeze through the porthole brought cooler air and the night's salty scents. But he still couldn't sleep.

Lani was becoming increasingly important to him, more than was safe. For either of them. He'd do his damnedest not to let harm come to her, although his track record kept his gut in knots. He flopped around on his flattened pillow.

He was just drifting off when the swish and whisper of sheets popped open his eyes. Agitated murmurs accompanied the continued shuffling. She groaned, first softly, then louder in clear distress. He'd be surprised if she *didn't* have nightmares. He swung around and lowered his bare feet to the deck. Maybe he should leave her alone.

*"Noooo!"*

Heart pounding, he launched himself off the bunk and flung aside the curtain. Lani sat upright. She gasped for breath. Her owl-wide eyes glinted in the porthole's dim light.

He stood by the berth and watched her as awareness kicked in. "You okay?"

She nodded and sucked in a deep breath. As pale as moonlight, she looked small and vulnerable in a long tee adorned with orange flip-flops. A bandage held a gauze pad to the back of her right hand, where the saline drip had fed her bloodstream. The reminder of how close she'd come to dying made his gut twist.

"Nightmare?"

She glared at him. "No, Sherlock. A murderer crawled through the porthole and attacked m-me." Her trembling lips negated her bravado.

"And you tossed him right back out. I heard the splash." He crossed to the edge of the berth and waited, unsure of his next move.

The shirt had slid to the side, baring her left shoulder and giving him a glimpse of the elusive tattoo. But only a curved shadow. He jerked his gaze up to her too-round eyes.

Easing onto the mattress, he propped up a pillow and leaned back. When he opened his arms, she snuggled against him and didn't object when he wrapped his arms around her. She rested her head on his shoulder. Draped her left arm across his chest.

She smelled of his deodorant soap as well as her shampoo. The combination was somehow more erotic and hardened him again—automatic where she was concerned, but at the moment not convenient. If he made a move on her, she'd dump him overboard. She was frightened and still healing. She needed him. For comfort and not for sex.

He pulled the sheet over his legs and lifted his right knee. "Yesterday's attack or the fire? The dream, I mean."

She shuddered. "The fire. It's always the fire. Lately with a new twist."

*Always*. Seemed she had nightmares on a regular basis. "Want to tell me about it?"

She pressed closer to him and he tightened his hold.

"Okay," she said on a deep breath. Her grip locked onto his ribs as if she were clinging to a life preserver. "There's not much to tell. I'm on the porch. I smell smoke and feel the heat. Then I see it—him."

He tensed, every cell alert. "*Him?* You saw the arsonist?"

Shaking her head, she leaned back and propped herself up on one elbow. Her eyes were luminous. "I don't know what I saw. If I saw anything."

"So what *did* you mean?"

"In the dream, I see a fire monster, a sort of dragon. Since the first dream after that night, always the same until now."

"What's different?"

"The dreams continue but no more dragon. Funny, now that I'm in Dragon Harbor."

"A dragon maybe originally *because* of Dragon Harbor." Maybe her return was transforming the imaginary dragon to the reality of memory. Not a good idea to lead her to that conclusion. "And now?"

"Since the threats—or maybe just since I came back to the farm—the fire monster has morphed into a giant flaming Bigfoot. He towers over me at the door to the barn. And then he roars and—" She sniffed and shook her head. Her dark mane curtained her face, hiding the facial scar.

Maybe she did see the arsonist. Maybe she *was* starting to remember. He swept her hair from her cheek. Tucked it behind her ear. Gently caressed her head. While trying not to notice the silkiness beneath his fingers or her softness against his side. He clenched his teeth so hard his jaw popped.

When she relaxed onto his shoulder, he gave her a minute, then said, "Is that what made you cry out, when you saw the monster?"

Releasing her grip on his side, she laid her hand on his sternum. "I cried out?"

"Loud enough to wake the guests up the hill at the inn."

He felt her smile against his chest. "I don't know what made me yell. The last thing I remember in the dream is seeing Gail on the barn floor. I start to run toward her but my legs won't move fast enough. Maybe I'm dragging her out and I can't make it. I don't…"

"It's all right, honey." He snuggled her closer. "You always second guess your bravery in trying to save your sister. Only natural, but you did all you could." More than most would. More than he did. "Grief eases with time but guilt is another matter. Even unwarranted guilt." He knew from experience. But Lani was tougher than he was.

"I know. Counseling after the fire helped me see the truth but the guilt never goes away completely. I've never told anyone but my counselor about the nightmare."

"Thanks for trusting me."

"Don't let it go to your head."

Smiling, he felt her settle into the bed, using his chest for her pillow. Her hand threaded through his chest hairs, rippling current along the skin. She hooked her left leg over his. Her smooth, slim, bare leg.

She was all relaxed now, soft and pliant. Never mind the blaze in her nightmare. He'd need the fire departments from three towns to extinguish the conflagration in his body. He was about to slide down and kiss her, but she'd fallen asleep. Her hand rested lightly on his chest. Her jaw was slack and her breathing regular and easy.

If he left now, she might wake up. Or the nightmare could return. He'd be back here anyway, so he might as well stay. He eased down in the bed and blinked, resigned to a night of no sleep.

Things between them had changed, but he should be careful of what new direction they went. He liked her. He wanted her. And vice versa. Probably. But he couldn't allow himself to mistake lust and respect for love.

Chapter Seventeen

LANI RECOVERED QUICKLY, and they skipped the Independence Day festivities in favor of continuing their interviews. The celebration in Dragon Harbor was low key, bunting and flags along Main Street and random pops and bangs from small fireworks. Nearly everyone went to nearby Thomaston, where the annual parade and fireworks drew tourists and Mainers from all over the Midcoast.

She agreed when Jake opined the lull for the noontime parade didn't mean the Wheelhouse regulars weren't on their usual stools. Sure enough, Ava Warren was at her post. He took Ava's hitting on him in stride. Later called it a game. *Game.* Bull. Lani felt like waving semaphore flags or maybe beaning the spike-haired chick with an empty beer bottle to announce her presence at his side, but she stifled her impulses. After all, she needed whatever Ava knew.

The flashy bartender allowed as how she'd worked side by side with Gail that summer, but the two of them didn't get along and didn't talk much. Ava said she knew some people who might be able to help, but wouldn't divulge names. She promised to talk to those anonymous *people,* and she'd get back to them. Jake supposed afterward she'd want money if and when she had anything for them.

Later they placed phone calls, disturbing the holiday

for some men Gail's friends had named. One was a dentist in Bayport who panted throughout the conversation. He barely remembered her sister among a series of girls he bedded that summer in a drunken stupor. Another whispered he'd been with Gail only one time and left the state for basic training afterward. He didn't even know she'd died.

And so it went through the entire list.

Disgusted, Jake said he wanted to give the new fire investigator all the names. Maybe he'd have more luck. But she insisted there was no reason to expose people to official scrutiny if the interviews resulted in no real suspect. His reaction probably had less to do with frustration than anger over Gail's promiscuity. Big-time blow to a guy's ego. Lani struggled to suppress her fury at her twin because she understood her pain. Hadn't she found her own way to combat pain? Granted, a tough chick act was less drastic.

The next morning, he dropped her off at the library while he went into Bayport for building supplies. She greeted the library volunteer and waved off her offer of assistance. "I know where to look." *And you just want to know my business.*

She settled down with the microfiche machine, a dinosaur in this Internet age, but these small-town newspapers hadn't yet been digitized. If they ever would be. Rather than reports on the fire, she was looking for something else. She flipped through issue after issue of the *Bayport Chronicle*. Nothing. She turned off the machine in favor of the computer, where she skimmed old issues of the Bangor and Portland papers. She rubbed her eyes, as scratchy as hundred-grit sandpaper, almost missing what she'd hoped to find. Then there it was.

*Galt lied.*

"Excuse me, dear, Millie said you were over here. You *are* Lani Cameron?"

She turned around to see a small white-haired woman in a peach pantsuit standing beside her. A familiar face, but she couldn't place her. "Yes, ma'am. Can I help you?"

A wide smile wreathed the woman's pink cheeks in wrinkles. "I came over to say how glad I am to see you. I used to see you all the time back when I managed the dining room at the Eastward Inn."

"Mrs. Verrill!" Lani stood and gave the woman a hug. Whoo hoo, a lucky coincidence. "Of course I remember you. Please sit down. We can have a nice chat." She pulled out the chair at the next computer.

****

"You look like you just hit a million in the lottery," Jake said an hour later when she hopped in the Jeep. "Or did you get Glenn Close's autograph while you were in there? I heard her yacht's in the harbor."

"Not even *close*." At his groan, she laughed. "Okay, you drive and I'll share."

"You wouldn't tell me what you were doing in there. More sleuthing?"

"And luck. I looked through the old news for any articles mentioning Galt, Sergeant Galt back then. I happened across a photo of J.T. Meagher giving a campaign speech in Portland. Guess who was standing behind him off to one side."

His mouth thinned and a frown crimped his forehead. "No kidding. But why?"

"The article mostly talked about J.T.'s policies, but at the end mentioned his entourage included his chief of security, Norman Galt, who also worked for the town of Dragon Harbor Police Department. You know what this means, don't you?"

"Damn good detecting."

She swatted his arm. "Thanks, but it means he must've met Gail. And me, but I don't remember him."

"He probably accompanied J.T. on the campaign trail. Didn't hang around stuffing envelopes and making phone calls. Or maybe he really doesn't remember you girls."

"I have another source. This is where the luck comes in. Emma Verrill."

More frowning. "Name's familiar but I can't—"

"She managed the Eastward Inn dining room when Gail waited tables that summer. She spoke to me in the library and I sat her down for a nice long talk. Seems after Galt's wife left him, he ate dinner at least four times a week at the inn. Gail worked dinner shifts most nights."

"So she'd have served him. Galt did lie."

"Question is why." Lani leaned back, pondering the angles.

"I'm having coffee with Otis and his pals Thursday. I'll see what they say about Galt and the ladies. Don't get too hopeful this will lead anywhere helpful." He gave her hand a squeeze.

She savored the warmth of his callused hand. He was right that nothing would happen soon. She had to be patient. A tall order, as desperately as she wanted her sister's murderer caught and punished. Her throat tightened with the familiar wave of sadness that rose and fell but never flattened to a calm sea.

For now she was content to accompany Jake to visit his mother. She could complain about his hovering but not about seeing the woman who'd always welcomed her and their group warmly into their home.

When they walked onto the terrace at the Pine View, she felt her stomach drop to her toes. This woman whose wheelchair was parked at a shaded table wasn't the Grace Wescott she knew. Seeing the frail body and vacant eyes broke Lani's heart.

Jake introduced her. "Maybe you remember Lani," he said. "She and her twin sister spent their summers at the old Cameron place, Birch Brook Farm."

Interest flicked across Grace's face, then vanished. "Hello, dear," was all she said.

Lani sat nearby, watching him help his mom do a simple jigsaw puzzle. Or rather, he found the pieces and pointed out where she should place them.

One day her father or mother, younger than Grace by several years, might be in such a predicament. If years from now Brody Cameron slipped into dementia, she could lose him twice. She felt as if a hard ball was stuck in her throat, and she blinked against the emotions crowding her. Maybe she ought to consider reconciling.

Jake pointed to the antics of goldfinches darting around the bird feeder. His laugh, a rich rumble of mirth, coaxed a smile from Grace. In spite of the torment of guilt he put himself through, he was a good man, still kind and funny. And, yes, protective.

And she was falling for him.

She envisioned no future for them. She trusted him with her life but not her heart. He would leave. He lived on a boat. She hardly blamed him since she would be leaving too. And the suspicion he wanted her because she resembled Gail left her chest feeling hollow.

She sure couldn't spend another day alone with him

while she organized their research on her laptop. Seeing him all the time just made her want him more. She'd go starkers, as the Brits said. Or she'd jump his bones. Besides, she was used to living alone and needed a day to herself to regroup, the same way she did after a crazy day at school.

She looked up to see his mom studying her.

"I remember you," Grace said. "You were too noisy in the library. I had to ask you to leave." She grinned, a mischievous glint in her eyes.

Lani laughed and Jake winked. In a few moments they rose to leave. She pressed a kiss to Grace's cheek. The papery skin was cool against her lips and smelled of lilies of the valley.

"Goodbye, Henry, love," Grace said, as her son kissed her goodbye. "Bring the boys tomorrow."

They left her with the birds and a completed jigsaw of a Maine harbor.

****

When they drove toward Dragon Harbor, Jake wondered if because Lani hadn't argued about accompanying him, she'd conceded staying together was the only way to keep her safe.

He reached for her hand and kissed it. "I'm glad you came with me today. I haven't been able to reach Ma in weeks and you managed."

"Only for a minute." Her shoulders twitched as if in embarrassment. "I did nothing but sit there. Her brain just needs time to work through the old memories. Trust her to latch onto the one about me misbehaving."

"What were you doing to get tossed out of the library? Mouthing off as usual?"

"Very funny."

"Come on. What? I can tell from your expression you remember."

She huffed. "I don't. Well, sort of. Back when I was a kid, before our crowd hung out together. We were noisy, like Grace said, but not just me. More than once, she had to ask Gail and me and our friends to leave."

Jake nearly choked. The good humor felt strange, as if he'd discovered a new emotion. In spite of their mission and their differences, she lightened his heart.

When the welcome sign greeted them at the village, he said, "I need to work on Gram's house. Part of my cover, remember."

"Fine. You can drop me off at the harbor."

Stubborn. She'd returned her rental car and depended on his chauffeuring but she resented giving up freedom. Too damn bad.

He slanted a glance her way but couldn't read her. "I suppose you'll phone me if the killer tries to get on board the *Amy Jo.*"

"I seem to recall you saying I'd be safe there because the harbor master and police station were nearby."

"I said it, true enough. But I've reconsidered since you brought up the possibility of Chief Galt being involved. Gram's house it is." He turned into the old cottage's driveway and cut the engine. "I have to get ready for the wallboard. For that, I'll hire a real carpenter. You can work on the files while I do more demo in the hallway and put in insulation." He got out, forcing her to exit as well if she wanted to keep mixing it up over her safety.

She glared at him over the hood. "No way. All that dust and fiberglass could gum up the laptop. If I can postpone painting the farmhouse, you can postpone this work."

The fire in her eyes tempted him to go over there and kiss away her objections, but she'd probably slug him. She was up to something. Ditching him again? He wouldn't let her. Odds were high the killer would strike again soon.

"My repairs won't wait," he said. "Uncle Joe's had three offers on his boat. It'll sell soon, and I can't stay here until the walls and floors are done." A white lie. He could camp out upstairs. "You can take the laptop to the back porch, away from dust."

She blinked, stared at him blankly. "The *Amy Jo*'s not your boat?"

He shook his head. "My uncle just lets me live on her until she sells."

Her cheeks pinked. "Then who's Amy Jo?"

He had to chuckle. Jealous? The notion gave him inordinate satisfaction. "My cousins. Uncle Joe's daughters, Amy and Jo Anne. Who'd you think?"

"No one." She ducked into the backseat to retrieve her laptop.

****

After he opened the door, Lani made a dash through the living room and kitchen, barely registering the rolls of pink insulation stacked in the living room and his warning to avoid the loose floorboards. She heard him chuckling as she slapped her laptop onto the bench. Sinking onto the wicker loveseat, she booted up.

Jake's cocky smirk seemed to stare at her from the screen. Her cheeks burned from her embarrassing blunder. Motor Mouth should be her moniker. She needed to rein in her impulsiveness as well as her emotions. She was an idiot.

The pounding and crunch of demolition inside made her shake off her musings and get back to work. If he could work, so could she. And she could focus without picturing the slide and bulge of the muscles in his arms and back as he wrenched out the old wall coverings and stuffed in insulation. Crap.

Entering the information from their interviews and Jake's background checks gave them a way to analyze suspects. According to him, anyway. She had her doubts, but the process at least gave her something positive to do.

An hour later, Jake's cell phone jangled. He spoke in a low voice to the caller. A few minutes later, she heard his confident steps coming her way. The happy blip of her pulse at his approach had her forehead crinkling. The screen door squawked as he joined her on the porch.

"Want a cola?" he asked, holding out a frosty can. The chalky odor of white plaster dust coating his gray tee-shirt, and the salty tang of his work rolled off him.

"Perfect. Thanks." Relishing rather than minding the smells, she told herself to ignore the warmth in his eyes and the trickle of sweat on his temple that needed wiping. She scooted the computer off her lap and onto the bench. "None of this makes much sense."

"It will. We'll see a pattern eventually. We have to."

He settled on one of the packing boxes that lined the walls and popped open his soda can. "My task force contact had some more news for me." His stony expression revealed nothing.

"Good or bad?" she asked.

"Depends." He took a long pull on the fizzing drink. "The team out west tackling the capture of El Águila picked up one of his men who gave over some info on Hector Vargas."

She scooted forward. "So why isn't that good?"

"Seems his real name isn't Vargas but Johnson. His mother was a Vargas. He's a cousin—big family—but that's all the guy knew. Apparently he looks as white bread as you and me. Is bilingual with no Spanish-accented English."

Lani sighed. "Rats. So much for spotting an obvious Mexican gun runner. He could be a tourist, a boater, anyone." From Independence Day on, tourists crowded the narrow coast roads, armed with cameras, backpacks, golf clubs, fishing gear, and maps to the historic lighthouses. Too many people.

"Not a tourist. If Hector Vargas or Johnson, or whoever the hell he is, is here, he's been here since spring. Winter weather was too chancy for gun smuggling. They've shipped out at least three boatloads of weapons and ammo that we know of. Now we're onto them, the task force figures they'll make one more shipment before moving their operation. God knows where. I have to nail this down before then."

She nodded. "Did this contact, Donovan, have any more on the background checks?'

"Some. They eliminate some people and add complications to others. Gail's college boyfriend's old alibi still checks out, but it doesn't matter now because he died in a car accident two years ago. Mike Spear at the marina's clean as a seagull's wing. No traffic violations, no drunken rampages, no hint of anything except being a family man and church elder. The harbormaster has a pristine employment record, Cape Cod before he came here. Same story on everyone else he checked on. He's sending a longer report by e-mail."

She hated to ask, but… "What about Kevin?"

"Nothing yet."

Not sure what that meant, she sipped her soda. "What's your next move?"

"Go back over the same people we've already checked out. See if I missed something. Correction, try to see *what* I missed." He leaned against the screening and closed his eyes. "After you've entered all our data, maybe you can look everyone over again. You have good instincts."

"Thank you, Mr. Agent Man, says the apprentice G-Woman." She gestured at the screen. "All this data can be helpful, but finding Gail's old secret lover has little to do with the kind of stuff a background check is likely to find, like financial difficulty or jail time or a substance abuse problem. From how she was acting the night of the fire, he was more than one of those casual hook-ups with the others. I like local gossip for leads in this situation."

"No argument here. But I see one area where the background checks might come in handy. If our killer has linked up with an arsonist for hire, we might find their association in what my ATF guy can come up with." He shifted on the box and rubbed his thigh. "Granted, nothing so far hints at criminal connections for anyone. So gossip and old history it is."

Gesturing at his less than comfy seat, she said, "What are all these boxes out here? Your grandmother's belongings?"

He wagged his head. "Some. The rest is from Ma's house. Hank and I packed up all the family stuff thinking we'd divvy it up sometime."

"Family stuff? Like pictures?"

"Photo albums, sports trophies, framed pictures. Old music albums, even some old vinyl LPs. Like that. Why?"

"Grace remembered me as a kid after her mind worked on it awhile. Maybe seeing family albums would jog her synapses. Even listening to familiar music. Without short-term memory, she might find it easier to talk about years ago. It might be a way for you to connect with her. And she with you."

He smacked himself in the forehead. "The nursing-home counselor mentioned something to me about that very thing when I first visited Ma. I was so blown away with how she was, I blanked on it afterward."

Sporting an elated grin, he set down his soda and pulled Lani to her feet. "Thank you. When I finish with this last wall, I'll dig through the boxes. You can help. And now I can do what I've wanted to do since we arrived at the house." After planting a searing kiss on her, he went back to work, whistling.

In peripheral vision, she saw him smiling. He'd put her off balance. How could she resist this man? And should she?

Chapter Eighteen

THE NEXT EVENING, Lani accompanied Jake to the Blueberry Head Resort as Kevin Meagher's fundraising gala was revving into high gear. The peninsula's only resort comprised a sprawling complex of hotel, conference center, condos, and golf course on a broad projection into the Gulf of Maine. The oldies sounds of a local combo and the clink of glasses floated from the ballroom's open windows.

"Thanks for the ticket," Lani said.

He slapped his chest. "You don't object to my paying? Not too much like a real date?"

She slanted a speaking look his way. He'd hit too close to the truth. "Doesn't matter. It's not a date. We're investigating."

"Remember it's *we*, G-Woman. Don't disappear by yourself."

"I won't leave your sight, *mi capitán.*"

Attending was essential, even at fifty dollars a ticket. And even if it meant support for Kevin the Wimp. She hadn't caught up to Ava Warren again since the bartender promised to ask around about Gail's affairs. Ava would be working the bar and Lani intended to corner her.

"Isn't this the same place J.T. had a fundraiser way back when?" Jake asked her as they stepped into the spill of light from the party.

"Afraid so. Déjà vu all over again." She heard the strain in her voice in spite of her flippant words.

He must've detected her unease too because he clasped her hand to stop her. Since the kiss yesterday, he'd kept hands off. Dammit.

"Hey, don't let being here get to you. You're safe with me."

"I know." She did. But inside she quaked. What if the killer tried again tonight? She'd just recovered from the carbon monoxide. "And most of our suspects are here where we can keep an eye on them."

"I'll have my eye on you. Especially the way you look in that dress." The appreciation showed in his heated gaze.

The cocktail dress flirted with her knees and dipped low in the back. The hot-pink silk did look good. Compliments from men always made her suspicious, but he wasn't paying lip service or lying. His admiration boosted her confidence.

"Thank you. Nora and I didn't have much time to shop today. I hit it lucky in Damariscotta." She surveyed him, lean and mean in a dark-blue suit, white shirt, and blue tie. "You look spiffy yourself."

"My court testifying suit." He ran an index finger around inside the shirt collar. "Give me a tee-shirt any day. Maybe I should ditch the ATF, take up carpentry."

"You'd starve."

His hearty laugh warmed her. No self-deprecating or reserved chuckle.

In the last few days he'd let down his guard. And so had she. But not tonight while they were here and maybe under scrutiny by Gail's killer. And maybe Hector Vargas. As if the Mexican gangster had touched her, a shiver lifted the fine hairs on the back of her neck.

She was ready to go inside, away from the evening breeze and the yen for Jake's strong embrace to warm her bare arms. "You ready to work the room?"

"Let's do it. Maybe a little booze'll shake loose some tongues and some memories." He turned her to face him, his hands on her elbows.

She wanted to lean in for a kiss, but said, "What?"

"The killer could be at this party. Or Vargas. Or both."

"Big shocker. But didn't you just say I was safe here?" She eased out of the temporary haven of his arm. Her nerves vibrated like live wires, but she'd be safe in the crowd. Definitely.

"Safe, yeah, but with me. For what it's worth."

She wanted to reassure him, but they'd arrived at the entrance with several other couples, so she merely squeezed his arm. Someday she'd get him to tell her the full story of what had happened in New Hampshire.

A teenage boy took their tickets and stamped their hands with a blue smiley face as they entered. From the stage at the far end of the room, the music segued from "Mack the Knife" to "Free Fallin'." Was the band onto something? "Karma Police" would suit her better.

The resort had set up cash bars on both sides of the room. No Ava at either station.

Before she could mention not seeing her quarry, Nora and Kevin greeted them, thanking them for coming. Nora looked the gracious political hostess in her new dress, green with a matching shrug. Kevin, on the other hand, looked nervous. Sweat beaded his brow and his eyes were glassy.

"Hey, old buddy." Jake clapped Kevin on the

shoulder. "Wouldn't miss it. The resort's food and helping you over the top."

"Let's get you two something to drink." Kevin led Jake off toward one of the bars.

"You'll have to excuse Kev," Nora said. "He's on edge about tonight."

"I can't imagine why," Lani replied. Excusing Kevin for anything, forcing any words remotely nice through her teeth ate acid into the enamel, although what she felt for him now resembled reluctant tolerance rather than anger. Fine with her if he couldn't wait to escape her presence. "Just look at all the people who've forked over fifty dollars."

Nora pruned her mouth. "I hope it's enough. Money's an issue. His dad can pull only so many strings."

Lani had other matters on her mind. Not Kevin's success in politics. "I need to talk to Ava Warren. I heard she was working here on her night off from the Wheelhouse."

"I haven't seen her." Nora tugged Lani into a corner. "Have you heard what she's been saying?"

That got Lani's attention. "No, but I'm listening."

"She bragged at the bar about knowing the identity of the other man in your sister's life."

Lani gasped, her pulse racing. What was Ava up to? A ploy to get money from her and Jake—or someone else—or were her claims only hot air stemming from jealousy? But maybe Lani was stampeding to conclusions. "What exactly do you mean?"

Nora leaned closer. "She claims to know who Gail saw after Jake left that night."

\*\*\*\*

Jake ordered a white wine for Lani and a club soda for himself. He edged to the side of the bar so he could keep an eye on her. She still stood talking with Nora but with her hands firmly planted on her hips and that tongue-on-teeth thoughtful expression. Agitated.

He turned back to pay for his drinks in time to see Kevin knock back a shot of whiskey. Judging from his friend's bleary eyes, he'd hoisted a few already.

"Take it easy, man," he said. "You have a speech to give later."

Kevin set down the shot glass and ordered a wine for Nora. He glanced toward J.T., who held court in the middle of a crowd. "Don't *you* start on me. I've spit out this speech so many times I'm a robotic recording." He pushed an imaginary button on his chest.

Chalk up Kevin's anxiety to his dad's presence. Jake had other issues to deal with. He surveyed the room but caught no one paying him or Lani any undue attention.

He leaned closer and spoke in a low voice. "I have more to ask you about Gail."

The other man held up a hand in protest. "Hey, man, I told you all I know."

"Maybe. You said she'd slept around. You didn't say where you stood in that lineup."

"*Me?*" Kevin shook his head hard enough to rattle his brain. His fleshy cheeks reddened. "No way. I didn't touch Gail. She was yours. I don't poach on my friends." But he wouldn't hold Jake's gaze. Dammit, he was lying.

Even if by remote possibility Kevin hadn't poached, Jake couldn't count him blameless. A slow boil worked its way up from his gut to his throat. "Apparently others *were*—poaching, I mean—and you didn't tell me."

His old buddy hiked a shoulder in defense and

picked up his wife's white wine. "I figured you knew. Or maybe you didn't want to know."

*Lame. And cowardly.* "And no one said anything when Gail was killed? Afraid for yourself? Afraid saying anything would implicate you?"

When Kevin sweated more and didn't reply, Jake had to force himself not to let the roiling inside him explode into physical violence. He jabbed a finger in his *former* friend's chest, backing him up. "Or did you think I was guilty, that I'd found out and killed her?"

"No, I never—"

"Forget the protest, man. Did you expect I'd be grateful you didn't rat me out? And I don't believe your damn denial about Gail. Not that it matters now."

A few people seemed to notice their raised voices. He didn't give a damn who listened. Leaving Kevin mopping splashes of Nora's wine from his shirt, Jake picked up his drink order and stalked off through the crowd. He needed to get to Lani.

Except she wasn't where he'd left her.

"Chill out, bro. She's over there by the other bar."

Jake wheeled on the source of the restraining voice. "What the hell are *you* doing here?"

Hank held up his beer as a shield. His expression was serious except for the glint in his eyes. "Don't dump your fury on me. I'm on your side."

Buoyed by his brother's support, Jake dipped his head and hauled in a breath to clear his brain. "I'd slug you or hug you but my hands are full." He indicated the drinks.

"No prob. I can't stay. Sure don't care to hang around long enough to be subjected to Meagher's tarnished-gold words."

Jake spotted Lani on the other side of the room with Steve Quimby. She had to angle her gaze toward the rafters to converse with him. Her brow was furrowed in irritation, and Steve looked ready to bolt. No memory still, none he'd admit to, Jake bet.

Although he wanted to cross to Lani, he made an effort to carry on a normal conversation. "Nicole with you?"

Hank shook his head. "She had a company party. Zack's with Uncle Paul and Aunt Beth. I'll stay with them in Thomaston tonight."

Jake knew there had to be more to the story. The couple's troubles over Nicole's disinterest in child raising seemed to have escalated. "You and Nicole okay?"

Hank made a throat-clearing sound. "Yeah, fine. Just fine. No worries here." But his words didn't ring with confidence.

His brother wasn't a Meagher fan any more than he was these days. "You didn't come to support Kevin."

Hank smiled. "Stopped to see Ma earlier. Marina customer gave me the ticket to this shindig. I came because I figured you'd be here. Wanted to see how you were holding up. No news?"

"Nothing helpful." Jake took a drink of his soda and turned to observe J.T.'s entourage. Kevin was glad-handing some fat-cat donors under his father's watchful—and critical—eye. "Waiting for info on Steve and our next U.S. Representative."

Hank snorted. "I've been observing Kevin since you guys were kids. He has a hot temper but not the brains to cover up a murder or keep it quiet this long. If he manages to get elected, he'll be a one-termer. For the arson-murder, my bet's on Steve."

****

"I told you all I can," Steve said, shaking his head.

Lani could only watch as the tall man stalked toward the stage area, where people were gyrating to "All I Wanna Do." All *he* wanted to do was escape. A big fat waste of her time and temper control.

She turned to see Jake weaving his way through the crowd toward her. Steely command in his jaw and shoulders, he looked determined.

"You were supposed to stay put." He handed her the wine.

She smiled sweetly. "I'm fine, as you can see."

The identity of the other man with him eluded her at first. A little taller and a little older than Jake, dark-blond hair. When he ambled closer, she saw the Wescott sky-blue eyes.

Jake's brother was six years her senior, older enough he'd no longer lived at home when she and Gail were teenagers. She'd seen him only a few times during her summers in Dragon Harbor.

"Hank," she said, "I haven't seen you since forever."

After shaking his hand, she felt Jake step to her side. She felt more secure with him near. He wasn't touching her, but she could feel the heat of his body, smell the lime of his aftershave.

Hank grinned and searched above as if his memory hung from the glittering chandelier. "Probably not since I was about seventeen. You announced at the annual dock party my alternative rock band sounded like instruments falling downstairs."

As if on cue, the band eased into lower decibels with a ballad.

192

Jake sputtered into his soda. When he recovered, he said, "Good thing someone told the truth. Honey, you saved the whole family from loss of hearing."

She took a sip of wine and offered a smile. "I call 'em as I see 'em—or hear 'em, in that case. Jake, looks like Kevin got some straight talk from you just now."

He rubbed his nape and worked his shoulders. "He denies being one of Gail's conquests. I'll tell you the rest later. You find Ava?"

"She's not here. The caterer said she never showed up for work tonight. He's pissed as hell. But I did learn something interesting from Nora." She explained Ava's boasting.

"Hope the woman told the cops or the fire investigator what she knows."

"*If* she knows anything," she said. "I have my doubts."

"Either way, mouthing off like that's risky," Jake added. "What about Steve?"

She shrugged in resignation. "I wormed no more out of him than you did the other day. Just made him more defensive."

"No sweat, you two," Hank said. "I have a feeling your background checks will help someone stand out."

"Well, no one's standing out at the moment." Lani waved a hand carelessly at the crowd.

The music stopped and a smattering of applause broke out. The county head of the political party stepped to the microphone. Time for Kevin's speech. Lani wrinkled her nose before schooling her features to neutral.

She stilled as her gaze landed on someone unexpected. Fortyish, bland looking, complexion rubescent from the sun or from drink.

"What is it?" Jake whispered in her ear.

His warm hand on her bare back moved her to lean into him. "That man at the right of the stage. Dark hair, jeans, checked shirt. Who is he?"

"Works for Meagher," Jake said. "I saw him at the Wheelhouse talking to Kevin about his paycheck. I see him around town some. Name's Brandon. First or last, I don't know. Why?"

A chill rippled down her spine. "That's the man who's been following me."

Chapter Nineteen

"WHY WOULD A dozer driver for Meagher be following you?" Jake asked later as he flipped on the *Amy Jo*'s cabin light.

He'd hustled Lani out of the party as soon as Kevin finished speaking. Hank had already left, so there was no reason to stay and every reason to move her where he had more control over her safety. As much safety as he could provide.

"Beats me." Lani kicked off her heeled sandals and perched on the padded bench beneath the starboard porthole. She propped a throw pillow in front of her and curled her bare feet beneath her. Armoring herself? "But maybe you could get that official contact of yours to look into his background."

"Already in the works." He hung up his suit jacket and dragged off the polyester noose. Seating himself beside her, he slid his left arm behind her and played with her hair. "Brandon's also one of the lobstermen involved in the trap war you saw in the newspaper the other day. No reason there I can imagine either. You're sure he was following you?"

She hunched a shoulder and squeezed the pillow tighter. At least she didn't pull away from him. "No way to be sure. But I saw him twice today, when Nora and I were shopping. Once in Bayport and again in Damariscotta. Hard to miss him in a truck with the

Meagher Enterprises logo on the side."

"Doesn't seem like he's too cool about it if he's tailing you." When she started to protest, he added, "Unless Kevin has something to do with it." On the way from the reception, he'd related his conversation—correction, confrontation—with Kevin.

"Kevin's excuses are lame, but who knows," she said, turning her head and leaning into his caress like a kitten. "I don't think he cares about this election as much as his dad does."

"J.T.'s living his dreams through his son. His failed dreams. And those for his lost son. J.T. knows Kevin is nothing like John Junior. And probably doesn't let Kevin forget it. He's had to deal with the comparison his whole life."

"He doesn't hold up under pressure. No wonder he couldn't stifle his revulsion at my injuries in the fire." Her eyes held sorrow but no bitterness.

Jake cupped the back of her head, wanting more than casual touching. Damn. High school nerves. No, junior high. "You've forgiven him for dumping you so cruelly?"

"Forgive? Not really, but I understand him better. The break-up was no big loss. I wasn't in love with him, so that helps."

Her blasé tone sounded forced. Even if she hadn't harbored strong feelings for Kevin, his and her father's rejections hurt her deeply. But she had soldiered on, thickening her shell against further pain.

Jake didn't want to hurt her, but what future could they have? Their pasts had changed them. Failing Gail and Soriano had warped him, creating a shell like hers. What did he have to give?

He looked down to see his hand caressing her bare knee.

She turned toward him, flattened a palm on his chest. The pillow shield was on the floor. She scraped a nail down his shirt front. That her nails were short and unpolished made the gesture no less arousing. "Why don't you just kiss me?"

So he did just that.

He pulled her into his arms and took her mouth with all the hunger that had been building for days. She tasted sweet and hot and he craved her beyond reason.

She wrapped her arms around him and opened to him like a flower, making no protest as he dragged her onto his lap. Lust shot through him, pulsing through his veins. He burned for her. She answered his desire with all the passion she'd channeled into protecting herself.

Then the taste and feel of her in his arms unlocked a mystery he'd puzzled over since that aborted kiss in her kitchen, a mystery he'd kept to himself for years. "Lani, there's something I have to know."

She opened her eyes, fogged over with desire. She withdrew her arms from around his neck and looked at him, sharpening her focus and her tongue. "What? You backing out? Afraid I have more scars?"

When she tried to scoot off his lap, he held her in place and kissed her nose. "Honey, I have plenty of scars. Scars don't scare me."

"What then?"

"Earlier that summer, I grabbed Gail in the dark barn one evening and kissed her. She answered me with more passion than I ever got from her any other time. I was drunk on that kiss and wanted more, but she ran off into the house. I chalked it up to the darkness or one of her

moods. But that wasn't Gail. The twin I kissed was you."
He peered into her eyes, searching for denial.

Color flooded her face. Her gaze fell, then returned
to meet his. "I never told anyone. Especially not Gail."

"It's the reason I said Gail's name when I kissed you
in the kitchen. I was drunk on your kiss the same way.
Why did you let me kiss you?"

She didn't embrace him as before, but letting her
hands rest on his shoulders was a step in the right
direction. "At first you surprised me."

"And I never suspected. Until this—you, me. The
girl I knew then would've knocked me on my ass,
verbally anyway. But no. You practically ripped off my
clothes."

She huffed. "Your ego's talking there, buster. I let
you kiss me because I was curious if you'd know the
difference. It's a twin thing. And then—"

"Yes?"

"The same chemistry we have now sort of took
over."

She walked her fingers up his shoulders and linked
them behind his head. Her eyes held mysteries he wanted
to solve.

Dark amber.

Sensual.

Irresistible.

She smiled. "Do you want to continue your *Sixty
Minutes* interview or can we return to that chemistry
experiment?"

As reply, he rocked his mouth over hers and sought
her tongue. The heat between them ignited again. He
hardened, aching for her as she leaned into him, pressing
her breasts against his chest. He cupped her bottom

beneath the short dress and dipped his tongue between her lips.

When she wriggled around to straddle his lap, he dragged his mouth from hers. "I want you in a bed, not on the couch grappling like teenagers."

She slid to her feet. "Your berth or mine?"

"Mine's bigger." He hustled her forward to his berth and followed her onto his queen-size mattress before she changed her mind.

The light above the table didn't reach the sleeping quarters. Moonlight through the porthole shed the only illumination, a wash of pale gold across her skin.

He partly unbuttoned, then peeled off his shirt and tossed it in a corner. "See, you're not the only one with scars."

She traced the jagged mark on his side. "How'd this happen?"

"During a sting to take down a gang for illegal arms dealing. Arrested the leader, biker with tattoos wallpapering his dome. He objected. Stabbed me." He tackled his belt with fingers made clumsy by passion. "I want you naked but I'm afraid I'd tear that flimsy dress if I tried to get it off you."

She started on the zipper, but her finger stilled. "I hope you won't be disappointed."

There she went again, doubting her appeal. He bent over and kissed her, a long tangling of tongues that poured heat through his body and swamped his system. Breath coming in short gasps, he lifted up on one elbow and finished sliding down the zipper. "Same goes. You're not the one who has to perform here."

She sputtered a laugh and stripped the dress over her head. With the barely there confection went whatever passed for a bra, leaving her clad only in pink bikini panties.

He smoothed his hands over her peaked nipples. "Never hide these from me again. Perfection."

His gaze veered to the mottled puckering that formed a wide strap on her left shoulder. Below it blue and red art swirled above the upper slope of her breast. The stylized design depicted Gemini. *The twins.*

"I've wanted to see this tattoo since the first time I caught a glimpse of the color." His heart pounded in rhythm with the water lapping against the hull. He had to get this right. He bent to kiss the scarring and the tattoo. "Your personal memorial."

Her wary gaze turned liquid as she appeared to accept his take on the marks. "Yes, a permanent one." She opened her arms. "Now come here."

He grabbed protection from a drawer by the berth and fell onto the covers with her. He covered her breasts with kisses. By the time he'd stripped off her panties and the rest of his clothing, there was only heat and hunger.

The need had never been so compelling, so complete. And as restrained as she had been moments before, she was as bold and sensual with him now. Every touch, every honeyed taste of her, every slide of skin drugged him, branded him, added to the pressure clawing at him. *But no, take it slow, make it good for her.* He started counting backwards from a thousand.

Lani was drowning in sensory overload. Her brain went on the fritz. She could only feel, not think or speak. He grazed his teeth across her shoulder muscle, and fire shot down to her toes. He laved her breasts with his tongue, and her nipples puckered. She shivered at the cool sensation left behind. He took her down in a kiss that was hard, hot, and hungry. He used his teeth and tongue, his dark male taste flowing into her, tingling through her, jolting her, triggering an ache deep in her body.

*Jake, Jake, Jake.*

How could this be just sex? This fevered urgency and shock waves of need, yes. But the softness and euphoric awareness were more than sex. They were only kissing, and yet she felt swamped with new sensations and emotions—like swallowing sunshine.

She felt the depth of his desire as he ran his palm, roughened by hard labor, down her belly. His touch sparked heat and longing that threatened to consume her. She rolled into him, wrapped one leg around his hard hips, and writhed against him, used her mouth on him, on his beard-roughened jaw, down the summer-warmed skin of his neck, to his flat nipples. She felt his heart thumping in tandem with hers. Heard only their ragged breathing and the slap of water against the hull, nature's rhythms. Ah, if only that harmony could last.

She breathed in his familiar scent. She loved the way his muscles quivered when she licked her way back up. She cupped him, closed her hand around him, and smiled when he groaned. When his fingers found her most sensitive spot, brushed, stroked, swirled, she nearly lifted off the berth.

"Now!" She arched her hips and pulled him closer, if it was possible to be closer.

"About time." His words gritted out like sandpaper on stone.

When he joined their bodies, she wrapped her legs around him to drive him more deeply. They both stilled, and then he was moving in her, with her, and they seemed to move as one. Tomorrow they would return to the quest but tonight he was hers, joined in passion that burned away all the danger and pain and secrets.

**\*\*\*\***

Lani woke to the sun streaming through the porthole and warming her face. She lifted her head from the pillow and found Jake beside her, his eyes still closed. She sprawled across the rumpled sheets, warm and sated. Her sleep had been deep and dreamless.

Opening herself, sharing herself with Jake had tipped her over the brink. Emotion and desire mixed in the heat of passion made a dangerous brew. She could no longer make herself push him away. *You play with fire, kid, you're going to get burned.* She winced at the imagery.

She couldn't read him. Most of the time he kept his emotions and his thoughts closed off. No longer the open boy she'd once known, he'd been taught by tragedy to build walls. Walls, she could relate to. She'd erected a few. Ones he was dismantling. And was it her he'd made love with? Or Gail? He claimed he'd said her twin's name because of that one time years ago she kissed him. How could that be true? No matter, she had to keep it just sex. Right.

*Men don't stay. He won't stay. So suck it up.*

"Good morning." Jake's deep, sleep-roughened voice pulled her from her reverie.

She blinked. "Good morning yourself."

"Regrets about last night?" He smoothed a finger across her forehead. "Or are those furrows about our bad guy?"

Busted. "Wondering if you had any regrets. My poker face must be no better than yours."

The stubble on his hard jaw lured her to touch him. Then she trailed her hand down to thread her fingers through the smattering of crisp hair on his chest. To her satisfaction, she saw his eyes darken.

"No regrets, and I have an idea how to prove it to you." He rolled over, covering her with his body. His hands framed her face. He stared at her, his expression serious. "Lani."

"What?"

He shook his head and kissed her in a way that made her pulse sing. His mouth—hot, firm and confident—branded her everywhere. Her throat, her breasts, her belly. One day he would leave but if this was all she had with him, she'd take it. She ran her hands over his back, loving the solidity of him in her arms, the way he made her feel wanted and, yes, loved.

Chapter Twenty

ON THE WAY back from visiting his mother, Jake stopped for gas at the convenience store north of Dragon Harbor.

Lani was safe with Nora and other political types working on the campaign's parade float for Saturday's Dragon Harbor Days celebrating the hundred and sixtieth anniversary of the village's settlement. If anything came up, she could call his cell.

He flipped up his windbreaker hood as protection from the fog that had rolled in during the night. He grimaced at the cost of the fill-up, then again when the read-out sent him inside with his debit card. He stood in line behind a woman selecting lottery tickets, two men with lidded foam cups, and a baby-faced teen in chain-decorated black denim bearing a twenty-ounce bottle of amped-up soda and a bag of tortilla chips.

A delay he didn't need.

His visit with Ma had gone well, the best in weeks. He didn't regret a second of that time.

Nor did he regret a second of the time spent making love with Lani. Instantly the memory renewed that sharp need for her that slugged him in the heart. In spite of his defenses, she knew him too well. She was bright and brave and had become his friend.

He liked talking things over with her. Not just their mutual cause, but other things. She had distinct opinions about everything, including ideas about modernizing Gram's bungalow. Some he agreed with, others he didn't. Those she just waved away in a manner than charmed him. She made him think, always challenging him. In spite of his defenses, she knew him too well. She'd invaded the very fiber of his being and made him feel emotions he'd avoided.

He enjoyed her, cared for her, enjoyed making love with her, and he liked waking up with her this morning. She did make the best coffee. But two people with too much baggage would make for a hazardous future.

*But a future without Lani?*

His pulse stumbled and he willed away the intruding emotions. Those he had *no* time for. He didn't want to be late for his meeting with Otis. Since other leads stymied him like dead ends in an autumn corn maze, he needed something that would point in a new direction.

After paying for his gas and a candy bar, he paused to open the candy wrapper. The aromas of chocolate and caramel dispelled the tang of gasoline on his fingers. A familiar face at the pump beside his caught his eye and he stepped aside to watch through the window. Beside a black pickup, Kevin Meagher stood talking to the man who'd been following Lani.

Anticipation quickened Jake's pulse. Maybe a lead had dropped in his lap. They kept their voices too low to carry into the store but Kevin's doubled fists and Brandon's angry face meant trouble. Another motorist gave them a wide berth as he returned the squeegee to its bin and hurried to drive away.

Abruptly the argument stopped when Kevin crossed to his company truck, idling off to the side, and zoomed off toward Bayport. Brandon appeared to shrug off his ire, then finished gassing up his black king cab. His own maybe, since it had no Meagher logo on the side like Kevin's did. When he climbed into the driver's seat, a smile replaced his scowl.

Did the two men meet by chance or did Kevin stop when he saw Brandon at the pump? Jake chewed the question along with the candy. Probably the latter.

His gut said the argument had nothing to do with Meagher Enterprises. The black pickup could be the same one he saw speeding away after the attack on Lani. Could also be the one that rammed her on the cliff. Suspicion sifted inside him. He needed to get a better look.

Dammit, he might be late but he couldn't miss this opportunity. So when Brandon drove toward the village, Jake followed, hanging back as another vehicle, a green van, passed the store.

After about a mile, the truck turned off, onto a private gravel drive that leading toward the shore. A post at the end of the drive bore the East Road address but no name. The green van continued on south, its taillights disappearing into the mist.

Jake studied the entrance for possible cover. He couldn't let himself be seen, but he had to give snooping a shot. If Brandon wasn't involved in the attacks on Lani or the arson-murders, no harm done. If he was, finding some evidence—a dent in the truck, paint from Lani's car—even a hint Jake was on the right track, merited the risk. He'd left his weapon in the lock box on board the *Amy Jo*, so he hoped he'd need none.

This stretch of the East Road lay parallel to the bay, less than a third of a mile away. He could go in on foot if he had a place to stash the truck. And he knew just the place.

Another hundred yards took him to a new house lot, where the builder had cleared trees and poured a foundation. No one in sight. Maybe an independent carpenter who worked this project after his day job. He turned onto the bulldozer-ridged drive and pulled behind a small construction trailer.

After locking the SUV, he plunged into the woods, his sneakers kicking up the spice of pine needles and dead leaves. He'd baked in the overheated nursing home but now welcomed the protection of his jeans and windbreaker. A dense thicket of wild blackberry canes and other underbrush snatched at his jacket, wet from the dripping leaves.

At the gravel drive, spruce and maple trees arched overhead. He trudged along by the narrow track, taking care to make no sound and stay in the cover of the underbrush.

A small frame house with gray cedar shakes and a new chimney came into sight and he caught the salt of the water and dampness of the thick fog. The drive opened into a well-tended yard and led to a closed two-car garage. Damn nice place for a part-time dozer driver—if it was Brandon's. He saw neither the ruddy-faced man nor his truck but heard voices.

The dark windbreaker should help conceal him in the shadows. He swiped water from the bridge of his nose and made his way around the dwelling toward the water side.

Two voices. One had to be Brandon, and the other he recognized—Ed Pascal. What the hell was the harbormaster doing here? The visit could be innocent. Jake had seen the two men together before. Maybe they were friends. Or maybe this was Pascal's house. Or one of them was Vargas.

He had to get close enough to hear their conversation. He crept along the right side of the black pickup, its engine ticking as it cooled. Keeping the vehicle between him and the men, he gave the side the once over. A few minor scrapes and dings, no foreign paint like the white of Lani's totaled Subaru. He couldn't work his way around to see the front bumper without being seen. Shaking his head, he peered at the men through the passenger window.

Brandon and Pascal stood on a long wooden dock attached to a boathouse with a wide overhanging roof like a pagoda. Tied to the dock was the harbor launch. With the wind whipping the water against the pilings, Jake still couldn't hear, but it was obvious this conversation was no argument. A hard plastic cooler sat between them. Brandon picked it up, examined the contents, then snapped it closed and set it back down.

A fish sale? Tools? Or a drug deal? Needing to hear better, he took a step forward. A metallic clatter at his feet jerked the men's heads around as though on trout lines.

"Who's there?" Brandon called.

*Shit!* Jake had kicked a beer can beside the truck's front tire. No way could he explain his presence.

When Brandon pulled a semiautomatic from his windbreaker pocket and began to walk toward him, his pulse revved into overdrive. A gunfight was out of the question, no matter what they were up to. He backed around the truck and ducked into the woods.

The harbormaster laughed. "Nothin' but a squirrel. You spook too easy."

Jake didn't wait for Brandon's reply or to thank the squirrel that covered his butt. He booked it for his pickup. What he'd seen hadn't been innocent. The pistol confirmed that much.

Cocaine? Heroin? Maybe that was how an ordinary workman could afford waterfront property with a deepwater dock and a boathouse. And maybe a connection to the smuggling centered in Portland. What if anything did Kevin have to do with the man's dirty deals? His head reeled with too many questions.

****

When Jake picked up Lani at noon, his expression stifled any objections she had to being yanked away two hours earlier than planned. Harsh and resolute, like the first day he'd showed up at the farm. Her stomach knotting with nerves, she would make herself wait. A few minutes anyway. She'd phoned her father earlier ,but telling Jake about that could wait too.

She eyed his profile. Eyes more intense than usual. Planes of his cheeks flat with suppressed emotion. And the muscle twitching in his cheek. What had happened?

No more than a mile away from the small development where the younger Meaghers lived, Jake stopped on the roadside. Before she could ask what was wrong, he reached for her and slanted his mouth across hers for a demanding kiss loaded with fierce emotion.

Something had happened to shake him up but she wasn't going to deny his need, no matter the reason. She leaned into the kiss, savoring and tasting him, chocolate and heat. When her rib cage hit the gearshift, the jolt reminded her they were parked beside a public road.

"Jake, we have to stop."

Breathing in deep gasps, he leaned his forehead

against hers. "You're right. I wasn't thinking."

She straightened her clothing and smoothed her hair. "What was that about?"

He laid his palm against her cheek. His dear, crooked grin melted her. "Your suggestion of sharing photos with Ma worked."

"Oh, I'm so glad. Tell me about it."

He shifted to first and steered back onto the road. "I took an old photo album from when Hank and I were in grade school. And I found a framed portrait of her and Dad. Her eyes lit up and she even talked about the pictures." As he spoke, his voice roughened and his eyes glistened.

Jake always tried to be so tough, but he cared deeply for his family, especially Grace. Tears burned her eyes and she turned to look out the window but barely registered the fields and houses visible dimly through the fog.

When he finished describing the rest of the visit, she realized he wasn't headed toward the harbor but up the peninsula. "Where are you taking me?"

The softer expression when he spoke of his mother reverted to grim. "Rangeley. To see Frank Tyson's ex-wife. How about lunch before we go any farther?"

He pulled into a gravel parking lot. The sign on the barn-red wooden shack read Fred's Eat's, the extra apostrophe for emphasis. Or possibly local color.

She tingled with the possibility of what he'd said as the delicious aroma of fried clams filtered into the SUV. "Your contact came through with a lead. Did you talk to her?"

He shook his head. "Her number's unlisted. I didn't want to waste time trying to get it. Or risk her telling me to shove it. They separated before the case, but she still might have some insights. I want to know why a man with an exemplary record suddenly slacked off."

They went to the window to place their orders. To reach Rangeley in Maine's western mountains meant a drive the width of the state via a series of two-lane highways through villages and farmland, proving the Maine saying that "you can't get theah from heah." A three-hour drive. On speculation the woman would talk to them. Lani couldn't get there fast enough.

When they returned to the vehicle to wait for their food order, she said, "Is there more?"

He slanted her an unreadable look. His hands gripped the wheel tightly enough to bend it.

When he didn't speak, a sliver of anxiety lodged in her. Already he was shutting her out. The sliver ignited like a matchstick. "What? I'm good enough to help investigate or for a good lay, but you're the Great Stone Face now you have leads? Crap! Forget lunch and Rangeley. I'm outta here. East Road goes two ways."

Jake's eyes widened and he clamped a hand on her shoulder. She tried and failed to ignore the buzz his warm palm sent through her. "Whoa, Lani. We're still partners. I was just figuring how to tell you. What to tell you first."

"Yeah?" She waited, still doubtful, fighting to hang onto her ire.

He caressed her shoulder as if in apology, then gripped the steering wheel with both hands again. He blew out a breath. "I followed the guy tailing you, David Brandon. A guy at the party the other night told me his first name."

"I'm waiting." She would *not* grind her molars. As

his story unfolded, a chill rippled through her. When he finished, she heaved a sigh of relief he hadn't been caught. "Dammit, Jake, if that *was* a drug deal..." She couldn't finish.

"Yeah, I know." Left unsaid was what they both knew. "The pickup didn't look like it'd had bodywork done, but it's worth checking. Maybe DHPD looked into him. And I need to find out who owns the house. Public information but I'd rather my checking on it wasn't public."

Before he could speculate further, the loudspeaker bellowed his name.

"Hold on." He bounded from the driver's seat. When he returned with the steaming paper baskets of food—burger and coleslaw for her, burger and onion rings for him—he reached behind his seat, then deposited his portfolio in her lap. "Notes from more background reports."

She nibbled on her food as she read. She looked up briefly when he turned toward Bayport at Route One. "Nothing interesting on Mike Spear or Steve Quimby."

"No surprise on those two upstanding citizens. Keep reading." His brow furrowed as he ate an onion ring.

Soon they left Bayport's strip malls and housing developments behind. In Augusta, they would pick up a smaller state route west.

Her stomach lurched when she read the next report. "Five years ago Kevin spent eight months in a private New Hampshire clinic. Kevin in drug rehab? Addiction to pain medication and tranquilizers? I can't believe it."

"I can. He may still be on something. In addition to alcohol. He was hitting the sauce pretty hard Saturday night."

"Like we agreed, he's under constant pressure from J.T. to succeed in the company, to win this election, and who knows what else."

"Having a father like J.T. could drive anyone to abuse legal *and* illegal substances."

She ran her finger down the page. "David Brandon has a couple drug convictions, small time, and an OUI. Sort of a red flag. He could be involved in selling drugs, I guess. Maybe to the harbormaster. To Kevin, if he's still using. But why's he following *me*? And how can he be involved in the arsons? I can't see the connection between those two and Gail's death unless he's Hector Vargas, which doesn't seem likely." She hung her head. This was so frustrating.

"Connection to Kevin, maybe. Otherwise, nothing obvious. Maybe the ex Mrs. Tyson will enlighten us and it'll all come together."

Lani stared at him. "Stop the motor and let me out now. Aliens have replaced the Jake I know with Little Mr. Sunshine."

He barked a laugh. "I have to think something'll break soon or I'll have to beat my head with a hammer to feel better."

"Then maybe I shouldn't tell you what I learned while we were building the float."

"I can still take you up on your offer to walk back."

When he was teasing and charming, he made her heart and her body flutter. She threw up her hands in a gesture more flippant than she felt.

"Okay, I'll fess up." Her smile faded as the implications of what she'd heard hit her. "Word is that Ava has disappeared. No one seems worried, since she has pulled a vanishing act before. Ran off with some guy for a few days last year without telling anyone. But this time seems to me too much of a coincidence."

"I'm no fan of coincidence." He tapped both index fingers on the steering wheel. "Could be our killer sent her a warning not to tell what she knows. She panicked and beat it."

"A warning? Maybe." Like the massive truck slamming her off the road and the carbon monoxide. Her stomach rebelled again and she set aside her lunch. "Or worse."

Chapter Twenty-One

WHEN THEY ARRIVED, Jake spotted the former Mrs. Tyson weeding a flower garden beside her cedar-shingled cottage. Despite white hair, her sun-tanned cheeks and brisk manner gave her an air younger than the seventy plus Jake's report had indicated.

When he explained why they'd come, she said, "I'm sorry I can't be of help. By the time you're talking about, Frank and I were divorced." After a beat she added, "Rest his soul." She appeared self-contained, her expression giving away little.

"Yes, ma'am, I know. But if you'll answer a few questions, you might help us head in the right direction."

Carolyn Tyson remembered the barn fire case, Frank's last before he retired, because the death of that *"poor girl affected him so."* When Lani informed her it was her twin who'd died, Carolyn, as she insisted they call her, became instantly sympathetic and offered drinks in the backyard.

When they were settled at a wooden picnic table, she brought a tray from inside the house and deposited it beside her orange gardening gloves. From a cut-glass pitcher, she poured lemonade into glasses.

Perspiring in the sun pouring down on her deck, Jake thanked her for the cool drink.

"You have a lovely place here, Carolyn." Lani smiled, gesturing at the bay window that looked out over

215

the lake's expanse.

Primo property. The lawn sloped to a short dock and a swim float that rocked on the wake kicked up by boats, one towing a water skier. The view was postcard quality. Directly across the lake rose the low hump of Bald Mountain and in the distance higher peaks that could be Sugarloaf and Bigelow.

"Thank you. This is my family's camp and has been for generations. My sons own it now. They let me play hostess in the summer. They live nearby, so it seemed natural to come here after I left Frank."

*Some news at last.* "You left *him*? Not a mutual split?" Jake felt Lani's hand on his thigh urging restraint.

A tiny frown creased the older woman's forehead. "Those are personal questions. Why should that matter to you?"

Lani flattened a palm on the rough tabletop as if reaching out to the woman on the other side. "That case may have been Frank's last because his investigation was sloppy. He missed important facts and didn't pursue clues. He reported the fire was accidental, but now that's in doubt. We're wondering what might've preoccupied him."

Lani sugar-coating questions into delicate diplomacy? Something she'd learned working with difficult kids. The woman constantly impressed him.

"Anything you can tell us could help." He crossed mental fingers.

The corners of Carolyn's mouth crimped as she seemed to reconsider. "I see. Well, I don't really, but I'll tell you anyway. I left Frank because he was losing our money, our savings."

"Losing it how?" Lani asked.

"At that big casino down in Connecticut and in risky investments, get-rich-quick schemes on the Internet. He kept telling me he was going to make up for the losses. When Global Paper Mill shut down, so did my office job. I still had my company retirement plan and I didn't want to lose everything if he owed big money. He became angry and secretive and wouldn't listen to me. So I left and filed for divorce. He sold the house in Augusta and I got half the proceeds."

Jake hadn't seen Frank Tyson's other house before the fire but the Oak Mills property seemed substantial, not that of a man who'd lost everything. "Sounds like a tough time. Did he pull out of his hole after the divorce?"

She nodded, her mouth drawing into a tight line that creased her lips and made her look every day of her age. "Bill—that's my oldest—said his dad hit it big and didn't need to work anymore. That's when he bought the property that burned around him."

A new possibility vibrated every nerve in Jake's body. "Do you remember when his fortunes turned around?"

Carolyn studied the garden loam embedded beneath her short fingernails for a long moment. When she looked up, a glint hardened her eyes. "I know exactly when it was."

\*\*\*\*

No wonder she remembered the damn date—the day after her divorce was final.

Lani cracked her knuckles until her fingers ached as they drove away from Carolyn Tyson's bungalow. "Frank Tyson came into money when his shallow investigation left the case at the conclusion he chose. Other fires needed investigating, so no one followed up later. He wasn't sloppy because he was freaking distracted. He took *money* to bungle that case."

Beside her, Jake said nothing but she saw tension in his shoulders and in the grip on the steering wheel. The same anger that boiled up from her stomach to her chest.

Narrow driveways led through the dense foliage to lakeside camps and houses. The gravel access road was private, so little traffic passed them. When they came to a hiking trail turnout, he pulled over and cut the engine.

She couldn't sit still a second longer. Storming out of the truck, she cursed and stomped around in the packed dirt. The knot whirled inside her until bile stung her throat. Before she knew it, she was puking up her burger in the roadside weeds. *Damn, not again.*

He ran to her side and laid his hand on her back. He offered the clean paper towel he kept in his pocket as a handkerchief. "Hey, you okay?"

She snatched the towel from him and mopped her mouth. Breathing hard as she straightened, she said, "Can't you tell, genius?" As soon as the words left her mouth, she waved a hand to erase them and shook her head. "Sorry. Kneejerk snark."

"An apology. Call the media." His arms enfolded her. "And don't think I missed what you said earlier."

"What?"

"A good lay? That's an insult. To us both. I care for you. A lot." He paused, then rushed on as if afraid she might want to dive into feelings. "So, seriously, you okay now?"

A pickup passed them but the occupants paid them no mind. Probably figured they were two lovers making up after an argument. Not too far off base.

She nodded against his thudding heart. "The

implications of what she said hit me like that stun gun. Because Tyson didn't pursue leads and push people, my twin sister's murderer is still out there. Free. He's trying to kill me. You must be angry too."

"Honey, I'm way beyond anger. A whole lot in this mess makes sense if someone paid off Tyson. Like why Tyson didn't search my house for condoms to match the unique lubricant or why he didn't keep asking questions. Not just sloppy investigating, but deliberate and criminal. I want this arsonist, this killer. I want him to pay."

"This information has to be enough cause for the fire marshal's office to re-open the case." She rubbed her chest, trying to massage the tightness inside.

"Maybe they can get a warrant to trace the sudden influx of funds into Tyson's bank account. I'll call Robichaud."

She leaned back, studying him. "Starting that investigation will take time. We still have a lot more questions unanswered."

"And you're still in danger."

"The Dragon Harbor Days parade and fair is this weekend. I promised Nora to help at the church booth making fried dough. She must know about Kevin's drug abuse."

He kissed her forehead. "Then make more than dough."

\*\*\*\*

At the police station the next afternoon, the dispatcher waved Jake back to Chief Galt's office. No time to waste, not after what he'd just heard from Otis and his pals over pie and coffee. He figured he'd get more out of Galt without Lani. He'd left her checking email on the boat. She'd be safe enough alone because it was only for a short time. He'd hurry.

"If you want to know about progress on finding Ms. Cameron's alleged assailant, I can't comment on an ongoing investigation," Galt said. He waved Jake to the battered wooden chair in front of his desk.

"Glad to hear it's ongoing." Jake settled in. "Not why I'm here."

"Got a case we're wrapping up, so get to it." The police chief smoothed his salt-and-pepper hair and leaned back in his chair.

"You said the other day you didn't remember ever speaking to Gail Cameron. Gail, Lani, Kevin, and I all worked on J.T. Meagher's congressional campaign that summer. So did you, moonlighting as his security." When Galt started to speak, Jake held up a hand. "I've also learned that after your wife—your *first* wife—left you, you ate regularly at the Eastward Inn, where Gail waited tables."

His gaze held steady but a cheek muscle twitched. "Doesn't mean I remember the girl."

"Come on, Galt," Jake said, a guy-to-guy grin on his face. "She was hot and a flirt. *I* should know. From what I've heard, you notice *all* the pretty girls. When you were in your prime, lots of them noticed right back. More than *noticed*. The reason both your wives split."

The big man leaned forward. His elbows hit the desk. "What's your point, Wescott?"

"I'm convinced Gail's death was no accident, but murder. That summer she was moody and depressed. Had sex with a long list of guys, some her age, some older. One of them killed her, maybe during an argument, and used the fire to cover up his crime."

Galt studied his desk blotter, appearing to consider his options. Jake's chair creaked as he leaned back to wait.

The mustache moved with Galt's grimace. "Okay, I do remember Gail. And yeah, she came on to me at the inn. Wagged her fanny at me, bent over so I couldn't miss her tits. I kidded around with her but didn't take the bait. Not because she was too young, but because I didn't want to give my soon-to-be ex ammunition for alimony. I walked a straight line until the divorce was done in September. You can believe me or not, but that's it."

He rolled his swivel chair away from his desk and stood, reaching for his chief's cap. "Have to cut this short. Like I said, I have a meeting and a case to wind up."

Jake pushed to his feet, gratified his leg didn't make the motion that of an old man. He needed a show of strength here. He held Galt's gaze, studying him. "Why'd you deny you remembered her?"

The chief's shoulders shifted as a sigh escaped him. "Her sister. I heard you and her were asking around about Gail's… lovers. Figured you'd reach me sooner or later. When it was Lani who asked, I saw the pain in her eyes. Just couldn't tell her. Thought claiming not to remember Gail meant an end to questions. Looks like I was wrong on that score. Long list of lovers? I'm sorry for the family. You know who?" He headed around his desk toward the door.

Galt had taken the interview exactly the direction Jake wanted. A small-town cop wouldn't have had the money to pay off Tyson, but the small-town cop knew someone who did. "Most. And you know someone not on my list who might've taken Gail up on her offer."

The chief's gaze shifted down to his left as he adjusted his cap.

"Someone who couldn't afford even a whisper about an affair," Jake continued. "Especially not with an eighteen-year-old girl who worked on his campaign."

"J.T. Meagher." Galt's mouth turned down. "Kevin maybe. Not J.T."

"But you suspected J.T. Your reaction when I asked said so." Jake edged around so Galt couldn't pass, had to face him. "I'll be giving my conclusions and the list of suspects to Sgt. Robichaud for use when the state re-opens the Cameron fire case. Looks like I'll have to leave your name on the list and add J.T."

****

Lani was sitting on the cabin's padded bench when Jake returned. She listened intently as he recounted his chat with Chief Galt. "Nice little bit of blackmail. How'd he react?"

Since galley clean-up was Jake's chore today, he loaded their lunch and breakfast dishes in the sink. Cooking odors mingled with dish soap in the cabin. Rather than domesticated, Jake looked lethally masculine in his jeans and a yellow polo, muscular forearms daubed with suds. She snapped to attention as he began to answer her.

He chuckled. "I readied myself to duck if Galt had swung a punch, but he acknowledged using the same technique with suspects. Even laughed about it. Then he told me *he* had asked J.T. about Gail."

Her jaw dropped. "No kidding. When? Twelve years ago or now?"

"As soon as he heard we were asking around about Gail and men. J.T. was shocked and said something

222

about all the college kids helping in his campaign, that he thought of us as kids."

"According to Galt," she scoffed, remembering the chief as unreadable. Typical cop. She'd seen the same blank mask on Jake. "You believe him?"

"About himself, yeah. About J.T., I don't know. Kevin's still a good bet even if he did deny hooking up with your sister. J.T. could've paid off Tyson to protect his son."

Lani lifted the laptop lid and opened their research file. She'd finished entering all their interviews and the background checks. "Too many suspects. More than a couple with the money to pay off Tyson. Mike Spear was the beneficiary of his grandfather's insurance and estate to the tune of six million. That money helped set him up in the marina business."

"And could've left enough to siphon off for Tyson."

She nodded, scrolling down the list. "Steve Quimby leads a modest life now as a kitchen designer but his family is old money, stocks and investments from a lumber company. Both parents are influential attorneys, and were back then."

"And Kevin and his father," added Jake. "After you talk to Nora at the church booth, we need to give all this information to Robichaud. Let them take over the investigation."

*And the danger*, words he'd left unsaid, understood. Only it wouldn't work that way. Until there was solid evidence against the arsonist, she remained in jeopardy. A winter chill slid down her spine, but she firmed her chin. She climbed the few steps to the deck to go check her email in the sun's warmth.

Jake stared into the sink as he scrubbed a plate. What

they knew and what they didn't might as well have been this jumble of soapsuds. Still no further information on Brandon's truck, and nothing in Ed Pascal's background even so much as hinted at illegal activity. He rinsed a dish and set it in the drying rack.

Lani had chatted with Pascal, who was open with about where he lived, a rental in the same development as Kevin and Nora. Brandon rented a mobile home not far from Ava Warren's. Their meeting could have been totally innocent. Except for two things. Brandon pulled a gun at the noise Jake made, and that house was supposed to be unoccupied because the owners were away. How the hell should he proceed? Follow the guy? Hard to be invisible in a rural area where people knew you and your vehicle.

"Jake, you better come up here. Something's going on."

At Lani's announcement, the commotion topside broke through Jake's thoughts. He joined her on deck.

The main dock near the harbormaster's building was lined with official boats of the Maine Marine Patrol. More official crafts surrounded two lobster boats at their moorings. Engine exhaust soured the more pleasant aromas of roasting beef and baking rolls from the inn's kitchen.

The dock swarmed with men and women in uniform. Chief Galt and his sergeant in their khakis and white shirts. Four or five others in the dark trousers and tan shirts of the Maine Marine Patrol. And two EMTs in jeans and blue shirts with epaulets. Police cars with their red lights rotating sat beside the open back doors of an ambulance.

Jake saw no crime-scene tape but the DHPD

sergeant and a couple of men with fire-department volunteer badges kept curious onlookers back from the action. He'd forgotten how small towns with five-man forces had to depend on partially trained volunteers. On land, more volunteers, self-important teenaged fire-department wannabes, herded the curious back and uphill toward the inn.

Two MMP officers hoisted a black body bag from their patrol boat onto a gurney held by the EMTs, who hustled up the hill with their burden. Onlookers' excited voices hushed as the body passed them.

"You think it's Ava?" Lani's whispered words conveyed her horror as the ambulance pulled away.

"A possibility. Could be a boating accident. Could be anything." He didn't want to scare her, but with the cops standing around, his bet was on the bartender. Her bragging might've gotten her killed.

"Over there. David Brandon." Lani pointed farther down the docks. She gripped his arm. "In handcuffs."

Three other men stood, their gazes downcast, with Brandon. He was the only one manacled. DHPD officers and an MMP officer then escorted them from a Marine Patrol boat along the docks, and to official cars.

As soon as the vehicles drove away with the apparent suspects, many people lost interest and wandered away. Others trailed down to the docks, apparently hoping for news or speculation. At a signal from Chief Galt, the volunteers ended their control and joined the crowd.

"Brandon is involved in the trap cutting," Jake said. "Probably so are the rest. Looks like the MMP has stepped in to stop it."

"Where's Ed Pascal? Is he mixed up in this?"

"There, by the harbormaster building," he said. "With Galt."

But not under arrest. Galt pumped Pascal's hand with both of his as if cranking a car jack. He beamed a smile for a woman holding up a mic. Jake recognized her as a classmate. Her byline regularly appeared in the Bayport paper.

"Let's get over there." He swung a leg over the side and reached for Lani's hand.

Chapter Twenty-Two

THEY RACED SINGLE file along the narrow finger dock and reached the press conference as Galt was launching into a speech.

"Thanks to our intrepid harbormaster, Ed Pascal," Galt announced, "at least two crimes and maybe three have been solved today. Disputes about fishing territory are centuries old. Generally we like to let lobstermen solve their own problems. But when trap wars turn nasty and dangerous, the law has to step in. Pascal here tipped off the Maine Marine Patrol. Surveillance yielded four arrests today, for allegedly cutting trap lines and firing shotgun blasts toward other boats."

Lani nudged Jake. "Didn't you tell me you had your contact report the trap cutting?"

He nodded. "No reason Pascal couldn't have reported it too." But Pascal didn't look happy at the praise and attention. His sun-lined features crimped deeper as he shrank back into the shadows of the building.

Jake had learned more about Pascal from his grandfather's buddies. The harbormaster had applied for the job after the previous guy retired. Had the necessary experience, having worked as deputy to a harbormaster on Cape Cod. Maine had no specific regulations for harbormasters, as far as Jake had been able to find out. All municipal hires, they managed the harbor moorings and dockage, organized search and rescue operations, and enforced coastal laws. Pascal's references checked out and no one else applied, so he was hired.

"Got up to speed fast on town ordinances and state laws," one of the old codgers had said. "Picked up where Murphy left off with managing the moorings and dock space. Don't interfere too much with workin' boats neither."

Except in this case, Jake mused now.

"One of the men may also be charged with drug possession," Galt continued. "David Brandon's pockets contained bags containing an unidentified powder and some capsules. I'll have more on that after DHPD searches his home."

"What about the body?" the reporter prompted. "Any identification?"

"Female in her thirties," Galt clipped out, suddenly all regs. "Have to notify the family before I can give you a name."

When she tried to ask more, he held up a hand. "MMP found the body washed up against the far side one of the smaller islands. Body'd been in the water a few days. Not clear yet if the death's an accident or connected to the trap wars. We're looking into the matter. If necessary, I'll call in Major Crimes."

"State detectives'll take over if it's murder," Jake murmured to Lani.

"Thank you, Chief." The reporter smiled. "I'd like a picture of you with Mr. Pascal before you go."

But the harbormaster had vanished. The harbor launch churned away from shore, its departing rumble floating back toward the docks. Ed Pascal, a cap pulled low over his forehead stood at the helm.

"Camera shy," Lani said. "What's up with that?"

Jake stared after the fleeing man. "I don't know but I aim to find out."

A trip to the library found no pictures of Ed Pascal in old newspapers, not even when the town had introduced him as the new harbormaster. He'd begged off, saying his ugly mug would break the camera.

Strange for such a gregarious man. One who'd placed himself in the limelight as a hero.

Later, Jake meandered around the docks, ostensibly gawking at the pleasure boats in town for the weekend's festivities. His cell phone captured more than one image of Pascal in conversation with boaters. Then he detoured around Donovan, who was out of the office with the smuggling task force, and made a call to a primary source.

\*\*\*\*

On Saturday, Lani sprinkled flour on her hands and on the makeshift counter behind the fried dough and pie booth. Fruity aromas of home-baked blueberry and apple pies mingled with the greasy odor of hot oil. Perspiration dripped down her backbone, and she eased farther beneath the canvas cover to escape the sun.

The denizens of Dragon Harbor worked hard on the annual festivities marking the village's founding. All year long, the Dragon Harbor Day Committee raised funds and organized the parade, fair, and fireworks. People from around the coastal area and beyond jammed village streets. On the truck-bed stage at one end of the middle school grounds, politicians pontificated between musical performances, but most people ignored them. They came to dunk the police chief or school principal in a water tank and to buy crafts and fair food.

"The parade was great," she said. "Just as I remembered."

Nora lifted one shoulder. "Not as good as it used to be. I miss the neighborhood floats." She sighed as she slapped a hunk of bread dough onto the flour-smeared counter. "Most floats represent businesses or churches. The spirit's there but folks don't have the time. I wouldn't have pushed myself to do a float either except for Kevin's campaign."

Lani grinned, wiping one floury hand on her cotton-duck apron. "Ours was the best, no matter what the judges say. And I loved the school bands and the Revolutionary War re-enactors with their muskets."

She mashed the dough between her palms and began stretching it into a flat, round shape. "Ah, there's a breeze." She tilted her face into the salt-laced air.

"Probably bringing in that rain they predicted."

"You two have enough ready for the fryolator? We have three orders waiting." Always in motion, the booth organizer was a tall woman with short gray hair framing a long, narrow face. She shifted back and forth on sneaker-clad feet.

"Enough to hold you for a while." Nora left a dusting of white as she pushed hair from her forehead. She handed a tray of flattened dough to the woman, who promptly slapped two into the bubbling oil.

Fried dough, doughboys, or elephant ears, whatever the name, Lani loved the decadent treat. Sprinkled with powdered sugar and cinnamon and eaten warm. Yum. Her mouth watered. Next break she'd have one. Maybe a snack would take the edge off her nerves, jangling from having to quiz Nora.

Her friend dusted off her hands and fanned herself

with the newspaper. "Did you see this morning's *Chronicle*?" She held up the front page with three-columns-wide pictures of the four men being taken into custody.

Lani'd read the story while she ate her cereal, but here was an opening. Her pulse kicked into an anxious two-step. "More developments?"

"Says they identified the dead woman as Ava Warren but—get this—'Chief Galt refused to state the cause of death pending an autopsy.' Unattended deaths require autopsies but maybe it wasn't an accident? Ava was a wild one but I'd hate to think some guy killed her." Nora looked up, her shoulders rigid. "Emergency room nurses see gruesome trauma to the human body. But not much is worse than what happens after several days in the ocean. I hope her mother didn't have to look at her dead daughter that way."

Lani had thought the same thing. "Maybe they used dental records. And Ava had lots of ink." Jake had said as much. "What about the men who were arrested?"

"Says here there's no evidence to connect them to the body. One of the MMP boats found Ava while they were observing the suspects. More than six hundred traps were cut loose in the fishing dispute. All four men are charged with criminal mischief, reckless endangerment with firearms, and vandalism of property. David Brandon faces further charges of trafficking scheduled drugs—oxycodone and other opiate pills—and cocaine."

People in shorts and tee-shirts chatted with neighbors in long lines to buy homemade pie or Italian sausage rolls or blooming onions, among other artery-clogging delights. Children darted among the adults and raced to the game booths. Lani saw Kevin in the middle of the crowd.

*Jump in, Coward.*

When Nora set down the paper to return to dough stretching, Lani tilted her head toward Kevin, who was walking toward the platform. "I see Kevin's headed to speak."

Nora glanced her husband's way. Her brows bunched together. "Yeah. He looks ready. Confident."

Something in her friend's tone and expression had the hairs on Lani's neck prickling. She picked up another dough chunk so she had something to do with her shaky hands. "He isn't always?"

Nora tilted her head as if deciding how much to say. She lowered her voice. "Being J.T.'s son isn't easy. Kev's had some problems, some… issues. There've been rocky times, but things are better now."

"And the arrests. Isn't David Brandon a Meagher employee?"

Nora sighed. "Disappointing blot on the company. Kevin prepared a statement, but the paper hasn't run it yet."

Lani swallowed. "Kevin know anything about Brandon's *issues*?"

The other woman's eyes narrowed at her anticipatory expression. Her fingers stilled on the still shapeless dough. "You're interrogating me, aren't you?"

The accusation burned her stomach, sending acid up her throat. "Nora, I—"

Nora's plump face was red now, and not from the sun or the fryolator. "No! I've heard about all the questions you and Jake are asking. You think Kevin does drugs? Or do you think he set that fire? Killed your sister?"

Behind the booth, a balloon popped and a child began to wail. The aroma of frying onions and hamburgers soured the salt breeze.

"No, I don't. I don't believe that. I'm just trying to get the truth. *All* of the truth." Her words sounded lame but the anguish of questioning her friend twisted her insides and short-circuited her brain.

Nora stepped close, fury glistening in her eyes. She jabbed her index finger against Lani's sternum. "I know Kevin hurt you. It was a long time ago. He was a boy. He has his faults but he's a good man. A good father. I thought you were my friend. I guess I was wrong." She tore off her apron and tossed it on the counter. "I'm taking a break," she said to no one in particular as she hurried from the booth.

Lani lowered her gaze. The white smear of accusation on her apron bib shamed her. Dough oozed between her clenched fingers.

****

Jake met Lani at the church booth when her shift ended. A man and woman he didn't know were donning flour-dusted aprons as she walked out into the afternoon sunlight. Her mouth was pinched.

He didn't see Nora anywhere around. Maybe she'd spilled some nugget that would help them. "What happened?"

Lani slipped her arm into his and led him away toward the harbor. She bit her lip. "I'll tell you later."

He squeezed her hand where it lay on his forearm. They fell silent as they joined others walking back into town.

On the docks, the aroma of salmon sizzling on a grill drifted from a neighboring boat. Glasses and beer bottles clinked. A cormorant dived, hunting a meal in the deep. All normal for a holiday weekend.

Peaceful. Innocent. Only on the surface, he mused. Somewhere a murderer watched and waited.

After they climbed aboard the *Amy Jo*, Lani dropped into a deck chair. Elbows on her knees and face in her hands. The picture of dejection. Not much different from how he felt. They had to make some progress, somehow. But now he needed to know what she found out. "Want to tell me about it?"

She lifted bleak eyes. "I couldn't find a way to ask about Kevin's drug use without sounding like a cop interrogating a perp. Nora may never speak to me again."

"I'm sorry. You two have been close for a long time. She'll change her mind and come around. Give her time." He managed to sound more confident than he felt. If Nora ever probed Kevin about Gail, she might find more than she bargained for.

"I hope you're right." She gave him a wobbly smile. "What about you?"

"I didn't have much luck either. After I helped barbecue chickens, I hunted down Mike Spear. For all the good it did."

"I'm ninety-nine percent sure he was one of my sister's one-night stands."

"Agreed. Although he could've acted in anger back then and covered up his crime, I can't picture him carrying out the attacks on you. I've checked on Steve Quimby's schedule. He was at work when the guy tried to asphyxiate you. Even if they have the money, I can't imagine either of those men *knowing* how to hire even a cut-rate hit man."

"So we have nothing. Still." She shook her head.

"Nora did mention Kevin's had some problems and they've had some rocky times. She didn't—wouldn't—elaborate but I got the feeling they spent some time apart. Maybe when Kevin was in rehab."

"He could've gotten into drugs after the fire, especially if he started it," he said.

"Or his substance abuse could be because of pressure from his dad, the loss of his mom. He's not strong like some people." Her pointed stare warmed him. "Who knows?"

"Back then he drank too much. We all did. Kevin more than most. Suppose Gail's latest wasn't an older guy. Suppose it was Kevin. And suppose they had a fight in the barn and he struck her in anger."

"I remember his temper. He could've killed her by accident, especially if he'd been drinking."

He nodded, picturing the scenario. "Then he panicked and splashed gas around and set the fire to cover what he did, like we said before. But Hank was speculating the other night. He doesn't think Kevin's clever enough to have kept the crime covered up by himself."

She sucked in a breath. "Good old dad. J.T. has both money and influence. He could pay someone else to take care of loose threads that might unravel a cover-up."

"Someone who didn't mind earning some extra dollars under the table. Don't forget Brandon's truck could've been the one I saw after someone zapped you last week."

Fear flashed in her eyes. "Murder for hire's a huge leap from small-time drug dealing. Unless he's involved with the Mexican cartel. Thank God he's in jail. Could he be Vargas?"

"I can't feature local fishermen being cozy with an outsider. But if it's true, he could've been the one who killed Frank Tyson. To keep him from spilling who paid him to bungle things. Suppose Kevin went to his dad for help, and J.T. paid Tyson to call the fire accidental."

She scraped her tongue against her teeth. "A big motive for his murder, preventing Tyson from squealing on him."

"I can't see either J.T. or Kevin committing murder directly. Brandon does work for Meagher. If J.T. knew about the drug dealing, he could've held that over Brandon and forced him to carry out the attacks on me and to kill Tyson."

He reached for her hand, enveloping its softness. "Damn smart. You could've been a detective."

Her cheeks flushed. "But I don't see how it ties to the smugglers."

"So far all we have is supposition. And only the C-4 to connect the arms smuggling and the arson."

"When the fire marshal's office re-opens the case, they'll connect it to Tyson's death and ask the tough questions. People will have to answer then. Including Kevin."

"All our efforts wouldn't be necessary if Frank Tyson had asked the tough questions twelve years ago. I might not have the C-4 link now. Small silver lining in a murky cloud." And he wouldn't have connected with Lani. Another silver lining.

"God, Jake, I hate all this. I hate grilling my old friends, alienating innocent people."

He drew her up and into his arms, inhaled her scent for comfort. "I know. I'm tired of it all too." Lifting her chin, he examined the crinkles fanning out by her eyes, fine lines more pronounced since this began. "You're scared. So am I. You could quit, leave town, and let me share the rest of what we have with Robichaud. We've drawn out the bad guys enough."

"Quit? Now? When we're so close? Stuff it, Wescott. I failed Gail twelve years ago. I won't fail her now."

He felt determination in her trembling shoulders. "You didn't fail her. *I* failed her. If I hadn't left, she'd be alive. You didn't know what she was doing."

She stepped out of his embrace. "Exactly. I should've pushed her to open up. Whenever I ragged her about her moods, she just snarked back or laughed away the issue."

"Your parents and Gail kept her secret from you. Even if you'd probed, she probably wouldn't have told you."

She flopped back into the deck chair and rocked. "You're right. But now I want justice for her. And evidence for you about the smugglers." She met his gaze, a fierceness in her hazel-gold eyes that pierced his chest. "I wish the fire marshal would *move*."

"The engines of officialdom crank up slowly. Being patient is hard. Remember Ed Pascal avoided having his picture taken?"

"Ran away is more like it. So?"

"I snapped his picture with my cell and sent it to the harbormaster on the Cape where he used to work. His office called me back and said he was busy, but he wanted to talk to me about the matter personally. Said he'd call. I haven't heard from him yet."

That brought her head up, snapped her out of her funk. "So our harbormaster might not be who he claims to be after all?"

"Something's off somewhere. Damned easy for a harbormaster to zip around all these little islands and inlets without suspicion. And he has access to waterfront properties."

"Are you thinking he's connected to the smuggling?"

"Ka-ching! Brandon could be the link between the arson and the drug-and-arms smuggling."

"But if they were working together, why would Pascal help bust Brandon?"

"I see a couple possibilities but nothing that makes sense in a big picture." He shook his head over the gaps in the puzzle. "When I saw them meet, both men seemed damned familiar with the property. The place belongs to some people from Pennsylvania who didn't come this summer. House and a couple outbuildings. Good place to stash contraband. "

"Or a pickup damaged in a hit and run."

"I texted Donovan—he's the Task Force Eagle agent I've used as contact on all this—about the property but he hasn't responded. I don't want to wait for them to search."

"I get it. Because evidence could be lost. We could take a boat ride this evening." Anxiety and excitement animated her words. She wanted answers as much or more than he did.

"Too dangerous for you if anyone's there. Who knows who else might be involved?" Protecting Lani while trying to search a dodgy location? Just like the disastrous search in New Hampshire. Not Lani. A wire twisted in his gut. "You're not going. Not gonna happen."

"Nora's not speaking to me. If the arsonist isn't Brandon, he could still be hunting me. The farm is as isolated as ever. You sure you want to leave me behind?" she said sweetly.

Chapter Twenty-Three

AT DUSK, LANI stood beside Jake at the wheel of the *Amy Jo* as they chugged out of the harbor. Moored craft around them rocked empty since most people were wending their way back to the school grounds for the fireworks display. Wind smelling of fish and dampness herded in clouds, bringing a weather change. She hoped the rain would hold off until after the fireworks.

She zipped her hoodie against the cool night air and jammed her hands in her pockets. She shouldn't be nervous. They weren't planning to do anything illegal. Or dangerous.

Out of the harbor, Jake steered in the growing gloom around the lighthouse and Dragon Rocks, then north along the peninsula. No moon shone to point out the colorful lobster buoys dotting the pitch-black waters.

Lighted houses among thinned trees alternated with thick stands of spruce and birch clumped near the rocks defining the shoreline. A fog bank, tall and wide as a cloud, crept in from the bay, muffling running lights—if anyone else dared venture out on the water. She had confidence in Jake's navigation skills, and they weren't far enough from shore to get lost in the murk. Still, the fog's eerie effect slid shivers over her back.

"How far up the peninsula is this place?" She raised her voice to be heard above the engine's growl.

"Not much farther," he replied. "Uncle Joe removed

most of the electronics to install in his new boat, but I checked a map against the chart. I'll head out toward the Mobcap. The island's directly offshore. Once I spot it, I'll turn toward shore."

"I know the Mobcap." Barely the size of the town baseball field, the windswept island was deserted except for a few scraggly trees and a tumbledown shack. "We used to sail around it. The water's plenty deep. No dangerous rocks either. Dad would let Gail and me swim ashore and look for shells on the little beach."

"You must be mellowing. You've called him *Dad* twice now."

Whoa, so she had. She blinked, not at Jake's perception but at her slip. "Maybe. I phoned him the day we went to see Tyson's wife. We talked about repairs to the house, a little about Gail's troubles that spring and summer. Our phone conversation wasn't easy but it made me realize how much I miss him."

"Long time to hold a grudge. Didn't your mom say the marriage was in trouble before the fire? You could sign a peace pact."

She was yielding to what her heart knew was right, to what her heart wanted. "How did you get to be so wise?"

The dim light of the control panel limned his strong profile. He flashed his crooked grin. "Had time to think since Mom's illness. Family's too important to blow off. So?"

"One thing at a time. After this is over. When the murderer is brought to justice." The weight of it seemed to lift, and she peered into the fog. Lace curtains of the swirling curtain dimmed the on-shore lights. "Houses look so different from the water. How will you recognize it?"

"The boat house has a distinctive roof line like a Chinese pagoda." His gaze swept her hunched stance. "You cold?"

She straightened her shoulders. "Hey, think I can't take a little Maine night outing? I'm nearly a native, you know. I even swim in the bay." Once a summer in the sixty-five degree water, just to make that claim. But she'd never admit the plunge turned her skin blue.

He laughed and curved an arm around her shoulders. "Nearly a native? No such thing here. You either go back several generations or you're *from away*."

She snuggled closer. A rough outline of humped land loomed just ahead. "There's the Mobcap."

A massive whomp from below pitched the boat askew.

She jerked sideways out of his arms. She slammed against the side of the wheelhouse and the safety rail dug into her back.

He spread his legs to steady himself and gripped the wheel with both hands. "What the hell?"

Another jolt and the running lights died as well as the instrument lights. The old lobster boat tipped steeply to port. Heart racing, she held on. "What's happening?"

"Not sure." She couldn't see him but knew his grim face from the tightness in his voice. "Get to the companionway if you can. Take a look below." He handed her a flashlight.

Staggering as the boat did another carnival-ride maneuver, she hand-held her way around him to the companionway. One look below with the flashlight had her gasping. "We're taking on water. Below deck is flooding."

He cursed and grabbed the radio mic. He clicked buttons. "Dead. Dammit, my uncle said this thing was giving out. Of all the rotten times." He bent to look below the console and swore again. When the engine coughed, he opened the locker in the cockpit and shoved a life vest at her. "She's sinking. We'll have to abandon ship. Put this on. Clip the light to it. It's waterproof."

*Abandon ship?* She stood frozen with the vest dangling in her arms. When she saw Jake whip into action, she shook the ice from her brain. She tore off her hoodie, which would be dead weight once wet, leaving her in a tee-shirt. Her arms went through the vest's arm slots. She clipped the bulky garment's clamps securely.

A gaze around the boat hit only a wall of gray. No lights from houses or other boats. The dense fog cut them off from the rest of the world.

Raindrops splatted on the windshield.

Jake shut off the dying engine and donned his life vest. He opened his cell phone. "Shit. No connection. Fog and rain or we're out of range."

Lani tried her cell. "No bars here. Why here? Why now?" She drew in a shaky breath.

He staggered aft. The ever-steeper angle forced him to hang on to whatever he could grab. Sea water sloshed over the low side onto the deck. In seconds, rain flattened his hair and plastered his tee-shirt to his skin. Her heart stumbled, but thank God for Jake. He looked so strong and in charge, she felt a fraction better. He threw open a storage locker and dragged out a yellow rubber blob.

"A lifeboat! Need help with it?" she called.

Muttered cursing. "Forget it. There's a big rip in the damn thing." Then strangely, he threw the useless item back into the locker and latched the lid before clawing his way back.

"Why—"

"Not now. We have to get off." He grabbed a waterproof plastic pack from a cubby behind the wheel. "My emergency kit."

He sealed the flashlight, his pistol, and both cell phones inside, then took her arm and helped her make it to the open deck. Icy pellets stung her face and soaked her hair. She shivered.

"Jump off the starboard side, the high side. It's a straight shot to the Mobcap. Fifty yards. Maybe less." He shouted above the rain and the gurgle of the sinking craft. He pointed away from shore. At least she thought it was away. "We have to swim for it. Lani, I wish—"

"Stifle it, Jake Wescott! Don't you dare apologize. I can swim that far with my eyes closed." She started to climb onto the rail, but he pulled her back and kissed her soundly.

"Keep your eyes open, Cameron. Works better that way." His crooked grin buoyed her. With another kiss, he helped her over the side. "Jump as far from the boat as you can. I'm right behind you."

She pushed out and hit the water.

Her whole body stiffened at the shock of the frigid water. Darkness closed over her head with the water. She braced herself not to struggle, to let the life vest's buoyancy lift her. When she bobbed to the surface, she gasped for breath.

A splash beside told her Jake had jumped in. He tugged on her vest to get her going as he struck out toward the tiny island.

Behind them, she heard the old *Amy Jo* give a final heave and gurgle as she sank.

What if they'd been farther out, away from land? What if they'd gone down with the boat? What if— Bile rose in her throat and she forced it down.

She kicked and stroked but wasn't sure she was making progress. She could barely feel her feet. Sucking in air above the chop was a chore. Even in the summer, hypothermia was a hazard in northern waters. Her heart bucked like a panicked pony.

*Stop it. Don't panic. Swim.* She spat out salt water and tried to capture the rhythm she'd developed swimming laps as part of her therapy. She kept her head up, kept her eyes ahead on Jake's yellow vest and the white emergency kit bobbing along beside him as she silently chanted in an even rhythm. *Stroke…stroke…stroke.*

After a dozen hours—in reality only a few minutes—she saw Jake standing in the water just off the Mobcap's beach. When she reached his side, he caught her arm. Lowering her feet to the rocky bottom, she managed to balance on her toes.

"We made it." He tugged her with him onto the shingle beach, the pebbles churning from beneath their feet with every lap of wave.

She stumbled, caught herself, and dragged in breaths. "Never thought…we wouldn't." But the mouth and whatever moxie she had were fading with her strength.

He wrapped an arm around her quaking shoulders. Her chilled body greedily absorbed his heat. The shack—dry shelter, whoo hoo!—was only steps away. "Let's get out of the rain. Then we'll see about sending for help."

They trooped up the small beach onto solid land.

Her athletic shoes squelched with every tread on the weed-and-rock-strewn soil. In spite of its rough board construction and sagging plank door, the rickety structure looming in the fog was a welcome sight.

When they reached the shack, Jake yanked the driftwood stick that functioned as a door latch. Once she was inside with him, he pushed the door closed.

"F-feels b-better just to be out of the wind and rain." She unclipped her life vest and chafed her arms with her hands.

He opened the emergency kit and tossed her a small towel. "Drying off will warm you up." He extracted a flare gun. "I'll shoot off this baby. Hope it's not a waste in this pea soup."

She toed out of her sopping sneakers, then mopped her hair and arms. The super-absorbent fabric dried her in no time. She wrung out the towel and finger-combed her hair. Someone had stuffed seaweed and old newspapers between the old barn boards to provide minimal insulation. Diffused light filtered in through salt-and-spider-web encrusted panes in two old house windows, showing her a nearly empty space little bigger than the farmhouse bathroom. Faint odors of mold and cigarettes hung in the air.

Someone, probably teenagers, had built the shack years ago as an overnight camping spot, a getaway from parent supervision. If an empty coffee can, cigarette butts, a newish ace of spades, and the folded blue tarp on the floor were any indication, the island still served that purpose.

Rain dripped through in the far corner, but the floor slanted enough that water drained between the floor boards there. Otherwise the roof—which had new but mismatched shingles—offered the protection they needed.

She searched in the emergency kit and set to work making herself useful.

****

Jake fired off a flare but the red sizzle disappeared in the gray curtain of rain and fog.

Useless damn thing.

He'd have to wait until the rain stopped to try again. Hell fucking damn. He should've foreseen another attack, prepared for something like this. Keeping Lani with him didn't keep her safe, as he'd feared. His belly roiled. The killer probably now had them both in his crosshairs.

His chest had tightened when he turned to see Lani stroking steadily, like a Channel swimmer, with the tide and the cold water depleting her strength. He'd sent up a silent prayer of thanks as he caught her arm. Man, she was game, strong and determined. Braver than him. No wonder she'd been able to drag Gail out of a burning barn.

He stumbled back to the shack in full darkness and pounding rain. When he pushed open the door, he found Lani had made the best of a worst-case scenario.

She was amazing. The battery lantern from his kit spread a halo of light on her, sitting cross legged on a tarpaulin. On the threadbare tarp were supplies from his kit—two of the energy bars, two bottles of water, the flashlight, and the space blanket.

She tossed him the other super-towel.

"Thanks." He shed his sneakers and dried off. Only then realized he was shivering. "I have three more flares but they're useless in this weather. I'll have to wait until the rain stops. You okay?"

"Sure, just big-time pissed. Again." She folded her arms and tilted her head. She was beautiful, dark hair loose and clinging to her neck. "The poor *Amy Jo*. That wasn't just an old tub springing a leak, was it?"

Hunkering down beside her, he pinched the bridge of his nose. "Not with that thumping noise. We didn't hit anything. I'm guessing our bad guy made use of his stash of C-4 again."

"A bomb," she whispered shakily. "On a timer?"

"Sounds about right. Maybe attached to the hull while we were at the festivities." Which was most of the day. "Padlock was still intact. So were my other security measures. Any bomb on that part of the hull had to be attached by a diver. The process would take too long without breathing equipment."

She absorbed that for a minute. "The life raft was no good but you locked it back up."

"The rip in it was no accident. A slice by a sharp knife. When the boat's raised, that slit will be evidence. The radio didn't die a natural death either. Son of a bitch yanked the wires loose."

"But who knew we'd be going out in the boat tonight?"

"No one. We didn't decide until after we left the fair. On second thought, the device could've been there for a couple days. You can do almost anything with electronics if you know what you're doing. Whoever did this could've watched and started the timer after we left the harbor. Or set it up to be activated by the engine's vibrations."

"Any of our suspects could be divers. We can figure that out when we're rescued. Who might know that much about electronics or explosives?"

A gust of wind flung waves of rain onto the shack's roof. The thrown-together building trembled but held.

He wagged his head. "More than you think. Construction crews need to blast granite ledge for foundations. Even Kevin must know how to control the timing."

"Then Brandon should be included in that list. He could've attached the bomb before he was arrested. I don't know about the harbormaster."

"Don't count out Mike Spear or Steve Quimby. Both of them work with construction supply outlets. That might include knowledge of explosives."

"As you so helpfully pointed out to me, you can find out on the Internet how to make a bomb. But timing the explosive tonight means whoever it is wanted to kill us both. Our bad guy is targeting you as well as me. We've both asked too many questions."

"Agreed." He dropped his head as his whole body sagged. "I sent some information to Robichaud, but all our notes are at the bottom of the bay."

"Our printouts and in my laptop. Do you suppose a tech wizard can retrieve my student progress charts from a wet hard drive?" Lani's eyes flashed with fury. "*I* will dry off, but someone's gonna pay for that."

He pounded a fist on the floor. "Keeping you with me to protect you, I only endangered you more."

"Oh, yeah, it's freaking *all* your fault, Jake Wescott. Trying to find Gail's killer just puts everyone in danger. You should just go back to Boston and forget the whole damn thing. Never mind the murderer should be caught and punished." She rolled her eyes.

In spite of himself, he had to grin. "Message

received. But if you'd stayed in town, you'd be enjoying the fireworks, not stuck out here in a leaky shed."

"I'd rather swim back to the mainland than watch fireworks."

Her shudder reminded him how traumatized the barn fire had left her. How she'd frozen at the sight of the smoldering cat. Her nightmares seemed to have fled since they'd been sleeping together but the fear remained. Probably always would linger in the recesses of her mind.

Her fierce expression softened. "And I'd rather be stuck out here *with* you than be worrying about you."

He scooted closer and curved an arm around her shoulders. Rain clattered harder on the shingled roof. "I'll have to phone Uncle Joe tomorrow to tell him about the *Amy Jo*."

"I'm sorry about your uncle's boat."

"Insurance should help him recoup the loss. I doubt he'd have gotten much for it anyway." Inhaling the scent of Lani's hair and feeling her softness made him prefer to forget he'd just lost his home. When she shivered for the fourth time, he said, "We should get out of these wet clothes and warm each other up."

She tilted her head and pursed her lips. "You wouldn't try anything, would you, Wescott?" Her eyes looked hopeful.

He affected a *who, me?* expression. "My intentions are pure, Cameron. I'm worried about a certain woman jumping my bones."

She laughed and started peeling off her sopping jeans.

Soon they were down to skin. Their clothing hung from nails on the walls or lay spread out on the hard floor. He stretched out and she lay beside him under the crinkly blanket. Orange polyester on one side and aluminum sheeting on the other, the emergency blanket wasn't soft or warm by itself. Instead it formed a reflective barrier to retain body heat.

"Survival blanket. I learned about these when I took a safety course for teacher recertification credit," Lani said, running her hand over the blanket's slick surface. "I don't know how good this one is. Feels chilly so far."

Jake smiled. "We need to increase our body heat. I have just the way."

"That should work." She turned her head and met his mouth.

Chapter Twenty-Four

JAKE SNUGGLED HER closer and nuzzled her ear, enjoying her sweet scent, laced with a salty tang. Sweet and salty. Like Lani herself.

When her index finger trailed a sizzling fuse down his chest to his navel, he drew back, sucking in a breath. His heart raced, but the cloud of doubt in her eyes snagged him. The past few days he'd been so hot for her he didn't think at all, knew only burning fever. He should've paid more attention to her belief she didn't measure up to her sister. Greedy bastard.

He had to clasp her shoulders to stop his hands from shaking with need. He should've said this sooner. "Lani, I sure as hell know you're not Gail. I never wanted Gail the way I want you. Whatever I wanted when I was a boy isn't what—or who—I want now."

"I want you too. I wanted you back then." With a smile as seductive as Eve's, she kissed him again and his heart turned over.

He exhaled the breath he'd been holding. Rolling atop her, he trapped her between his arms. "I want to take it slowly tonight. I want a leisurely journey of anticipation, but you make restraint near impossible."

"Well, then. The challenge is on."

Her flirtatious air softened as his index finger traced the plump upper curves of her breasts. She sucked in a breath when he stroked one nipple to pebbled arousal.

He bent to her left breast, and the right, first brushing his lips over the peaked nipples, then laving and tasting the salty coating and unique taste of her skin.

When he opened his mouth and suckled her, she arched upward with a small cry of pleasure. He kissed down to her flat stomach. Dizziness pulsed in his head, in his loins. In his heart. His need for her overwhelmed him.

That she trusted him touched him more deeply than her desire for him. Lani had journeyed from fearing his intentions to reliance on his skills and honor and finally to trust. In spite of the doubts remaining between them and the danger facing them, she opened herself to him. It humbled him.

She opened her arms. He craved her with an ache as powerful as a fever. "Sure you still want to take your time?"

He donned protection so fast she laughed.

"You had a condom in your pocket?"

"With you, I need to be prepared at all times."

She laughed again until he silenced her with his mouth. They kissed with all the hunger and passion and intensity in their souls. He stroked her body as she moved beneath him and their insulating cover crinkled and slid off.

She caressed his skin, traced the contours of his muscles and rubbed his sensitive nipples until he ground his teeth. She kissed him as if he was the hottest guy on the planet and they weren't lying on a plank floor in a cold, damp shack. As if she couldn't help herself. As if he was the only thing in her world.

Hell. He'd never been anything special. She was the one who was special. She made him feel like the king of the world. As if he could give her everything, do anything, be anything. With her, for her. If only he could live up to the way she made him feel.

He murmured with excitement and turned for better access to her. He massaged between her legs, first in gentle circles, then deeply.

Moaning, she reached for him, explored and circled, cupping him and stroking him. "Now, Jake, now."

When they joined, he groaned at the exquisite sensation. Slowly, he pushed deeper, and the wonder of it, the joy of the deep oneness he felt with her stilled him. Stunned him. Awed him. She locked her legs around him. Ancient rhythms rocked them, and they kissed endlessly as the need for release built.

He stiffened, fire surging in his blood, poised on the edge, straining to hold back until she joined him. And then she cried out, her strong legs gripping him, her body rippling beneath him, and he joined her in release.

Later when they found the space blanket kicked against the far wall, they laughed. He retrieved it and doused the lantern. Holding each other beneath its reflective warmth, they talked in the dark.

"Your student charts," he said, relishing the tickle of her hair on his chin, "do you have hard copies?"

She sighed. "Doubles. In each student's file and my working copies. But losing the computer file means filling in new forms and starting from scratch. I'll manage."

"All may not be lost. Hard drives are glass, enclosed in plastic. Your student data and some of our notes may be retrievable."

She gazed up at him. "Small comfort at the moment, but thanks."

He urged her to tell him more about her students. Some she couldn't help, and those tore at her heart but she smiled at her successes. A learning disabled boy named Scott whose reading and spelling struggles had led to anger issues. Sometimes he just needed a place where he could be quiet, she said. Her resource room offered him that space. A girl named Joy with ADHD who daily lost pens and pencils, books, and lunch money had resisted help, but finally accepted her as "manager." And a boy named Michael with cerebral palsy, who could barely make his speech understood and used a walker but who wrote beautiful poetry on the computer.

"You're amazing, honey. But it shouldn't surprise me you can reach insecure kids."

"You're amazing too," she said, dropping a kiss on his chest. "You've saved my life several times, maybe some we don't even know about. Not being able to protect anyone is a load of crap. Why don't you tell me about what happened in New Hampshire?"

Maybe it was being cocooned in the dark beneath the emergency blanket, or maybe it was Lani's gentle hand on his body. But he began talking.

"Some kids on ATVs saw tire tracks leading to a defunct old sawmill outside the little burg of Grafton. Out in nowhere. The local cop knew to be on the lookout, passed on the info to the task force. The place didn't seem to be guarded so no raid, only a scouting mission to check out the site. Maria Soriano was my only partner that day."

"ATF or DEA?" she asked.

"ATF. We'd worked together before. Were friends. I'd been to her house for cookouts, played golf with her husband." He sucked in a breath as he allowed himself to think about Tom's grief. About their two daughters.

"Anyway. We left our car in some bushes on a side road. Checked the woods and made sure the place was really deserted. Found the tire tracks and where some big crates had been stored inside but nothing incriminating." He could smell the moldy sawdust clumped on the floor and oily residue on the machinery, hear the skitter of rats in the corners.

"When we gave it up as a bad tip, we headed back to the car. Soriano" —calling her Maria made the telling too painfully personal— "went ahead of me to check under the car for explosives while I stood watch. Standard procedure. But the weeds underfoot were wet and she slipped. Grabbed for the door handle to break her fall. The car exploded in a ball of flame and shooting shrapnel. She was killed instantly."

"Oh, God, Jake, I'm so sorry. And you?" Her hand pressed the leg scar.

"The blast threw me back into the trees. The only reason I didn't die, I guess. Knocked me out cold. Jagged metal from the car impaled my leg. Lucky I didn't bleed out. Either the smugglers had just returned or the whole thing was a trap. When we didn't report in, the task force sent help."

"You were partners. She slipped. Maybe her grabbing the handle triggered the blast. You weren't responsible for what happened. It could've easily been you."

"That's what the task-force leader said." The words hadn't helped then, but for some reason, hearing them from Lani did.

"You can't help trying to protect everyone, but try not to feel responsible for everything that goes wrong."

She smiled. "Unless you want to try to take responsibility for all that goes right." She kissed him, first on the jagged scar, then on the lips, before vowing she wouldn't be able to sleep. In moments she was breathing evenly, head pillowed on his left arm.

He lay back, head on his linked hands, careful not to disturb her. He listened to the rain drumming on the roof, every rat-tat a reproach. The boat sabotage meant they had concrete evidence proving the attacks on Lani, and now him. The time they had together was coming to an end, and soon. Every day spent together, every time she made him smile or laugh, every time they held each other made that harder to imagine. He'd wanted to avoid getting involved, afraid he'd fail her. She'd pointed out he saved her life more than once already. But he was still afraid. Look how close they came tonight.

Now that he'd acknowledged his feelings for her weren't fleeting, what the hell was he going to do about it? If he lived to do something about it. If he *could* do something about it.

The bomber might come around in the morning looking for debris and bodies. Jake had his sidearm, a multi-tool, and a couple of flares. Hardly enough if their attacker had major firepower.

****

Lani woke to silence except for the squawk of a seagull. No rain. Thank goodness. The front had swirled on to torment tourists Down-East. She tried to finger-comb her hair but dried salt held a shape better than industrial-strength hairspray. It didn't bear thinking about how she must look, since she could do nothing about it.

She struggled into her still-damp jeans. "Yow, these

feel like an evil laundry demon starched and sprinkled them with gravel for extra abrasion."

"I wouldn't want to be our mad bomber when you get in his face." Jake chuckled as he too did battle with his stiff jeans. His salt-crusted hair stood up on end as if the sight of her witchy hair terrified him.

Crap, still no coverage on either cell phone. She could no longer blame the weather. Both phones' batteries were too weak. They ate the last of the energy bars and shared a bottle of water, careful to preserve the other in case they had to wait a long time for rescue. Lobstermen and others fishing should be out and about by dawn.

She donned her life vest—the bright yellow should make them more visible—and joined Jake outside as he prepared to send up a flare. The lifting fog revealed swatches of blue overhead and splashes of green on the mainland. At low tide, the water spread out as smooth and shiny as new paint.

Her gaze went to Jake as if on a homing device, to the tense set of his lean jaw, to the determined set of his wide shoulders. Last night he'd been different, more contemplative and intense. Thanks to their situation, stranded on an island and stalked by a murderer.

He was her match. He *got* her. They understood each other, could talk about anything, and did. More than physical attraction, they had a link. He was always present in her thoughts. Did he care for her? Maybe, but their only *real* links were sex and their searches. Anything more was in only in her mind. She'd always known the end would come, had steeled herself. She was too much work, too outspoken, and too defensive. Men always left. But the anticipated loss hurt like razorblades lacerating her insides.

Her heart beat with slow, hard thumps as she watched Jake extract a flare from the emergency kit. He cocked the flare gun and raised it.

A faint rumble ghosted through the drifts of fog.

She grabbed his arm. "Wait. I hear an engine."

He turned toward the sound, louder now and coming from down the peninsula. "Some lobsterman heading out to haul traps. If he misses seeing us, I'll shoot off the flare."

Through the fog shredding like torn sheets, she spied the long Dragon Harbor launch, with the harbormaster standing in the open at the helm.

"It's Pascal. He's headed around the other side of the island!" She sped across the rock-strewn terrain.

"I see him," Jake replied. "He may be involved but we have to get off this island. Take off your vest and wave it."

She tore at the clasps. Jake's steps clattered the loose shingle as he jogged along the narrow beach, widened by low tide.

A sizzling flare arced into the blue. "Ahoy the boat!"

When the launch's prow turned toward them, she whooped, then joined Jake where he stood with their meager belongings. Soon the familiar flat-nosed, weathered features of Ed Pascal came into focus.

"What're you folks doin' out here with no boat?" His disapproving scowl seemed to lump them in with the partying teenagers he must've sometimes rousted from the Mobcap.

"The *Amy Jo* sank last night," Jake called. To Lani he whispered, "I've got my sidearm. Watch him. Don't mention the explosion."

When Pascal beached the flat-bottomed launch, she accepted his callused hand and scrambled aboard. Metal seats ringed the gunwales around a raised storage box in the deck's center. She clambered to starboard while Jake took a port seat, to balance the craft.

As their rescuer pulled away from their rustic haven and picked up speed, the rushing air cut into her skin like sleet. She shivered and rubbed her arms, bare beneath the cap sleeve of her tee-shirt.

Pascal tossed them each a fleece blanket. "I got no extra jackets."

She and Jake thanked him in unison. The blanket's soft warmth went a long way toward cheering her.

Pascal tucked one hand in his windbreaker pocket and turned toward them. "How'd you folks come to be over by the Mobcap?"

"Out for an evening cruise." Jake's tone remained casual, although his face held a wary look. "Got lost in the weather. Must've hit a rock."

Pascal wagged his head in commiseration. His eyes crinkled as he squinted beneath his billed cap emblazoned with the town's dragon logo. He returned his attention to the waters ahead.

When she heard a crackling sound, she looked up to see Pascal talking into his ship-to-shore radio. "What now?" he said before the motor's roar and the air rushing past her ears drowned out his next words. In a moment, he set the unit back in its cradle.

He steered the launch back the way he'd come, toward Dragon Harbor. The craft barely bounced as it skimmed the swells.

Jake was staring aft. Just like a man, ogling the horsepower—twin Mercury two hundreds. But no, he was looking at something else. On the deck beneath the engines lay diving gear—a scuba tank and a wetsuit. Her eyes widened as she met his grim gaze. His head shake of warning was barely perceptible. He withdrew his pistol from the small of his back and concealed it beneath the blanket.

Was Pascal truly involved? He'd moved to the peninsula a couple of years ago. Jeez, he was a harbormaster. Maybe their suspicion was only paranoia. But as the saying went, it's not paranoia when they're really out to get you. Her heart gave a thump trying to leap out of her chest. She bit her lower lip and wished Jake could sit beside her instead of miles away.

As they neared the harbor entrance, she saw other boats heading out. A couple of sailboats dodged the wake of a speedboat. When Pascal passed the lighthouse, he didn't slow. Instead of steering around Dragon Rocks and into the harbor, he slapped the throttle forward and continued down the peninsula.

"Where are you taking us?" she demanded, half out of her seat. Jake raised a hand in caution but she ignored him. She wanted an answer.

Pascal set the wheel and turned. The hand in his jacket pocket came out with a pistol. He pointed its black barrel at her.

She emitted an involuntary squeak and began to scoot farther aft.

"You bastard!" Jake dumped the blanket, pointed his pistol at Pascal's chest.

The older man jerked the wheel, slewing Jake off balance. Pascal yanked Lani to him, jammed his pistol under her jaw. She swung her elbow but he deflected the blow. "Stay put, Wescott. Toss the pistol overboard or she'll pay for your stupidity."

Jake subsided as he seemed to weigh his options. His mouth a taut line, he complied. The engine muffled the pistol's splash. "What the fuck is this about? Who do you work for, Pascal? Or is it Hector Vargas aka Hector Johnson?"

The other man's jaw didn't drop but his eyebrows shot up nearly to his cap brim. "So you checked on me. Vargas it is. You'll find out the rest soon enough. For all the good it'll do you." He barked a laugh with no humor.

He jerked Lani around and made her take the wheel. The warning—at the point of his lethal pistol—to steer where he said brooked no transgression, no slips.

The barrel tip bit painfully into her flesh where he jabbed it against her neck. Her insides cartwheeled. *Vargas.* She couldn't get her mind around Pascal as Vargas. Not only the arsonist, but the smuggling gang intended to kill them. Somehow it all tied together. A bubble rose in her throat that nearly choked off her breath. But no. She needed logic, needed to think. To bide her time.

Jake was poised to attack, his grip on the seat so tense his knuckles were white. When they reached wherever Pascal—no, Vargas—was taking them, maybe they would have a chance.

Chapter Twenty-Five

JAKE SEETHED, EVERY fiber vibrating with adrenaline. But as long as Hector Vargas held that semiautomatic on Lani, all he could do was wait.

Fifteen minutes of high speed across the bay took them to a familiar landing—the crumbling dock at Lani's farmhouse. Vargas couldn't tie up there. He'd have to change his plans, whatever the hell they were.

But the harbormaster took the wheel, pulled back on the throttle and beached the launch, as he'd done on the Mobcap. He forced Lani to jump out, then followed, keeping the pistol trained on her and one eye on Jake.

Jake's pulse jolted, his heart knocking against his sternum, as he shed his life vest and tossed it next to Lani's. When Vargas ordered him to jump out and tie the boat to a low-hanging tree, he had no choice but to comply.

"Be sure you tie up proper, now, gringo Fed," he ordered with a nasty cackle. "We wouldn't want the town launch to drift away."

The beach, accessible only at low tide, lay several feet down from the dock and grassy shore level. Lani climbed the steep bank first, followed by their captor and Jake.

When Vargas slipped on a loose stone, Jake grabbed his gun arm, but the other man was stronger than he looked. He backhanded Jake with the gun. The blow to his jaw sent him to his knees. Through the agony shooting sparks inside his skull, he heard Lani cry out his name.

When he shook away the fog, he looked up to see Vargas and Lani on the grass above him. The Mexican aimed the pistol at Jake and his free hand gripped her upper arm. Painfully, if her pinched expression was any indication. He saw fear shadowing her eyes, but defiance setting her jaw. *Good for you, Lani. Hang on.*

"Don't try anything again," Vargas said.

Still reeling from the receding pain, Jake worked his jaw. Skin broken. Nothing else. He'd live. The metallic taste of blood where he'd bit his cheek would focus him. Remind him to cool his temper so he didn't tip his hand. Or show emotion. This bastard would make Lani pay and Jake wouldn't allow that.

Vargas forced Jake to walk ahead of him and Lani through the white pines. A muscle in Jake's back twitched as if he could feel the pistol jabbed between his shoulder blades.

The green scent of fresh-cut grass filled his nostrils. Lani'd told him a lawn service was coming to mow the lawn and the field. If someone was there, they had a chance. He didn't want to endanger anyone, but even the sight of a truck might put Vargas at a disadvantage. He'd have to back off with a witness present.

But when they reached the grassy path through the field, he saw only the finished mowing, no one on a tractor. Now what?

And at the farmhouse, what he saw in the driveway stopped him in his tracks. He whirled on his captor. "What the hell? How did my SUV get here?"

Vargas didn't answer, only raised the gun higher.

"Keep moving."

Lani's eyes were owl wide. He could almost smell the fear emanating from her. Her eyes seemed to plead with him not to rile their captor. He tried to reassure her silently, but he had no plan other than to watch for an opening.

Hector Vargas ordered him to open the kitchen door. Jake immediately saw why they needed no key. Broken window. He had a pretty good idea who they'd find inside. The man with the money. The man with the most to lose.

Vargas shoved Lani at Jake. "Get over there by the sink."

He caught her in his arms and felt her shaking. But her mutinous expression said the tremors stemmed as much from fury as from fear.

On the kitchen table lay his spare Jeep key, the one he kept in a magnet box under the back bumper. One small mystery solved. The bigger answers were to come. If only they could survive them.

*Lani.* He couldn't lose her, not when she'd helped him find himself, the self he'd lost for twelve years. A spasm gripped his throat and he swallowed it, determined to stay focused.

"What is going on?" Lani demanded. "Who's behind this?"

"I'm amazed you haven't figured it out by now, my dear."

J.T. Meagher stepped into the room. Cool and calm in sharply creased khakis and a pink button-down. Not a pewter hair out of place. "Apparently you haven't remembered."

Jake squeezed her hand. *We were right.* Only they'd

had no evidence, only hunches. Until now. When it might be too late. Vargas hadn't shot them already because Meagher planned something here. That's why he'd driven to the farmhouse.

"Maybe not yet," she declared. "But I will."

Meagher ignored her bravado. He pocketed the key and magnet box. Slipped on thin deerskin gloves and took the pistol from his man.

"Wescott knows who I am," Vargas said. "The ATF's been looking for me. This has to end today."

"I'll handle these two. You delayed and bungled enough," Meagher said.

Dissention. Jake might be able to work that.

Vargas turned his back on his accomplice and disappeared down the hall. His tread thumped on the stairs, then a metallic thunk sounded above.

A carving knife sat in the dish drainer to his left. Jake began to edge that way.

Lani stepped forward, her hands fisted at her sides. She glared at Meagher with toxic contempt. "Is your cover-up worth murder? All this to protect your baby son and get him the House seat you couldn't win?" Her voice was as dry as ashes.

Meagher moved nearer. He bent close enough to them both that Jake could see the red web of capillaries in his cheeks.

J.T. gaped at Lani in amazement. "Kevin?" He barked a laugh. "So you really don't remember that night. No matter. You would eventually. And your poking around has raised too many questions. I have too much at stake. But my son? Not that milquetoast. He wouldn't have the guts to kill your bitch of a sister."

The pieces fell into place. "It was you," Jake said.

Gail's lover had been older after all. Much older. Meagher had lied to Galt. All those late nights at campaign headquarters must've led to an affair. One that got out of hand. "*You* killed Gail."

Meagher didn't deny the accusation. Merely held the gun steady on them, his expression cold as the North Atlantic.

"But why?" Lani's voice broke on a sob. Jake's gut twisted at the strain he heard in her voice and the ivory pallor beneath her tan. "My sister was… troubled that summer." She flicked an apologetic glance toward Jake. "There were… several guys. She never told. Even I didn't know back then."

Jake nudged her, hoping she understood his signal. *Move away.* The farther they were apart, the harder to shoot them both. He edged another step toward the knife. She seemed to catch on and sidled right, away from him and toward the hallway.

Meagher's gun hand trembled, and he added his other in a two-hand grip. "Other men, yeah. She didn't tell me but I found out anyway. That night, I left the campaign party. Had my Bayliner at the resort dock so I could come and go unseen. When I told her I wanted to end it between us, she had a hissy fit. Claimed to be pregnant. Threatened to tell my wife."

"So you killed her and set fire to the barn," Jake said quietly. And all this time J.T. thought Lani saw him.

"An accident." Meagher seemed to look inward, although he kept the gun high. "I only meant to scare her. She made me lose my temper. I hit her with a board. She was unconscious but she'd tell when she came to. She gave me no choice."

The egotistical gall of the man. Making it Gail's

fault. Hatred prowled inside Jake, fury that Meagher had cheated on his ill wife with Gail, then killed Gail and was killing again to keep his secret. His murderous recklessness had ruined lives, tainted others.

"The gasoline was right there, handy," Jake said. "Lining the pockets of Frank Tyson took care of the rest."

The other man shrugged in concession. "Until now. Our harbormaster is a man of many talents. He's been quite useful in tying up loose ends. In both our mutual projects. Except he wasn't content with arson, had to use his new toy."

*The C-4.* Pascal/Vargas must've been the one who torched Tyson's house and tried to kill Lani. Jake's vision went red around the edges. He couldn't let these monsters get away scot-free.

"Scratching each other's back. He helps you cover up your old crime and you provide a hiding place for his contraband. Let me guess, one of your old warehouses."

"I suspected you were here for more than recuperation and carpentry. Looks like I was right." J.T.'s long, seamed face looked drawn and tired.

Gasoline fumes stung Jake's nostrils. Vargas entered the kitchen with a gasoline can in his hands. It sloshed—only partly full—as he set it down by the refrigerator.

Where had he been spreading the accelerant?

Lani stood closer to the hall than he did. She swung her gaze to him, panic flaring in her eyes. She smelled the gas. Knew what came next.

Shooting them was only part of the plan. Or not part of the plan at all. Lani needed him. His throat was cotton-dry, but he swallowed and forced the tension from his body. He couldn't function without calm.

"It's time. You got the matches?" Meagher said to Vargas.

"This old place'll fucking go up like dry timber." Vargas tossed over a matchbook. He slid a small stun gun from his pocket and started toward Lani. "We have to get out fast."

"All my troubles will go away with a little murder-suicide," Meagher said to Jake. "Folks will assume Lani snapped when she realized you were the one who killed her sister." His smile was icy, but sweat beaded along his hair line. He waved the pistol. "Stand over there with her."

Jake didn't budge. Neither did Lani. Would J.T. be able to kill in cold blood?

The slam of a car door turned everyone's head.

Meagher dipped his head, and the Mexican crossed to the mud-room door.

Kevin Meagher burst in, anxiety furrowing his brow. "I know what's going on. Dad, I know about you and Gail." Voice shaking, he gestured toward Jake. "You can't kill them. They're my friends." He started toward his father but Vargas blocked his way.

J.T.'s face darkened to purple. "Get out of here, Kevin. How did you… What—" He sputtered, unable to formulate anything coherent.

Kevin tried to skirt Vargas, but the other man clamped an arm around his chest and jammed the stun gun against his neck. He struggled against the grip to no avail. "Never mind how I know. Give yourself up, Dad. It's over."

J.T. yelled back that he wasn't going to prison. He erupted in a harangue about Kevin's failings.

The acrid scent of smoke stung Jake's nose. Black fumes snaked in from the hall. The living room ceiling smoldered, which meant the fire had already started upstairs. A crash jolted him. He backed against the counter as a cloud of smoke and dust billowed from the living room, stinging his nose with smoke and a musty smell.

He coughed and pulled his shirt up to cover his nose and mouth as he looked for an opening. Lani remained pressed into the small nook between the cabinets and the refrigerator.

With a great thump, like a wave crashing into a cavern, the living room exploded in flames. Flames crackled and roared and licked toward the kitchen. Glass panes burst their window frames. *More oxygen for the fire triangle.*

Fifteen, maybe twenty feet for the fire to reach the kitchen.

The can of gasoline. Open. If the fire reached its fumes, the place would explode. They had little time before all hell broke loose. They had to make their move.

But Lani stood as rigid as a two-by-four, staring at the fire. Frozen, in a trance.

He couldn't help her, couldn't save her unless he got that damn gun away from J.T.

"You dumb *Americanos* can stay in this fucking inferno if you want." Vargas coughed and shoved Kevin away. "I'm not getting burned up for nobody." He went for the door.

J.T. swung the gun toward Vargas. "Come back here!"

Jake tackled J.T. with the momentum that had once propelled him to second base. They went down hard below the increasing smoke. J.T. was fit and strong. Jake kicked him in the balls, felt no pain in his thigh. When the older man doubled over, Jake went for the gun. J.T.'s grip held. They tangoed in and out of the noxious fumes. Breathing smoke sapped their strength. They gasped.

The pistol coughed once.

And again. Jake heard a cry of pain. If the bastard had shot Lani…

Rage gave him new strength. He wrested the gun loose. Stepped back, ready for J.T.'s next attack, but the other man only looked behind him. Jake followed his horrified gaze. Kevin lay crumpled on the floor, a red stain soaking the Meagher Enterprises logo on his shirt.

An animal roar erupted from J.T. He charged Jake, his face mottled with fury. "You made me shoot my own son!"

When he grabbed for the pistol, it slipped from Jake's hold and went flying across the room. The gun disappeared with a clatter somewhere in the fire's smoky haze. A clip on the chin deflated J.T. to a heap on the floor.

Coughing, Jake stumbled across the room to Lani.

Chapter Twenty-Six

MEMORIES STIRRED IN Lani's head like dark shadows in the smoke. *Fire monster. Outside the barn. Clawing for her. "Help! Help us!" But he vanished. Red. Yellow. Chimneys of black. Choking clouds. Gail! Gail!*

*There, face down on the floor. All the smoke. Have to move, have to get my sister out. The heat, fumes, eyes streaming. Hauling her up, dragging her. Cool air on my face. Stumbling into nothing... all black.*

She tried to suck in air but could manage only shallow pants. Heat and pain clamped her lungs. Fear rose like bubbles in boiling broth. Her legs threatened to buckle.

"Lani! We have to get out of here."

She knew that voice. Gentle, soothing. Trusted. Jake. But why did she feel so weak? So lightheaded?

She felt his arm around her shoulders. "Listen to me, Lani! You have to get moving. You were right. I couldn't have saved Gail from herself and neither could you. But we can save each other now. Come with me."

His words, his deep voice, tight and sandpaper rough, spun through her addled brain.

But she couldn't drag her gaze from the fire. The mocking roar, the blanket of smoke, the grasping flames held her in thrall. *The hungry flames. They reach for me.* If she moved, the fire would take her. Crazy thoughts, but she couldn't make herself move. Couldn't speak.

His hand gripped her shoulder, gave her a sharp shake. "*Lani!* Let's get out of here. We can make it out together. I won't leave you, I promise. You have to trust me." He took her hands, began pulling her along with him.

She managed a small nod, but her voice was locked in her throat.

Suddenly the fire wrenched Jake away from her. Not the fire. A man. *J.T. Meagher.* She could only watch as the two exchanged blows.

Jake's gaze sought hers. Something flared in his eyes that called to her. Broke through the smoke in her brain. And the world sharpened into reality. The two men twisted and turned just out of the fire's grasping claws. By the door through the soupy haze she could make out another form on the floor. *Kevin?*

The beamed ceiling creaked and groaned. Burning debris rained down upon the grappling men. Seeing flames descending on Jake stripped away the remnants of paralysis still gripping her. Panic turned to anger.

She grabbed a pan from the dish drainer. Her backhand swing nailed J.T. on the temple, making a sickening thwack. He fell to the side and on his knees.

Jake's tee-shirt shirt smoked. Tongues of flame licked across one shoulder.

"Jake!" She plucked the small rag rug from in front of the sink and flung it over him. Desperately she pounded out the fire. She helped him to his feet. "We… outside."

He brushed the smoldering rug from his shoulders as he pushed to his feet. "Need to take J.T. He's got to admit—" A bout of coughing cut off his words.

Lani could find no one. J.T. Meagher was gone.

She saw only the wall of flame eating its way into the kitchen. And the fire's roar of rage. Over it all, the screaming of sirens. "Help is coming," she managed.

Holding onto each other, they bent double beneath the smoke and stumbled toward the door. They hoisted up Kevin's dead weight between them and trudged out to the porch.

Two firefighters in full gear met them on the steps.

Lani collapsed against one of them.

"J.T. Meagher... in there somewhere," Jake rasped out.

A great boom from the house threw them all forward off the porch.

\*\*\*\*

Solving the arson-murder of Gail Cameron and a major Northeast smuggling case, plus the scandal of J.T. Meagher's guilt in both was the biggest story any news organization in Maine had ever covered. The *Boston Globe* sent reporters, and all the state's TV channels swarmed Dragon Harbor. Over the next two days in her hospital bed, Lani pored over the news in every paper she could get the nurses to bring her and flipped through every TV broadcast.

A passing motorist had called the fire department, but the trucks arrived too late to save the structure. Nothing remained of the farmhouse but charred beams and a pile of ash-coated debris. Like the barn, she noted with a shudder.

The firefighters found J.T. Meagher's body in the ruins. He'd apparently been trying to escape through the garage when timbers fell on him.

Kevin Meagher needed surgery to repair the damage to his shoulder muscle but after physical therapy, he would recover. The day after the fire, he dropped out of the political race, sending the party scrambling for a new Congressional candidate.

Ed Pascal aka Hector Vargas aka Hector Johnson was implicated in the fire that killed the former fire investigator, the death of Ava Warren, and the attacks on Lani and Jake. Vargas had recruited David Brandon to follow Lani, but that was Brandon's only involvement in the murders. In an effort at a plea bargain, Brandon named names, leading Task Force Eagle to more of the Mexican cartel in northern New England.

All well and good, but Lani had too many questions unanswered by the scant details in print and on screen. So when Chief Galt dropped in to apologize for not listening to her, she grabbed her chance.

"You owe me, Chief," she croaked, her voice as rough as lava. Never mind that the attacks on her played a big role in ending two major crime sprees.

"Looks like I do."

"What about Vargas aka Pascal?"

Galt heaved a resigned sigh and settled in a chair by her bed. "My sergeant and I picked up the man calling himself Ed Pascal. Claimed he'd been at the town dock all morning. ATF agents from that smuggling task force and the state fire investigator tag-teamed him with evidence. They didn't let on J.T. was dead, and when they intimated J.T. blamed him for everything, the man spilled some of the story. Seems J.T. bribed the fire investigator to conduct a cursory investigation and rule the barn fire an accident."

"Exactly what Jake and I concluded. What about the attacks on me?"

"Interesting these recent attacks weren't the first.

Vargas said J.T. told him he'd paid another man years ago to kill you but the attempts failed."

She nodded. "There were a couple of incidents. Then nothing. I think he dropped his plot when he decided I wasn't going to return and remembered nothing.

"Your return to Dragon Harbor changed that. So then Meagher got Vargas to scare you away or kill you and make it look like an accident."

"Or suicide."

He nodded. "Vargas admitted forcing you off the shore road. He stashed his damaged truck at the house where Jake saw him talking with Brandon. He claims his dealings with Brandon were all about discovering who the other trap cutters were. Says he was just doing his job as harbormaster." Galt snorted his disbelief. "More'n likely he wanted the Marine Patrol out of the way for his next arms delivery."

"One thing I haven't heard in the news is why David Brandon didn't rat out Vargas as soon as he was arrested. If he didn't know our erstwhile harbormaster was part of the smugglers, he knew Vargas paid him to follow me."

"Seems Brandon had dealings with the drug side of the cartel. Vargas put the fear of El Águila in the guy. Threatened him into silence." Chief Galt grinned, deepening the creases in his cheeks. "That is, until charges started piling up on him. One of the Feds allowed as how they'd see Brandon went to a prison far away from the kingpin's reach."

From what Lani understood, no prison was out of El Águila's reach. She shuddered, shifting to a more comfortable position in the bed. "What about Tyson and Ava? And the smuggling?"

"Vargas would cop to none of those. Clammed up as soon as the questions were asked, Agent Donovan told me. But the barbs embedded in Ava's arm matched the design of the ones in Vargas's stun gun. A search of his house found C-4 and more than one timing device. A closed Meagher warehouse contained enough weaponry and explosives to arm a small country. Whether Vargas ever utters another word, he's cooked and cracked like a lobster. He'll go away for a very long time."

"About the smuggling, I'll bet he's not talking because he fears his cousin El Águila more than a U.S. federal prison." Lani lay back into her stacked pillows. "How did J.T. get Vargas involved in his cover-up?"

"We may never know for sure. But Jake Wescott's and the Eagle Task Force's research on him suggest J.T. had the goods on Vargas. Knew he wasn't Ed Pascal. Wescott told me the harbormaster on Cape Cod said both the real Ed Pascal and a man he knew as Hector Johnson worked for him. Both men left about the same time. He wondered why Pascal had requested a referral but not Johnson. Possible Vargas did away with Pascal so he could take his place in Dragon Harbor. The cops there are looking for a body. And turns out about two years ago, that area experienced a rash of arson fires."

She thanked Chief Galt for being so candid with her, and he left.

Lani tilted up her water glass. The cold liquid felt good on her raw throat. Jake and she had escaped the burning house before they could become victims of smoke inhalation like Gail. The eerie similarity brought tears to her eyes. She'd wept so much these last two day the nursing assistant brought extra boxes of tissues. All the tears she'd refused to shed since Gail's death were pouring out of her with no end in sight.

She hadn't seen Jake since the ambulance brought her to the hospital. Minor brachial damage was the diagnosis of her injury. Nothing life threatening, only irritating. A tube flowed oxygen into her nose and down her throat in case her seared airways swelled too much.

She chafed at being tethered to her bed, unable to go see Jake. The nurses told her he'd asked about her but that only made her more anxious. He was on oxygen too, the reason he didn't come to her room. If only she could see him, see he was all right, the fist clamping her heart would ease.

The door swung inward. Nora entered with a tentative step.

"I brought you some clothes," her friend said, crossing to the hospital bed and holding up a canvas tote. "Pajamas, underwear, jeans, and a shirt. They're from Kevin's sister. Mine would fall off you." She smoothed her tunic top over her ample hips. "The sandals are mine. We wear the same size."

Lani was surprised to see her. Not disappointed, really, but Nora wasn't Jake. She scooted higher on the bed and tucked the wad of damp tissues beneath one of her pillows.

"Thanks," she croaked. After her long conversation with Galt, even one word felt as if she were swallowing crushed charcoal briquettes. She lifted the glass from her bedside table and sucked down some ice water. "I need something other than this doll-size johnny. I think Nurse Ratched stole it from the pediatric ward."

Nora laughed. Color rose to her cheeks and a rueful smile played on her lips. "Peace offering. I'm sorry I popped off on you at the fair. I—"

"It's all right." Lani reached for her friend, and they hugged for a long moment, comforting each other.

Lani offered her a tissue from the box at her side. "A wife has to defend her husband." She mopped her puffy eyes. "I was insensitive."

"No, you were right to ask." Nora dabbed at her tears. "I still have trouble believing it was J.T. I don't know what to tell the boys." She sniffled as she stepped back.

Oh my, how difficult it would be to explain to two little guys their grandfather was a murderer. "Kevin's had a rough time of it too. To discover what his father did. How's he doing?"

"Resting. Lost some blood but he's out of danger."

Lani smiled. "I'm relieved for him. And proud. He tried to save us, to convince J.T. to turn himself in. I might not be here if Kevin hadn't showed up. Tell him I'm so sorry for him, about his father. And thank him for me."

Nora sniffled and blew her nose. "I'll tell him. He wishes he'd figured things out faster and been able to stop J.T. Seems he overheard his dad talking to that man Pascal, or Vargas, whoever he is." She lifted one shoulder in a shrug of indulgent affection. "Kev's not the sharpest scalpel on the tray, but he means well."

Lani waited while Nora stowed the clothes in the room's small locker. "Brandon was selling drugs to Kevin, wasn't he?"

Tears again filled Nora's eyes. "Yes, the bastard. Kevin always drank too much, even more after his brother died. Still does sometimes. Several years ago he wrecked his car, hurt his back, and lost his license. That's when he got hooked on painkillers. After the pain ended and doctors stopped prescribing, he found other addicts who'd sell him more. He got help a few years ago, but this run for Congress put him over the edge. Brandon was only too happy to help."

"He can get the right kind of help now," Lani said, reaching for her friend's hand.

She couldn't find it in her heart to feel one bit sorry for J.T.'s death. Everything was his fault. *Everything.* The murders and attempted murders, the bribery, and the mental abuse of his own son. He'd belittled Kevin for not being his older, "perfect" brother and badgered him into striving for more than he could handle.

Nora looked at her watch. "I should get back to my husband. Call me if you need me."

"I will." Lani bit her lower lip. Talking was making her throat sorer and sorer but she had to know. "Nora, before you go, tell me. How's Jake?"

"No better shape than you. Smoke inhalation. Plus first and second-degree burns on his back."

Her heart turned over at the thought of the pain he must be in. She knew all too well. She had to see him, to tell him how she felt. "Where is he?"

Nora propped her hands on her hips, a stern nurse expression pursing her mouth. "Gone. He checked himself out of the hospital. Against doctor's orders. But that's a man for you. His brother brought him some clothes and off they went."

Chapter Twenty-Seven

AFTER NORA LEFT, the nurse came in to check on Lani. She said the doctor would be in to see her later. Maybe he would release her. But what if *later* was *too late* for her and Jake?

Outside the window in the courtyard, a hummingbird hovered above a red geranium. She marveled at the blur of its wings, at the quick movements as the tiny jewel hung in midair. It backed off, then dipped again as if fearful, then made its decision and swooped down to sip nectar. Quick as a blink, the creature darted away in a flash of iridescent green.

*No more indecision for me.* She had to see Jake before he left Dragon Harbor. He'd said he needed to be here for his mother, but Hank could handle things, and the house renovation was nearly ready for a carpenter. Jake had no reason to stick around. He might head back to Boston.

If she waited, he would leave not knowing she loved him. She'd spent so much of her life behind walls. Jake had broken through her defenses and she had to take this chance. Yes, men left, but so did women. Look at Jake's brother's marriage. His wife was away more than she was at home, on her way out. Lani's fear had wrapped everyone in the same package. Leave when the going gets tough? It couldn't have gotten much tougher than the last few weeks, and Jake was there for her time and time again.

She swung her legs around and sat on the edge of the bed. Could she remove the oxygen herself? Then she had to get dressed and hoof it down the hall before someone caught her like a kid playing hooky.

When her door opened again, she tucked her bare legs beneath the covers. Her pulse did a little happy dance. *Jake?*

But the man entering her room with an armful of yellow roses wasn't Jake.

"I'll understand if you don't want to see me, but I had to come see for myself if my baby was all right."

When she saw her father's face and heard the familiar rolling cadence of his voice, her breath stalled. Brody Cameron looked almost the same as the last time she'd seen him, when her mom had tried to reconcile them five years before. A little grayer, a little sadder, a little heavier, but dapper in crisp blue pants and a collared shirt.

She managed a shaky breath. "Come in, Dad."

He approached her, but without his usual confident stride. His hazel gaze, so like hers, searched her face, caught on the crumpled tissues in her lap. "This is too reminiscent of... hell, you know." His fingers fretted the paper sleeve wrapping the roses.

"You'd better put those flowers in water before you shred them."

His gaze dropped to the golden blooms as if he didn't know where they'd come from. Then paper and all, he plunged them into the pitcher.

They'd probably die in the ice water. But no matter. Her father had come. *Dad.* "Thank you for the flowers."

He squared his chin. "After your phone call, Serena

called me a jackass and a bad father. Not for the first time. This has gone on way too long."

She joined him in a small smile of agreement and amazement at his usually meek wife's assertiveness. "I've been partly to blame."

"No." He shook his head with vehemence. "No. I was supposed to be the adult. But I let guilt drive me into a corner. So I left your mother and you to handle everything. Serena is right. And I'm profoundly sorry."

She trembled, her heart tripping over itself. "Oh, Dad, I'm sorry too."

When she opened her arms, he gathered her in. "Lanibug, I've missed you."

"I've missed you too." *Crap, more tears.* As she sopped up the new flood, something he'd said penetrated her addled brain. "What did you mean, guilt drove you into a corner?"

He propped a hip on the edge of her bed and gripped her hand as if he were afraid to lose her again. "I'll tell you about it later. Long story."

After her short chat with her mom, she'd known there was more to the divorce than she'd believed. Jake had suggested that, but she ignored him. But she would let it go until her dad was ready.

"I'm sorry about the farmhouse." In spite of her sore throat and chest, she couldn't seem to stop. "I nearly had the repairs done except for the plumbing. Jake repaired the banisters. They're gone. The house is gone. Everything's gone. Granddad would—"

He shushed her and kissed her forehead. "It was just a house. Granddad would be proud of you as much as I am. I phoned your mother. She's on her way home."

She settled back against the pillows again and

mopped her eyes. Again. "How did you know to come?"

"Nora phoned my office and informed me what's been going on." He eased onto the bed's edge and affected a stern expression. "More than you told me, I might add."

She shrugged off the reprimand. "I didn't want to worry you."

"It doesn't matter now. I see you're going to be all right. And Gail's murderer has at last been punished." He rubbed his nape. "All those years between you and me wasted."

Her heart turned over at his genuine remorse and she had to swallow past the hot lump in her raw throat. "If you want to help, I have an idea. Can you get me out of here?"

"Honey, I'd like to, but don't you think—"

"Just can't stay out of trouble, can you, Ms. Cameron?" A smiling Dr. Laurenz strode into the room, a stethoscope stuffed in his shirt pocket. Baseball bats and red socks frolicked across his necktie.

Lani sank back on the pillows. "Why whatever do you mean, Doctor?"

\*\*\*\*

"Didn't know you had talent at carpentry, Wescott." Holt Donovan's blue gaze perused the bungalow's exposed studs and wiring, the rolls of insulation. The smell of new maple boards mingled with the dusty scent of sawdust.

"Some talent at demolition," Jake said, "but none at carpentry. My brother and some other guys helped out earlier today. The rest of this job is waiting for somebody who knows how to swing a hammer. I got a few calls in." He trailed to the fridge and got both of them a beer.

"Thanks." Donovan accepted the brew. He sank onto a sawhorse and tipped back his Broncos cap. A brawny man taller than Jake, he looked like he belonged on his Colorado ranch instead of wrangling smugglers in New England.

He withdrew a spiral notepad from his shirt pocket. "Speaking of calls, I got one just now. At dawn, agents took down a compound in Massachusetts and a warehouse outside Portland. Arrested about twelve bad guys, all illegals. Confiscated drugs, crates of weapons. The arrest of David Brandon set us up to end El Águila's entire northeast operation. You did good here."

"Thanks. If Lani Cameron's return to town hadn't threatened Meagher so he sicced Hector Vargas on her, we might still be chasing our tails." *And Lani wouldn't have nearly been burned to death.*

"Maybe. You sound like a foghorn, Wescott. Better take it easy. Boss says you're to take a couple more weeks off to heal."

"I'll get work squared away on this house, and then I'll be back at work. I got no reason to stick around here anymore." Except for Ma, and he'd drive up on weekends to see her.

"We'll need you. Boston's shorthanded. Two task-force guys already went to California to round up El Águila himself. I'm leaving tomorrow. They another agent who speaks Mexican Spanish."

After the other man left, Jake wandered the empty room with his half-finished beer. He touched an index finger to the age-darkened studs. Modern wallboard would alter the character of the old bungalow, but a guy had to move on. Out with the old, in with the new.

Or was he thinking of himself?

"You're a damn fool, Wescott." He downed the rest of the beer. He ought to be happy, celebrating his success. Lani had survived all J.T.'s plots and schemes. But it was no thanks to him. He'd led her right into Vargas and J.T.'s trap. A hell of a Fed he was. He nearly got her killed. *She'll be better off without me.*

He stared at the expanse of bare wall, colorless and empty as he felt. He peeled off his shirt—one with buttons because a pullover hurt his burned back like hell—and grabbed the broom. He couldn't do much work, but he could sweep up the sawdust the guys had left.

The doc had let him leave the hospital only if he promised to return for the nurse to change the dressing on his burned shoulder and to remove the stitches on his jaw. He was hoarse but hadn't sucked down as much smoke as Lani, who didn't cover her nose and mouth. After visiting Ma in the nursing home, he returned to his grandmother's with some supplies—sleeping bag, clothes, food—and found Hank and a crew of drop-ins hard at work finishing the essentials so he could camp out in the house.

One drop-in was Steve Quimby, who confessed his alibi the night of the fire had been his gay lover, who was now his life partner. He was still in the closet. ABC was a conservative family company.

After announcing he and his wife were separated, probably getting divorced, Hank left. Jake wanted to console his brother but couldn't find the words. Could only pound him on the back and say he'd be there for him and Zack.

"Lani's good for you," Hank said. "What are you going to do about that?"

Jake avoided the question. What he was going to do was leave her alone. In the midst of the fire, she'd snapped out of her fog enough to bean J.T. and escape with him. She'd saved him, for God's sake.

Even Ma asked about her. *"Where's the noisy girl?"* When he said she'd gone away, Ma shook her head vehemently. *No. She wouldn't leave you,"* Ma had insisted.

*But I left her.* The words fissured his heart. His hands grew clammy. He set down the bottle and wiped his palms on his jeans. Rubbed his sternum. Shit, he shouldn't have left the hospital without seeing her. Her belief everyone deserted her had left her defensive and alone. And he'd proved her right.

*Coward. I'm a fucking coward.* The squeak of the door yanked him from his funk.

When he recognized the footsteps on the new floorboards, his heart revved to third gear. Her face was drawn and pale from her ordeal. His chest grew too tight to breathe.

Chapter Twenty-Eight

LANI NEARLY TURNED and ran when she saw the injuries on Jake's face. She'd argued with herself since learning he left the hospital. He'd defended her and tried to stop Vargas and J.T. and paid with searing pain.

*"I won't leave you. You have to trust me."*

He meant what he said—to get her moving—but did he mean more? Could he have meant more?

His jaw was purple and the gauze bandage gave him a rakish air. Stripped to the waistband of new jeans, torso glistening with the sweat of his labor, he looked so strong and handsome she could barely restrain herself from rushing over to throw herself at his chest. But she had words to get off hers first. *Don't wimp out now. Offense, remember?*

She cocked her head. "Wescott, I never knew you were a coward. You slunk out of the hospital and came here to hide in your cave." Talking didn't hurt as much now but the croak did detract from her snarky act.

His mouth twitched as if he might grin, but then he schooled his expression into that wary mask he'd discarded. It twisted her insides to see his defenses up. Against her.

He propped his left foot on a sawhorse, leaned an elbow on his knee and scratched his ear. "And I never knew you could do such a good Kathleen Turner imitation."

Hell, if he wanted to dance around the elephant in the room, she could do that. For now. But he didn't deny the cowardice accusation. She'd get back to that. "You have a little Eastwood thing going for you. Or else you've been secretly smoking a pack a day. How're the burns?"

"Sting enough to remind me not to lean against the wall. I'll live. You okay?"

She nodded. She took another step closer and clasped her hands behind her so he wouldn't see them shaking. "I see your SUV survived the fire."

"Only some heat damage to the paint." He ambled away from the wallboard he'd been installing and toward her. At first she thought he was going to let her off the hook and take her in his arms. But he planted his feet more than a foot away and kept his hands at his sides.

Then she remembered the plastic grocery bag. She held it up. "I have Greek pasta salad and pork chops to cook on the grill. One of your granddad's old buddies offered me four lobsters right off his boat for free, but—"

"You remembered my aversion." His bemused expression at her babbling morphed into an unguarded smile. "Thank you." He took the bag of groceries from her and strode to the kitchen to stow them. He turned to her with a determined look. Her pulse leaped into next week.

He handed her a beer and opened one for himself. "You come here to drop off food or can you stay and eat with me? I can put these on the grill now."

She tore her gaze from him, so he wouldn't see how desperately eager she was. "Definitely. I mean, I can stay. Thanks." Grateful for the distraction and the soothing coldness in her throat, she hovered in the kitchen doorway.

New maple strips replaced the last of the holes in the floor, which was cleared of the old lath and plaster. And he'd installed a new sink and faucet in the kitchen. The house smelled of new wood and fresh air, not moldy and dank.

"You've come a long way in a day. What happened here? Elves?"

"Close." He unwrapped the chops and collected a paper plate, then led the way through the back porch and into the yard, where a gas grill awaited. "My brother and some friends. And Kevin's sister sent over a work crew to finish the demolition and the floors."

Lani chose one of the plastic deck chairs nearby while Jake started the grill.

"I can't imagine how bad J.T.'s family must feel," she said. "Now that Vargas is in the slammer, the town needs a new harbormaster. Maybe you could apply for that job." If he stayed, maybe she could. She set the beer down and popped the knuckles on her right hand.

Using his thumbnail to pick at the beer label, he shook his head. "Nailing bad guys is my calling, not haranguing spoiled teenagers who speed in the harbor. Funny thing though. ABC delivered a bunch of wood flooring. Steve said it was donated anonymously. You wouldn't know anything about that?"

Lani felt her cheeks heat. "I think my dad took care of that. He wanted to atone for all his neglect. Since I don't have a house to fix up anymore, you were elected for his largesse."

"The one who really needs to atone will have eons of time for that where he went. But I appreciate your dad's generosity." He took the next chair, scooted close enough to smell his honest sweat, masculine and salty. When he reached over to tuck a stray strand of hair behind her ear, she wanted to jump into his lap. "So he's really *Dad* again?"

"He came to the hospital to see me. He's going to handle the land trust deal, and he thinks I can get a better price for the property without a drafty old house. Even if it had new locks."

He grinned, tugged on that lock of hair. "Won't there be insurance money?"

"Eventually. We talked for the first time in a long time. You were right about the divorce. He and Mom were having problems anyway, and he couldn't deal with Gail's abortion and her emotional implosion. The fire just exacerbated their differences."

"I'm guessing he felt helpless."

She nodded. "Then he blamed himself for the fire killing her and burning me. He felt if he'd been able to help her, she wouldn't have gotten in too deep with— well, at the time, he thought it was you."

"He's human. I hope you straightened him out like you've done your fix on me."

Seeing his gaze soften and heat, she longed to lean into his caress. But she had her apology to say first. "I want to atone too. I accused you of being a coward."

"You were right. I didn't know what to say. How to say it, but I'll say it now." His features seemed to darken with pain. "I failed you. I let those bastards grab us. You almost died. I should've known they'd sabotage the boat. I did a damned lousy job of—"

She pressed a finger to his lips. "Just stop the recriminations, Wescott. What happened wasn't your fault. It was J.T. It was the smuggling gang. I'm alive. *We're* alive." Tears slipped down her cheeks and she let them come, ordering herself to be soft and not defensive.

"Yes, ma'am." He touched a finger to her wet cheek. "I didn't know if you'd ever let yourself cry."

She wanted to step into his arms, let it all go. She managed a wobbly smile. "The dam burst. It was time."

"Past time."

Stiffening her shoulders, she launched into her speech. "The fire. It made me remember. Everything. I saw J.T. that night but only through the flames. He was the towering fire monster in my dreams, but I couldn't have identified him in a line-up. I called for help and he ran away. But I heard *you* say you wouldn't leave me, that I could trust you. Was that just about the fire?"

His blue eyes seemed to laser into her soul. "I meant that and more. Much more. I didn't know the truth of it until the words were out. I love you, Lani."

Those words swept through her, dizzying her. She was a mess, and that low voice vibrating with intensity nearly undid her. But she forced herself to continue. "I never want to hear you say you can't be trusted to protect anyone. You saved me."

"I know better than to argue with you, but we saved each other."

"The smoke, the flames, they paralyzed me. I couldn't move. Until I saw the flaming ceiling collapse. Until I saw the man I love on fire."

"You love me." He breathed it like a prayer. "Enough to trust me to stay?"

She eased closer, placed her hands on his chest. "You and I have been tested by fire a second time."

"All these years alone I'm not sure I know how to

love." Then he grinned, deflating her incipient panic. "You'll have to zing me when I screw up."

"That's a given." She swatted him on the biceps. "You have to know I'm not easy. Not high maintenance, like diamonds or designer shoes, but guys tell me I'm too much work."

"Nothing I don't already know. One of the things about you that intrigue me. You challenge me, honey, and I do love that mouth, whether you're zinging me or turning me on. You like control but so do I. And I know how to get around you."

His arms came around her and she yielded happily as he pulled her to her feet. She smiled, pressing her cheek against his chest. She sighed as he gathered her in and tipped up her chin with a finger.

"Lani, what I felt for your sister was more lust than love."

"You don't have to—"

"Shush, but I do. I want you to never wonder again if I compare you two. Gail was flash and smoke, but there was nothing to hold onto. You're flame, warm and steady and enduring. A genuine woman with humor and honesty. I want to keep you in my arms if you'll let me."

Tears flowed again. Tears of joy. "You've thought a lot about this. Us."

"Since I knew I had feelings for you. Wanted to know what I felt was real. And I had some things to work through."

"Oh, Jake, I accused you of cowardice, but you're not a coward. I'm the emotional coward, have been for years. Not trusting anyone. Not letting anyone in."

"No, you're the bravest person I know. The barn fire was a defining moment for both of us, but neither of us let it be a dead end. And now we can move ahead together."

She touched a finger gingerly to the bandage on his cheek. "You'll have a new scar."

"Makes us a matching pair." He swiped a tear from the corner of her eye with his index finger. "The ATF sends me into danger. I work rotten hours and deal with slime."

She grabbed his finger and kissed it. "After this, piece of cake."

He crushed her to him but when their lips met, it was the sweetest kiss imaginable. If hadn't been holding on so tight, she'd have slithered into a puddle at his feet. The two of them had survived a past that devastated her entire family and turned both their lives upside down. Coming through the fire a second time annealed them into stronger fiber, made tougher still because they would face the future together.

She smiled at him through her tears. "The *Amy Jo* is gone. The farmhouse is gone. I have no place to stay. Don't suppose you have room for me in this house?"

"If you don't mind camping gear. The bedroom upstairs has a couple of sleeping bags we can put together." His expression turned serious. "But not for long. I have to return to Boston as soon as I get a crew started finishing the house. My place is north of Boston, but forty-five minutes from Concord is still too far from you."

"I've kinda gotten used to waking up with you in the morning. I'll bet some school district nearby can use a special education teacher."

"I can't offer you much," he said against her cheek. "Only my love."

"That's all I want."

Before their lips could meet again, wings flapped and fluttered behind Jake. She peered around him to see a great black-backed seagull perched beside the chops.

"Hey, you thief! Get away from there! Shoo!" Waving her hands, she rushed at the big black-and-white scavenger.

Looking offended, the gull swooped into the air, its beak empty.

"Of all the damn nerve!"

Laughing, Jake swung her around. He planted another kiss on her mouth.

"*What*?"

## A word about the author...

Occasional bouts of insomnia led to Susan Vaughan's writing career. When she couldn't sleep, she made up stories to fill the long dark nights. Her stories throw the hero and heroine together under extraordinary circumstances and pit them against a clever villain. Besides curling up with a good mystery or romance, Susan enjoys walking her dog, boating, traveling, and gardening. A former teacher, she is a West Virginia native, but she and her husband have lived in Maine for many years. She is the author of 16 novels and one children's book. Find her at www.susanvaughan.com, where you can contact her, or at www.facebook.com/susanvaughanbooks.

www.susanvaughan.com

www.ingramcontent.com/pod-product-compliance
Lightning Source LLC
Chambersburg PA
CBHW052003020726
47501CB00004B/986